A TINY STEP

BY KATHERINE A. KITCHIN

McKnight
& Bishop
Ltd

About The Publisher

McKnight & Bishop are always on the look-out for new authors and ideas for new books. If you write or if you have an idea for a book, please e-mail **info@mcknightbishop.com**

Some things we love are undiscovered authors, open-source software, Creative Commons, crowd-funding, Amazon/Kindle, social networking, faith, laughter & new ideas.

Visit us at **www.mcknightbishop.com**

About The Author

Katherine Kitchin is both a midwife and reflexologist.
She is married with four children and lives in North Yorkshire.

Cover Images:

'Park in Dublin St Stephen's Green aerial' by dronepicr is licensed under CC BY 2.0. http://tinyurl.com/hw635mo (Image has been edited)

'Overhead KAP Shot of Arbor Low Henge, showing Stone Circle' Copyright © 2012 Jim Knowles. Used with permission. http://tinyurl.com/zqyjuvg (Image has been edited)

'Newborn baby boy asleep on a blanket' Copyright © Hannamariah | Dreamstime.com http://tinyurl.com/zxprebe (Image has been edited)

ISBN 978-1-905691-45-6
A CIP catalogue record for this book is available from the British Library

First published in 2015 by McKnight & Bishop:

McKnight & Bishop Ltd. | 28 Griffiths Court, Bowburn, Co. Durham, DH6 5FD
http://www.mcknightbishop.com | info@mcknightbishop.com

This book has been typeset in Garamond-Normal and *Chopin Script*.

Printed and bound in Great Britain by Lightning Source Inc, Milton Keynes. The paper used in this book has been made from wood independently certified as having come from sustainable forests.

This book is dedicated to
all the madwives out there;
only you can know what it is really like!

Acknowledgements

To my brother, Simon Edwards, for his brilliance as an editor.
To my brother-in-law, Stephen Finegold, for his helpful advice.
To all of my family for listening to me

and especially my husband Darcy for his patience
and research on the Arrol-Johnston starting handle.

Table of Contents

PART ONE

Prologue

31ˢᵗ December 1999.

"What day is today?" The aged brittle voice cracked the silence and made Maria take a pause from her nursing duties. She knew the question well, for it was always the same, like a record stuck in its track and supposed that it gave comfort by its repetition; a sense of security in its familiarity. More often than not Maria ignored the question for if an answer were to be offered, the phrase was still repeated moments later. Today however, enthusiastic about what day it actually was, she responded playfully, regardless of her busy schedule in the care-home.

"And what day do you think it is Rose?" Warming to her subject she continued in oratory fashion. "Today is the very day when the world as we know it might end. Today is the day when everything could change. It just may be that nothing will ever be the same again, after this day." With mounting vibrancy her voice became louder and more frenzied as she spoke, the monotony of her work forgotten momentarily as she pirouetted around the room as if an actress on a stage. "...or so they say," she concluded. Her proclamation finished, she paused and took a deep breath through her nose, as if to absorb what she had just said. After a loud exhale she was brought back to the business in hand, to dress Rose and take her down for breakfast. Dismissing the frail and shaking fingers out of the way, Maria deftly buttoned Rose's cardigan with her firm authoritative hands.

Rose yielded in surrender. Buttoning cardigans, indeed the whole task of getting dressed and toileted was far too tricky and quite beyond her capabilities now. There was a time when she would have remonstrated about all the intrusions; was all this necessary? Was she going out? Did she go out? Couldn't she stay in bed? But not anymore.

Days blended into other days, moments in time blurring into other moments. Life was a constant moment, no beginning, and no end, in a circle around and around and far too much unnecessary effort. She was so old now; too old to be bothered with anything really, everything was a struggle, but yet there was something that made her stay just a little longer.

For most of her life, Rose had waited for this day, and through the long monotonous years, it gave her the strength to keep on going.

"What day is today?" Maria raised her eyebrows to the ceiling as the fragile voice in its strained repetition reverberated inside her ears adding echoes to her exasperation. When she had finished asking the Lord to give her strength, she held Rose's face in her hands and looked into the clouded eyes in front of her, faded and expressionless. Maria implored "Rose! Oh Rose. Don't you know? Don't you understand? It's arrived; New Year's Eve. It's the millennium. It's here!" Seeing nothing other than that Rose's cataracts seemed worse than ever, she gave up, sniffed again and shouted to her workmate she was almost finished. The mostly one-sided conversation concluded, Maria trundled the wheelchair towards the dining room no longer aware of its feeble occupant, her thoughts now elsewhere and onto her next task. Thoughts of computer meltdowns or millennium bugs were now forgotten and Rose was placed at the breakfast table, her job was done. If Maria had taken the trouble to look at her again, she would not have failed to miss the sparkle that had appeared in the usually lifeless eyes and it would have gladdened her heart.

Rose would never ask the question again. In all her bewilderment and fuzziness the meaning had got through. It's time. It had been so long in coming but the day had come, it was finally here and she could not help but smile.

Chapter One

A New Century.

The street lights had never been good in that part of town and tonight only half were lit and of no useful purpose. It was the brilliant streaks flashing above that served to light up the night. The young woman trudged on, trying to ignore the heavenly display, wary of what would come next. As expected, the rumbling explosions, like giant foreboding tympani clapped out. She felt tired and vulnerable, her head hurt and it was late. She ought to move more quickly, she only had a few hours before... well, she didn't want to think of that. Nonetheless her mind kept turning over the recent events and soon came back to it. She had known for a while it would come to this and there was nothing she could change, but that hadn't stopped her finding it difficult to come to terms with the situation. 'Why did it have to be like this?' she moaned inwardly. But life's foibles can be so undeserved sometimes.

Then their parting; so unexpectedly quick in the end. She had wanted to say how much she loved him, but how could she under the circumstances; seeing him with her had ruined that. She hadn't even said goodbye; it had all been too much when finally she had walked away. Her footsteps slowed again at the thought. She rubbed at a bump on her head where a step ladder had fallen on top of her but half an hour ago, she was sure it was growing bigger. How mortifying, how ridiculous; a step ladder of all things. But she hadn't seen it and now she was bearing the consequences and had a great lump which was hurting badly. Miserable and alone, she wished she had been able to talk with someone, but the situation had made that impossible. She tried to cheer herself up by remembering better times and even raised a smile, but it was to be short lived.

The solitary woman had been going along the road that edged around the park, and had first thought to walk through, but peering into its shadowy depths her mind changed. It was not the place to be alone at night. She looked about; most people had returned back behind their doors and apart from the intermittent light show from above, everywhere was dark and deserted. It served to reflect her mood and facing forward again, clumped one heavy foot in front of the other.

She wasn't making much in the way of progress when she felt a wave of nausea. Nausea always made her feel giddy and she began to lurch about. She felt a rushing sound in her ears and a haze appeared in front of her eyes, swirling. Everything seemed distorted, she couldn't understand what was happening; it was only a silly bump to the head, nothing at all. Trying to get a grip on herself she carried on as best she could placing her feet apprehensively, fumbling her way forward. Nothing seemed clear now, her hearing was affected, even her footsteps were muffled and so remote she had to persuade herself they were really hers. An occasional explosion, far off in the distance now, was her only reassurance that she was still in the land of the living. Her hands continued to feel about for any obstacles in her way as she inched along but the isolating murk was thickening and she had no idea in which direction she was heading,

She wished he had come with her; she wanted him now; needed him; she loved him so much, but he had deserted her, preferring to stay there. Her anger returned and distorted her reflections; she hated him for doing this to her but she hated herself even more for feeling like this. Her body shivered as it tried to rid itself of resentment. This present predicament had nothing to do with him and something was definitely wrong and she was scared.

She stood in the silence rubbing at the bump on her head and trying to fathom what was happening, and began to hear a noise. The frightened woman listened; it became louder and louder; strangely different from the previous rumbles. It was coming towards her and it was growing to such a pitch, her whole body began to sway to it, and her head hurt so much. Her breath came shallow and fast, her heart thumped as if making a break for freedom from her chest but the thunderous sounds still clamoured in her head. She clasped her hands to her ears as they resonated violently, trying to shut them out. The whole street appeared to be shaking; everything seemed so jumbled up. She tried to distinguish something, anything familiar. There was nothing. The deafening noise, the pall, the dense dark fog and her vibrating head made her distraction complete. She was completely disorientated and hopelessly defenceless against the approaching danger.

It happened rapidly. The pounding noise rose into a stunning crescendo, hitting her with an almighty force just as she took a step to steady herself. The unfortunate woman fell backwards and lost all consciousness.

Chapter Two

She started to shiver with the cold as she lay on the ground trying to gather her thoughts. She did not understand what had happened, nothing was clear, her head felt very thick and pain resounded inside her skull. Never one for liking the winter months; dark days, cold nights, always feeling chilled to the bone. 'Well what you would expect for the time of year' she remonstrated with herself. At least she had on the long thick cloak that her mother had once given her. It was unusual, but she loved wearing it when the weather was like this. She always felt she could tuck herself away inside it as if it were a cosy blanket. Standing up tentatively, trying to get warm, she looked about her. The fog had lifted, she tried but could not quite recognise where she was and began to stumble about feeling dizzy and peculiar. She felt as if she ought to know this place but her mind would not focus properly and her body felt heavy; she could remember nothing clearly.

Hardly bothering to see in the new year at the hospital, with a heavy heart, John walked home. He had been attending a particularly difficult maternity case that had concluded with the use of some rotational forceps, a stillborn infant and a hefty blood haemorrhage following the afterbirth. The woman's painful ordeal was over at least and she would recover given time. He had witnessed similar events many times.

John, who had followed his father into the medical profession, once stood tall and proud, but since the death of his beloved wife Eleanor, he had developed the stooped appearance of a man much older than his still relatively youthful self. She had died following the birth of their first child, George, three years ago. Bearing witness to the unforgettably harrowing experience of child-bed fever, John looked as though he had borne the weight of the world on his shoulders ever since. Apart from the delightful 'little Georgie' who captured everyone's heart with his big brown eyes, the same as his father's, and lashes that women adored, some good came out of her death as it caused John to develop a life-long interest in the field of midwifery. Ever since, he had doggedly set about trying to make a difference.

Dejected and weary, he had reached the road alongside the park when his attention focussed on a coach; horseshoes and wheels clattering noisily on the cobbled street. It was passing at speed; too fast, he thought, for the sharp bend ahead. It managed the manoeuvre, just, but John felt something was amiss as he watched it disappear out of sight. Inquisitive by nature, he followed its path around the corner and quickened his stride.

The poor light made it difficult to see clearly but peering intently, he detected a dark form coming in and out of his focus. As he moved nearer, he could make out a female shape; unusual, given the time of night. She appeared unsteady. He wondered if she had had too much to drink and was about to continue on his way but then felt enough concern to persuade himself not to. "Are you all right Miss?" he called out to her. The young woman was taken by surprise not realising she was not entirely alone.

"Sorry?" she replied tentatively not sure if it would be safe to engage in conversation with a disembodied voice in the dead of night.

"Begging your pardon, I said are you all right? I couldn't help notice you having a bit of difficulty getting about." The woman, feeling that the voice showed genuine concern, replied.

"Oh yes. I mean no, I'm not sure. I think I might have fallen. I have banged my head and I admit I'm feeling rather odd."

The woman looked around trying to locate the owner of the voice. Everything was strange; fuzzy round the edges; she was feeling dizzy again and she started swaying. John ran towards her and was just in time to catch her and break her fall. There was no smell of alcohol on her, even though, he surmised, she would have had an excuse, given the occasion. Even he had eventually been persuaded into a small drop as a toast on leaving the hospital.

"For your own sake Doctor, take it," the night porter had implored whilst taking out his hip flask. He needed a drink himself after returning from the hospital's mortuary. There, among its lifeless company, he had laid the tiny corpse of the stillborn infant wrapped only in sheeting and quiet on the cold stone table. Before leaving he placed a flower over the innocent cloth having plucked it from a posy in the hospital entrance. He felt it was the least he could do. He hated that part of his job; he had lost two of his own and was no stranger to the suffering and grief. "Oh come on, it's a new year, a new century," said the porter. He took a quick nip then offered it up to the doctor who accepted unenthusiastically.

Well if not drink, what else could be causing her distress and confusion? He always enjoyed the process of diagnosis. There was definitely an art to it; asking the correct questions, performing a thorough examination; noticing anything unusual. He would forget his own personal grief when others were in need of his skills. He noticed that her nose was bleeding and at first thought she may have been the victim of some form of attack, but then recalled the coach and horse and deduced she had been clipped by it.

The woman regained consciousness quickly and John spared no time. "Why didn't you get out of the way, did you not see it?" he asked her, pleased he had solved the puzzle. "Out of the way of the coach," he added as he could see her confusion. "You shouldn't be out on your own." John was annoyed she had put herself at risk. His temper was always short when he was fatigued.

"No, I shouldn't," she replied bowing her head in contrition, she knew the dangers of being alone at night, "but I had no choice, I had to get... What coach?" She stopped herself from finishing by asking another question.

"Well, you could hardly miss it," he said incredulously. "It was causing such a din, far too much for this time of night; hooves crashing down in their gallop. The speed it was going at, how dangerous," he continued, preferring to believe that the accident was the fault of the driver taking things too fast rather than the woman not seeing where she was going.

She managed to focus for a moment and started to look around, her eyes slowly coming to rest on him. She saw the creases in his forehead and his eyes beneath, full of care and concern and it made her feel quite safe but being in a state of confusion, needed to get her head straight. 'Yes, she remembered noise; it was a coach?' She managed to stand up and started pacing about, pondering. 'What on earth happened? She had stepped in front of a coach? Why was it making her so uneasy?'

"Careful," said John as he saw her swaying. He caught her again as she fell unconscious. He knew she needed his help whoever she was and whatever she was doing here alone at this time of the night. There was only one thing he could do, only one place he could take her, but should he? It did not take him long to reach a decision. Was there a decision to be made, he could hardly leave her there, to be found in the morning, dead with the cold?

In that one thought of his, her future was set. The future of John too, considering that if he had passed her by in the street, he would never have known her, she would never have been a part of his life. He would never have progressed in life in the way that he would now. How easily it can happen for a life to change because of a single moment in time. He caught her in his arms as she fell and carried her, his vigour renewed, back to his home.

Once inside the wide Georgian hallway of his house John flicked the switch by the door and the newly installed electric lighting turned on instantly. He regarded the limp and insensible woman draped across his arms. She may feel vulnerable and afraid when she woke and would need to feel protected. Where ought he to put her for the best? He decided she required a cloistered bed upstairs rather than a public couch in the parlour. He looked up at the galleried landing high above and changed his hold of her, grasping her securely in readiness for the ascent upstairs. With heavy breath he mounted each step, arriving at the arched passageway at the top and onto the landing. John paused only briefly to decide which room to take his now moaning and semi conscious load. The decision swiftly made he progressed along the corridor and on arrival, managed to locate the doorknob by reaching between her legs. The door creaked open as he pushed it with his aching shoulder and he placed her as gently as he could upon the heavily-draped bed before dropping next to her. After a few moments of recuperation John rose to turn on the light and then went back over to the four-poster. 'Where to start?' he thought. He began by carefully undoing her cloak. He would not know that she had conceived a child that night.

John was not going to bed. Pleased with his long unpractised fire-making skills he had stood back to watch the flicker of flames develop in the long-cold and lifeless grate. He was soon forced to place the fire-guard in front as the wood started to spit frightfully, and satisfied that the girl was safely asleep rather than still unconscious, he went to the library to begin searching through some of his father's old papers. He found what he was looking for. Only now in the mood for a proper drink he reached for the decanter. He paced the floor for some time, deep in thought until Polly, the housemaid disturbed him. She had come in to lay the fire for the morning but now hovered in the doorway. The long fingers of her left hand flustering to brush away an imaginary lock of her thin brown hair behind her ear whilst her right hand clutched at an overly full coal scuttle.

"Oh! Doctor I'm sorry, I didn't realise you were here," she exclaimed through pursed lips that spoiled her otherwise pretty heart-shaped face.

"Nor would you Polly, it is not my usual hour. Please, do carry on. Oh and please would you tell the rest of the staff there is a lady guest in the blue room and to make necessary arrangements. She will require rest and recuperation at the moment. I believe she has suffered a small blow to the head."

"Madam's room?" she replied with some surprise after a short pause. John had barely given it a second thought last night; it had been the nearest room; he could not have carried her any further. How dare a maid question him? So, it had not been used since... time moves on after all. Polly felt a pain in her stomach as if she had been kicked. For the last three years she had lovingly tended that room in reverence to her mistress. Every time, she had wept when adjusting the green enamelled hair brushes in their places on the dressing table and imagining she had been brushing her lady's beautiful chestnut hair.

"Yes, the blue room, as I said," he replied abruptly. Polly, uncharacteristically lost for words even when it was not her place to speak, busied herself with her work as quickly as she could and left hurriedly. John took some notes, finished the whisky in one gulp and went down to the kitchen and ate breakfast there, something he had done as a boy and only occasionally since. When in need of comfort, the kitchen was always where he had gone to find it.

As the morning wore on, the woman John had plucked from the night woke and stretched out lazily. It was dark outside but she was able to make out the shapes in the room by the light from the fire. How on earth, she wondered, had the bedroom fire been lit? Slowly, she began to remember the events of the previous night in the street and then sat up abruptly as she looked around, and made sense out of what she saw. "Good grief!" she exclaimed. It was unbelievable, this room, its contents, the fire burning. The man from last night, he had brought her here, she remembered that, but the rest, it was all such a blur. What had happened? But wasn't she supposed to be somewhere else? Nothing was making any sense. She sat hugging her knees and watched the dancing flames in the grate not quite sure what to do.

Footsteps sounded noisily on the landing floorboards and brought her attention back to the present. She listened warily. The footsteps stopped outside the door and she heard someone give a small knock. She watched nervously as it creaked open. Someone entered in what appeared to be a maid's uniform and she trembled as two dark and deep-set eyes cut into her. She could only feel relief as the apparition turned about and went the way she had come. Still clutching her knees she stared at the closed door, hardly daring to breathe. Before long there were more footsteps, heavier and more slow and as they stopped, the creaking door opened a second time. Filling the doorway with a lofty height and wide shoulders was the man that had helped her during the night. He was holding a tray and entered carefully, the crockery upon it rattling precariously as he set it down. "Polly informed me you had woken. How are you feeling? I have brought you a cup of tea." Instead of answering his question she came back with her own.

"What has happened to me? What are you doing here?" John looked at the way she was sitting clutching at her knees and considered how frightened she must be feeling. Breathing in deeply he thought it best to start from the beginning and gave a low bow. On straightening back up to full height, his stoop having inexplicably disappeared, he began.

"Please allow me to introduce myself." My name is Brown, Doctor John Brown. I brought you into my home during the night following your collision with a coach and horse."

"Your home?"

"Yes, this is where I live. I was on my way here late last night when I came across you in the road."

"The road?"

"Yes, Meadowsring Road, next to the park. It was I who er, removed your clothing, it was covered with mud from the road," he added as he saw her looking at what she was wearing. His lingering glance over her captivating upper body left him wondering how exposed she would be if her softly curling hair wasn't tumbling over his unbuttoned nightshirt. He should have searched for a night cap to keep it up and out of the way. "It's one of mine, I'm sorry I could not find anything else and did not want to disturb anyone owing to the hour." She absent-mindedly pulled the shirt across her chest and accepted the tea and sipped it whilst wondering what to say.

"What day is it today please?" Her voice wavered when she eventually thought of something.

"Ha! You haven't been asleep that long," John laughed as he paced around the room eagerly. "It's still the same day, you tell me."

"Then it is January the first?" she asked tentatively.

"Yes that's right! And what a wonderful day, the dawn of the twentieth century and your memory, so far, is intact." He watched the girl's pinched expression change to one of blind panic. She tried to get out of the bed but was so shaky on her feet she needed his help to lie back down.

"No, this is all wrong, I shouldn't be here, I don't know what's happened, I need to be somewhere else," she protested wildly.

"Yes of course, all in good time. Right now you need to rest." John remained calm; he was used to confused and disoriented patients. "Tell me now, as I have introduced myself to you, perhaps you would do the same. Here is the next question, what is your name, you do remember, don't you?" John added the last phrase as she seemed to hesitate. She took some time before she answered trying to make sense of it all.

Was this a dream? She hoped it was just a dream. She wanted to close and open her eyes and see someone else looking at her and asking after her well-being. Manifestly, this was no dream; it was all very very real. Tell him the truth? Where could she start, what could she say? Her mind explored the events of the previous night. Had it been the right thing to leave just when she did? Surely she had no choice but to go, duty had demanded it, her damned duty. Whatever would he think when he realised she'd gone? He would never come for her; she would be dead to him. It was all so final. She watched as the cold light of the new day peeped through gaps at the heavily curtained window and wished to turn time around and go back. It could have been her own bed she was sitting in and in her own room, not this one, wearing her own clothes and not some stranger's and, horror of horrors, he had obviously stripped her naked! How did it happen to her?

The fact remained that here she was and no, she could never tell him the truth; he would think her quite idiotic, unbalanced, ridiculous even. Finding some inner strength she managed to calm herself; she needed to think fast and to formulate what to say. There was nothing she could do to change things at this moment in time; she would have to make the best of it and anyway she needed somewhere to stay. Right here seemed to be a good place. What else was she to do? She needed time to search for some sort of clarity as she was so confused, and she would be hopeless on her own. Without further deliberations, her mind was made up and just as John thought he needed to break the long silence she started to speak. The sentence was delivered slowly and deliberately measured, almost as if it had been rehearsed.

"Unfortunately, I am unable to remember who I am, or at least what my name is although I have been trying very hard. Thank you very much for taking care of me." It did the trick.

John switched into work mode and put a thumb under each of her eyebrows, lifted them up so her eyelids would follow and looked at her pupils for signs of concussion. "Close your eyes, and open. Again please." She obeyed all his instructions passively.

"This must all seem very strange for you," John continued when he had finished a thorough examination. "I expect your memory to return after plenty of rest. Meanwhile I will endeavour to help as much as I can. The first thing I can do to help is to bring you breakfast and the second is to ask my sister to sort you out with something to wear, as your clothing was filthy, as I said. There is no question that you remain here to recover, at least until someone comes to claim you. We must also decide what to call you. Now then, let me think." He put his hand over his mouth, rubbed his jaw and looked her straight in the eye as if he knew something. "Stella springs to mind, what do you think?" He turned about after giving her a mischievous look and left the room, leaving her to reflect on her surroundings and upon the name he had given her, and what she had been wearing the night before.

'Stella? What sort of a name is that?' She was fairly sure why he had thought of that name, and she blushed at the thought. On her left buttock was a birth mark about three inches across which looked remarkably like a star in its appearance. 'He must have seen it last night. Oh God!' The considered connotations made her body shudder; he must have scrutinised every bit of her. "Estelle?" she said as an alternative when he returned; it had to be better than Stella.

"Ah yes of course, in the French manner; Estelle it shall be," John replied with enthusiasm, preferring the sound of the French name.

After several days, it seemed that 'Estelle' might have started to recover a little from her ordeal. Her strangeness, the apparent loss of memory, her clumsiness, her fearfulness of anything and everything, had been rather disquieting. Doctor John, as he was affectionately called by the domestic staff when in their own company, had told them that Miss Estelle was both a patient and a guest in his house, and to treat her respectfully. He had done his best to reassure them her strange behaviour was due to the accident and would be only a temporary disposition. In spite of this they showed little regard for her and were restrained from the moment she arrived. Constant tittle-tattle only heightened their reservations and they began to wonder just who she really was and what she was doing in their house. Tongues wagged and made gossip, especially when Polly was involved. She had an axe to grind.

"She's no different from one of us. In fact she's worse, acting all mysterious like. I found her in the library this morning looking for writing materials. That was her excuse anyway, said it might help if she wrote things down, snooping around more like I'd say." Polly had just arrived in the kitchen after clearing away breakfast.

"You stop right there girl!" said Cookie sharply. "I won't have a thing said about them that pays our wages; they've always looked after me and mine. Anyway, Master John said it was on account of her accident and her memory will take time to come back." Mrs. Cook, or Cookie as she was known behind her back, had had employment within the household for most of her adult life and known John from when he was a small boy. She found it hard to call him by any other name. Thinking that was enough she went back to what she had been doing previously, shouting at Fay, the kitchen and tweeny maid for not getting her table ready quickly enough and muttering under her breath.

"Lord knows where she came from," Polly continued in a whisper to Charlie the valet making sure Cookie was out of earshot first. "I think Doctor John's taken a fancy to her, have you seen the way he looks at her?"

"That's enough!" They could tell Cookie was cross. Before its colour had faded, her hair had been such a fiery shade of red, as a child, she had been known as Carrot-top. She had a temper to match; it never took much to make her lose her composure; exchanging smirks they got on with the morning's tasks.

John, oblivious to the feelings of the staff, brought his sister in to help in Estelle's convalescence. Vicky had not long ago arrived back from a honeymoon that had been something of a disappointment. Glad for something to do, she arrived directly with a stack of clothes for Estelle to try on and spent a supportive afternoon helping her new-found companion to choose what was suitable to wear.

When John thought that Estelle was well enough to go outside for some air, Vicky came to the rescue again, but both women found this much more of a challenge. To stay in the house with disapproving staff was taxing, but going outside proved far worse. Every time Estelle stepped from the front door she started to feel giddy. Her heart beats galloped wildly and great globules of perspiration appeared on her forehead as she tried to catch her breath. The further she ventured from the house, the worse she felt. Vicky, normally used to frivolity and frippery, treated Estelle's behaviour as if it were another mere triviality. Naturally possessed with a caring and compassionate nature like her brother, Vicky encouraged her with calmness and gentleness and found her new employment liberating.

As the days grew to weeks she gradually and patiently coaxed Estelle around the garden. They rested every few steps and pondered unhurriedly, every leafless tree and every frozen shrub and bush in the otherwise empty borders. Even the pile of rotting leaves in the corner left from autumn was deliberated over. Vicky reminded her to take in deep breaths of the fresh January air and when Estelle felt ready, they moved on, passing the tiny green and yellow leaves of the neatly trimmed privet hedge, the crimson hips of the climbing rose and the winter flowering jasmine and its delicate perfume. Estelle began to improve.

As time advanced so did their strolls, out into the street and down the road. They walked away from John's red-brick Georgian house and passed the long stone terrace of Victorian properties and onward around the bend in the road where the park came into view. Through it all Estelle clung on to Vicky's arm for her strength and support. However, no matter how hard she tried she could not bring herself to go across to the other side of the road and walk through the entrance and into the park. Vicky could not understand why Estelle shook uncontrollably and was unable to advance any further every time they got to this point. John reminded her that this was the place where he had found her and perhaps something in her lost memory was being activated but was still too painful for her to remember. They solved the problem by entering the park by the south gates farther along.

Apart from her anxieties by the bend in the road, Estelle increasingly enjoyed her outings with Vicky into the parkland. They got on well together benefiting from one another's company. The young women were more or less of the same age and appearance; average height and build, similar hair colour; perhaps Estelle's slightly more fair and Vickie's more lank, and Vickie's facial features the more delicate. Whatever their similarities in looks and their differences in nature, which they would discover as they became more acquainted, they both shared a sense of escapism. Estelle and Vicky slipped their way around the icy paths, giggling as they held each other up trying to stay warm by linking arms and keeping each other close. Their new-found comradeship helped cement the fissures that were evident in both their lives but which neither would admit to.

The area that the park occupied used to be open grassland on the fringe of town. It had been left to pasture for centuries, touched only by its wildlife. For some reason, despite its beauty, nobody was ever moved to go there, save for the farmers down the ages to herd their flocks. The cycles of time moved on unnoticed, and little changed. Season pursued season, year chased year and the grazing sheep carried on bleating their unrelenting narrative in the lush-green meadows. But when the nearby industrial town prospered and rapidly increased in size, it engulfed Meadowsring, as it was known colloquially, almost into its centre. The once calm haven became a convenient open space for town gatherings, public shows and galas when it was leased out by the local landowners. Heaven knew how the animals continued to graze unperturbed by the intrusion.

No local could have anticipated how things were to evolve when the town corporation eventually purchased all fifteen acres thanks to the sterling efforts of the town mayor. The ancient meadows gave way to formal bedding, Italian gardens, fountains, a bandstand, lodges and the crowning glory was to be a great glass pavilion. Planning and responsibility for every aspect of the design was placed in the hands of the borough surveyor. However, not everything went as planned and the building of the glass pavilion hit an obstacle. During site preparation a discovery was made that outshone all other news of the progress of the park's construction and fortuitously for the planners, reached headline news. The borough surveyor had breathed a silent sigh of relief at the information as it provided a valid excuse for the pavilion not to be built. The cost of construction of the park was already far more than originally planned and his sleep had been regularly disturbed as a result.

One after the other, megalithic stones were exposed, usurping the glass pavilion's intended spot by way of being there first. As they were uncovered, it became clear they formed two concentric circles, the majority still in an upright position. They were of varying size and not very tall, the biggest only around two feet high but their exposure managed to raise havoc at the railway station with the sudden influx of sightseers, spiritualists and seers. No-one in living memory had known the stones existed.

The archaeologists moved in and the mobile stall holders and street traders jumped on the bandwagon. They each did a roaring trade even after the town council recognised a new rental opportunity and charged by the day. Onlookers could purchase all their 'indispensable' requirements from hot food, to satisfy physical needs, to ouija boards, to satisfy their spiritual wants, and alcohol for both. There were alleged ancient relics to ward off danger, dowsing rods purporting to discover phantoms; pendulums and bric-a-brac for all to haggle over. Any works in that area of the park were suspended apart from that of the archaeologists who, in the end, began to outstay their welcome. In due course, they returned to their homes, the people grew tired of looking at stones that didn't really do anything and were very small anyway, and the stall holders packed up. The grass grew back and was kept neatly manicured in between the mystical boulders by dedicated groundsmen rather than sheep. The park's construction finished, it finally opened with great formality and ceremony in the same year as the cornerstone for the Statue of Liberty was laid.

Everyone loved the park, especially in the daylight hours when it was always a lively place with plenty to do and see. The gardens and arbours were a constant delight for walks in any of the seasons with the changing flora and fauna, and children would be forever drawn to the ornamental lakes to feed the ducks scraps after the dizzy exhilarations of the swings and roundabouts. Much of community life happened there, concerts, public meetings, displays and it attracted people in droves, drawing them in, making them feel relaxed and content. They sensed ownership and connectedness; true common ground.

As the popularity of the park grew, events were organised during the evening hours and yet more people flocked in. However, the twilight hours attracted another breed, not sheep anymore, but those who were intent on 'doing mischief' and 'wilful damage' as councillors reported to the chief constable when asking for a stronger police presence. Looking forward a hundred years, when the park was closed at night because of too much unruly behaviour, a letter of complaint to the local press stated 'The Victorians never envisaged the heritage they left us would be abused in the way it is these days.' How little did the writer know!

The people came and went; growing up and growing old; new generations took their place but their practices, good and bad, remained unchanged. Ice-creams were purchased, tea was taken, music was listened to, lovers stole their kisses, litter was dropped, and pockets were picked, and all at the same place. By way of the stone circles and grand Gothic statues, the past had infiltrated the park from the start, enabling moments to intertwine and blur the lines of past and present, adding to the timeless feel of the moment.

Chapter Three

Little by little Estelle was getting more accustomed to her new environment even though Vicky, who was now spending a large part of her day in her childhood home, was not always there. Estelle spent more and more of her time with little Georgie, Doctor John's son. She found him easy company and felt no awkwardness with him; no difficult questions. In fact it was she who was doing all the enquiry making and he had been a mine of information. She was in awe of him, for even at his young age he had a full grasp on how one was supposed to live within the house; what one could do and where one was allowed to go. Estelle had gleaned much and Georgie had quickly taken to this new lady who would readily play with him or read him stories. This, at least, had gone down well with all the staff. Her untimely arrival had brought blessed relief as Nanny had to leave suddenly due to a family crisis, leaving anyone and everyone to attend him. Although they all loved him, looking after him meant the chores were never properly finished, causing backlog and mayhem in the normally well-run house.

John also took pleasure in Estelle's company; he was intrigued by this attractive woman who had arrived in his life in such an unexpected manner. She filled his thoughts constantly and had done so from the start. Thankfully he hadn't ignored her and walked away on that new year's night. Who was she really? How had she got there? Why could she not remember? It was such a glorious puzzle to solve and although she was improving thanks to his attentive little sister, for some unknown motive he rather wanted her not to leave. After all, he reasoned, she was excellent for George just when Nanny had left them so unexpectedly. 'Nanny... of course!' he thought, 'she could be his new Nanny.' He almost leaped with joy at the thought; it was the perfect excuse for her to stay.

The staff were less than pleased when they were told but had no choice but accept the decision, albeit reluctantly, until Nanny got back. For Estelle, it was a valid role within the household. She did not delay in grasping the opportunity, moving into the nursery immediately and making it her domain.

Vicky and Estelle's companionship flourished even though Estelle wondered whether it was an acceptable thing to be seen with the nanny. "We won't be able to do this when I start to wear my uniform; I imagine you will think it unseemly."

"Nonsense!" Vicky replied. "I am Georgie's aunt and I can spend as much time as I like with him and his nanny and no one can say otherwise." She was enjoying her afternoon in the park, watching the skaters on the frozen paddling pool practising their moves. Georgie wanted to do the same and pulled at his aunt's hand to go. She obliged him and he happily skidded around the edge of the slippery ice while keeping a firm grip of Vicky's hand. She kept her feet steady and walked, having no intention of falling. Estelle smiled as she watched from a nearby bench, lost in the wonderment of the moment. She noticed two women of smallish stature pass in front of her, presumably mother and daughter. Estelle was struck by the way they walked, or waddled; their gait governed by legs so bowed it must have been an achievement in itself for them to remain upright. They sat down alongside her and she moved up to give them more room noting the younger one was heavily pregnant. Estelle, taken aback by their deformity, put her reticence aside as she listened to their voices, full of hope for the safe arrival of the child. She felt moved to speak with them but Georgie and Vicky had finished skating and requested to go to Colleta's for some ice-cream.

"Who were they?" asked Vicky as they ate their hokey pokeys out of waxed paper on the bench outside the ice-cream parlour.

"I have no idea. They just sat down and started chatting. Surely something can be done to help women in that sort of state?"

"No, nothing." Vicky replied unemotionally and carried on eating her ice-cream in silence until it had all gone. "I feel as though I am nine years old again," she said licking her fingers before putting her gloves back on to warm her hands.

"Vicky, is it really that long since you ate ice-cream in the park?"

"I think it must be, Mother thought it beneath us to eat outside like the common people, as she put it. The park wasn't here when we were small though, I'm thinking about other outings. "

"I am sure it can't be that long ago since I ate ice-cream in a park, if I could remember. I must be one of those common people." Estelle replied.

Vicky looked thoughtfully at her companion and replied with meaning, "Common or not, it's jolly nice to eat ice-cream and pass the time of day here with you and Georgie. Come on, let's make a move before those louts pulling out the shrubs over there decide to make mischief over here." Whether Vicky was still curious about Estelle or not, their friendship was growing and any reservations Estelle may have had over class and status were seemingly of no consequence to this liberal minded young woman.

As soon as she had her brother's approval, Vicky took Estelle into town to shop for clothes of her own. What fun it was choosing dresses for someone else and all on John's account! How hugely generous of him, and so very uncharacteristic.

Chapter Four

John was not listening to what his patient was telling him. He had already come to a probable diagnosis and was dutifully going through the motions of examination in order to confirm it. He had found it difficult to concentrate properly on his work lately, his mind always wandering towards the young woman who had entered his life. The same questions repeated themselves in his head. Who was she? Where on earth had she come from and why was she always in his thoughts?

As John had put her to bed that auspicious night, as he had placed her down onto the bed, checking her body for cuts and bruises, as he had looked a little longer than necessary at the swell of her full breasts, the curve of her rounded hips, as he had turned her over, and as he had reluctantly removed his left hand from the softness of her left buttock, that was when he had seen it and it had taken his breath away. It was why, afterwards, he had been unable to sleep, why he had seized the decanter and drunk straight from it, and why he had gone through his father's archives. He remembered seeing a picture of what looked like that very birthmark before, many years ago. If he could prove it was the same one, then a twenty-eight year-old missing person mystery might be solved.

She must have been somewhere in the intervening years. Surely someone knew where she came from. He had made some general enquiries and placed adverts in the press about her in the hope that someone might come forward with information, but there had been no response. Not one 'missing person' had fitted her description and he had got no further forward. He wondered if he should have included the presence of the birthmark in her description but thought it may provoke too much of the wrong kind of response.

He suddenly remembered where he was. "It's your bronchitis back again. It's that time of year. Just take your usual medicine and keep warm."

"Thank you doctor, I wanted to be sure it wasn't anything else after losing me missus last winter. It was her chest that did for her."

"Just wrap up well, it's very cold and damp at this time of year." John did not mind calling on this particular patient. He had found life hard when his wife died, something John could relate to, and just needed a little more support than others, something he did not mind giving, and it helped with his own grief. However, he was glad it was his last call and he could go back to sitting behind his desk and letting his mind wander.

She fascinated him, there was just something about her and he was trying to put his finger on it. He found her seemingly well educated and intelligent but at the same time there was so much she did not know or understand. His sister, whom he had instructed to help in trying to jog her memory, stated that for all her good manners and charm, Estelle appeared unfamiliar with even the simplest of matters. Yet she was so forward in the way she spoke to him, not daunted by his position and so opinionated. Always ready to say just what she thought of everything, even including how he should treat his patients.

He had been surprised at her response when he happened to mention his desire for opening a hospital for poor women. She had seen it as providing an endless supply of defenceless women on whom males could practice birthing techniques 'with their grubby little hands'. He tried to argue that it wouldn't harm them as they would be heavily drugged and a first hand learning approach would improve students' skills and confidence. She argued back that too much chloroform would surely make the women delirious and unaware of what was going on. 'Quite,' he had retorted but she fenced back that drugs would anaesthetise the infants as well and they wouldn't know they had to breathe as they would be so sleep-induced. The only way he was able to appease her was to agree that a maternity hospital should be for all women, rich as well as poor, and that midwives would always be in attendance, especially when any medical staff were around. These were exactly where his thoughts were in the first place! What a tonic! She had forced him to think what his vision for change really was.

Something was happening, feelings, stirrings, things he had not felt for a long time. And her birthmark; he continued to be intrigued by it and could not stop thinking about it. It looked so pretty, just there in that place, its position so perfect and the very reason why he had chosen her name.

John, while sitting at his desk at the dispensary, had been scribbling absent-mindedly with his pen. He looked down at his note pad. "A star, oh my beautiful star!" he exclaimed as he observed star shapes all over the paper.

It was uncharacteristic of him; his usual restraint had vanished and he could not ignore what was bursting out of him. The door of the cage had opened and the grieving cavernous void was filled with a glorious light, John felt it shining right from the centre of his heart.

That mysterious woman had arrived in his life at a perfect moment; a new century had dawned; a catalyst for new beginnings. John had been grieving his late wife for well over three years now. George needed a mother. It was time, he was ready to move on. Perhaps providence had a hand in that portentous night.

Even the staff had noticed the changes in him. Charlie had heard him singing many a morning while dressing, Polly noticed him sniffing the perfume of the flowers in the arrangements and Cookie was ruffled by his ever more frequent visits to her kitchen. "Always foraging for tit bits he is!" she grumbled to Fay, after she had lately managed to tactically steer him out of her larder, her short and well-rounded stature dwarfed by his, tall and lean. "Same as when he was a boy, always hungry and always down in my kitchen looking for leftovers, cramming them in his mouth like there was no tomorrow. Oh well, I suppose it's good to see he's got his appetite back. He hasn't been the same since Madam passed, God rest her soul." Pausing briefly, she continued in good humour, "I think I'll change tonight's menu and make one of his favourites. Come closer girl and I'll teach you how I do it." Fay looked up from polishing the pans in shock. Something must be pleasing Cookie if she was going to share one of her precious recipes. "Look sharp then or you'll catch too many flies if you stay like that much longer," she added as Fay stood rigid and open-mouthed.

It was obvious to the staff that Doctor John was in love but whether they approved of the direction of his affections was a different matter. The intrigue however got the better of them and the tittle tattle was endless, especially when Cookie was out of ear shot. "Anyway," Polly began, "her position of Nanny was only invented as a reason so she could stay here with a legitimate excuse, Miss Hoity Toity. I'm sure she's in the family way too," she said, using her hand to cover her mouth for the last sentence.

"How can you tell?" Charlie asked.

"Because I just know these things."

"That's ridiculous, and stop standing there with your nose in the air. You'll be saying you're one of them mystic medium thingamajigs next."

"Don't you dare scoff at me Charlie boy." She started to swipe gently across his face with a cloth. He caught hold of her wrist to stop her.

"You deserve a spanking for that, little Miss Know-It-All." Charlie started to chase her round the kitchen table laughing with her. Neither small nor tall and with athletic frame, he was quite agile, but Polly managed to keep out of reach. How he ached to catch her.

"Shhhh! C-Cookie's coming along the passage, Charlie stop it, Mrs Cook's coming," Fay implored as the side door opened.

Estelle's new position of nanny meant she did not need to come into contact with the other staff, eating the majority of her meals with little Georgie, and this suited her nicely. It had not been easy to know how to behave, as she was still unsure of her position within the house. It was difficult to answer all their questions satisfactorily and in staying upstairs she did not have to hear all their whisperings and snubs and sneers. She was aware that it was going on and was rather bemused by it. She did not understand why people could be so horrid; this was unfamiliar behaviour to her and it was hard to adjust. On the outside, Estelle managed to hide how she felt but inwardly, things were completely different.

She was still full of remorse about her feelings when she had walked away from her old life. It was painful for Estelle to think about how she had arrived here, she was still trying to work it all out. Had she got it wrong? So much had happened since she got here, she couldn't be sure of anything any more, everything was muddled. But she had seen them together in an embrace, so it must be true. Yet she still loved him, despite his transgression, how could she ever not? He was her life! Yet she knew the gaping space that was now between them could never be filled. Her boat was burned, there was no way back.

There was no one she could speak to, not even Vicky, she was completely at a loss, not knowing what to do next. Hiding behind closed doors in the nursery seemed a solution for now. Maybe it was better that her account of things be never told, nobody would believe her. She knew she would never return; never go back to the life she had led before. She sighed deeply. 'Best I just forget then' she thought, trying to convince herself. But as she tried to forget, she felt something inside her, a pain coming from a place deep within, somewhere she could never have known to exist suddenly stirring up through her body. It burst out of her mouth, shocking her both in its unexpectedness and in its ferocity. Estelle could hear moaning but it was as if it were coming from somewhere else, not from her. The flood gates had been opened, sparing no tears. Her prolonged howls had made her hoarse. She did not know how long she had cried; nor that the whole household had heard her, turning a collective deaf ear. Only Fay understood her lonely cry. Exhausted finally and with no tears left, Estelle felt some relief in the release of it all and lay there quiescent amongst her memories. The emotion had taken her back to a time when she had once before felt such a loss. That had been so long ago; a different time, a different place far away from here. She had been so young then, so raw, but her naive heart still had feelings, it knew what grief felt like, it had already felt the hopelessness that she felt now.

"Nanny hurting?" Georgie asked hesitantly, when her weeping was reduced to occasional sobs. She looked up to see his big brown eyes framed with a frown of concern. She smoothed the creases out of his forehead. They reminded her of the permanent lines in his father's forehead and for a split second imagined herself caressing John's brow smooth. She managed to erase the picture from her mind's eye straight away, hesitant to think why the image may have manifested.

"I'm much better now for seeing you. Did I wake you? I am so sorry."

"Nanny not cry, Georgie make better." He said climbing up onto her lap. They sat there for some time, Georgie asking for songs, Estelle, clapping out the rhythms while Georgie sang his own versions. Yes, it was good to hide out in the nursery. Over the next weeks, Estelle cocooned herself within its walls, developing her own routines and rules and carving out her reason for being.

The nursery was situated at the back of the house looking into the garden and consisted of three rooms. The largest of which was where she and little Georgie spent the majority of their day. It had two large windows, both with window seats, where Estelle would read or tell stories as they looked down at the garden. She liked the nursery, it was where she felt safe and secure, and it was the part of the house she could call her own; no other self-respecting staff member would dream of entering in.

John had lately taken to eating meals in the nursery with his son and of course with his new nanny. One evening, as they were both seeing Georgie into bed, another increasingly common occurrence, John made his move. Being so close and yet so far from Estelle was driving him to distraction. Estelle's hands were resting on Georgie's cot as she was singing him a lullaby when she felt John's hand resting on one of them. There was a slight hesitation in the song as she sucked in her breath, but she carried on until the verse was finished. Her hand stayed where it was, her heart had missed a beat.

"We get on well together don't we?" he asked as he gestured Estelle to sit down.

"Yes, I think so," she replied, wondering what was coming next.

John had been turning up as if by accident when she took little Georgie out in the afternoons and then insisted that he should take both of them on various excursions. Those occasions had been full of fun and laughter and had made Estelle feel happy, as if she belonged. Only the previous week there had been a visit to the seaside by rail. They had stopped at York station and seen the Flying Scotsman getting ready to pull out after they had rested for lunch. They went for a closer look and what a sight it was. Georgie had cried at the noise when the driver let off steam and things appeared to go from bad to worse as they were completely enveloped in the vapour. Estelle had to cling onto John's arm for support; she was feeling queasy; she didn't like mist, fog, or even steam. John had immediately put his other hand over hers for reassurance but as soon as the steam dissipated she had retrieved her arm; her pulse was racing and she knew it wasn't the train causing it now. Georgie had clung onto them both and could only be persuaded to get back into their Pullman coach by the assurance that it was not a real dragon, that it was just trying to behave like one and that all brave boys got a penny lick at the seaside and could fill their buckets to the brim with treasure from the beach.

"...I thought we might take some refreshment in the little tea shop that has just opened at the other end of the park," he said. Estelle did not think this particular invitation was of a similar nature to the others. She tried to remain calm but instinctively knew what was coming.

"I'm not sure if Georgie would like that much, he can't bear to sit still for any length of time." She was trying to appear unperturbed as if the inevitable was not happening.

"Oh, I didn't mean with my son. I meant the two of us, by ourselves, alone." He was making advances but he could see she was hesitant. He sat down next to her and took hold of her hand, he took it to his lips and kissed it; his desire palpable. She withdrew it hastily, unnerved by his directness.

"I'm sorry, I'm not ready, I don't think I can, it's not the right time for me."

"Please, I should not have been so presumptuous, forgive me."

"It's not that I don't like you, you have been so kind to me, so trusting and I am forever in your debt, but I just cannot."

"I understand your reticence, it has been such a short time, but I thought that you, I thought that we..." He stopped in mid sentence and stood up. "I should never have asked. I am sorry to have embarrassed you. I shall see you in the morning as I should like to take breakfast with my son."

"But of course!" Estelle watched his brisk strides as he left the room wondering what to think. She liked John, she admired him, she felt a kind of empowerment when they were together with little Georgie, as if they were a family, but did she love him? She had never thought about it, she was always thinking of her lost love, or at least trying not to, but he kept appearing in her mind. She had not been oblivious to John's interest in her, it had been flattering, but she had not dwelt on it. What was she to do? She realised exactly what the doctor's intentions were; it would be nothing short of marriage. Estelle went to bed that night bewildered and confused. It would certainly be a good way to get to stay here permanently, but was it a moral way? Tied up in knots, she had forgotten that she had not actually received a proposal. Tossing and turning in anguish, it was a long time before she eventually succumbed to sleep.

The church clock chimed seven. Estelle turned over and pulled the bed covers around her, having to wake all too soon and face the cold dark morning. She felt sick and pulled the chamber pot from under the bed. "Not again," she moaned aloud. Estelle spent several uncomfortable minutes lying half on, half off the bed, her head almost inside the chamber pot which still rested on the floor. These repeated episodes of early morning could only mean one thing. Scrambling back on the bed into a sitting position, she puzzled at why it had taken her so long to realise. How on earth could she have got into such a situation? Head in hands, she massaged her brow, but was not able to work it out. So much had happened recently, she had not thought about what time of the month it was, she had been so ill that it could have altered everything. Reluctantly, Estelle forced herself up to face the bleakness of the day while the bitter truth overwhelmed her in wave after nauseous wave.

Letting her hands rest over her abdomen, she raised her eyes up thoughtfully. A hazy recollection came to her slowly at first but which became suddenly clearer as it burst explosively and vividly into her memory.

"We made a baby before I left!" she exclaimed. "In the nick of time! My love, oh my love!" was all she could utter until Georgie woke and needed her attention. Estelle had to think fast, she was not stupid; being pregnant and single was not good and John would surely begin to notice something. Polly had probably put two and two together already; she had taken it upon herself to empty the chamber pot when she came to change the bed sheets the day before; at least she assumed it had been Polly, no one else ever came into the nursery. Estelle took the pot and emptied it down the toilet before 'little miss prying Polly' could find it. She decided she had no choice now but to accept the good Doctor John, were he to dare to ask again after she had put him off last night.

John came into the nursery to have breakfast with little Georgie who ran straight towards him before he had time to get into the room. "Good morning my little chap, how are we today?"

"Daddy Daddy, are we going to the park today?" Georgie implored; his big brown eyes fixed on John.

"No not today son," John replied, glancing rapidly at Estelle who was attempting to look busy. She stopped and turned round clutching a laundry basket as a protective shield. She knew she had to think quickly, she took a breath and announced:

"I am sure we can go to the park if the weather fines up enough Georgie, but right now it's far too wintry. Perhaps later on, when your father is less occupied with other matters, he could spend some time with you here with your new train. Now go back to the table and finish your meal." Georgie trotted next door and went back to his breakfast happy now he had something exciting to look forward to. Estelle turned to look at his father, her eyes wide and bright.

"About last night," she began more hesitantly than she had wanted. "I was, it all came as a, what I'm trying to say is if you would care to ask me the same question, then I might care to say yes." There, she had done it and panting slightly with the anguish of anticipation she watched him lower his knee to the ground.

"Marry me," he said rather brusquely.

"Yes, I will," she replied, her voice wavering imperceptibly. She had not expected it to have been that easy. She saw John complete his genuflection as if it were in slow motion and noticed how long his fingers were, as unhurriedly, he raised his right hand towards her. How commanding it felt at her jaw as he lifted it upwards. She saw no more as with eyes closed she felt his earthy kiss on her waiting lips, another powerful hand at the back of her head. As unexpectedly as it had begun, the potent moment ended and her eyes opened questioningly as John took an awkward step backwards and left abruptly with a muttered apology. He believed himself an honourable man, his enthusiasm could wait. Estelle was left wanting and could only wait until the next opportunity, hopefully that same day. She did think, after all, she might be able to love him just a little, just enough, just once, it was all she considered necessary, all she desired at that moment. Georgie ate his porridge quietly, a little crestfallen by his father leaving without saying goodbye.

There was an awkwardness between them as John helped put Georgie to bed that evening. Estelle had watched them play together with the toy train, the confident little boy instructing his accommodating father how to lay the clothes pegs to make train tracks and use only the big books for the tunnels. A happy little scene usually, but now she was more and more impatient for the time to pass. With rising eagerness she heard the long-case clock in the hall chime the quarter hours. "Time for bed Georgie," Estelle called out when finally the hour struck. She jumped up anxious to perform this task before the ringing had ceased, scooping up the reluctant little boy. Coaxed by the promise of his father to read his favourite and longest story, he was finally safely tucked up. Estelle, who all day had thought of nothing else, was now to fulfill a mission.

They moved from Georgie's room and shut the door. With a plan in mind she decided to take control. She took hold of John's now seemingly weak hands and positioned them with intent, one by one at the very base of her spine and held them there until she could feel them squeezing her flesh of their own accord.

John stayed in the nursery that night, delighting in its attractions. He found Estelle's insistence and persuasive manner too tempting to decline, after all, they were engaged to be married now so he was obliged not to refuse her. He spent his time indulgently, studying her little starry mark as it gyrated vigorously beneath him. It was a consummate remedy for any feeling of apprehension or embarrassment at the sudden turn in their relationship.

The next morning John felt fully charged to take on the challenges of his working day. He had instructed Charles not to start up the motorcar that morning, with the warmth in his loins fuelling an energetic stride, he arrived at The Royal full of exuberance for life's little delectations. Preferring to walk the mile and a half to his workplace, he had taken pleasure amongst the snowdrops and aconites that carpeted the greens of the park, and recalled the events of the previous night.

He could hear the moans as he entered through the ward doors and a relieved looking nurse almost pushed him along as they bypassed the rows of occupied beds to the left and right before reaching the side ward. "She came in last night and has kept everyone awake with her expulsive noises for hours."

"Who told her to come here?" John asked.

"No idea," was the reply.

"Well if she can make a noise like that there is still plenty of strength left in her, which is a blessing. Are my forceps ready for use?" The question was more of an instruction and one of the nurses rushed off to retrieve them from the steamer. However, as soon as John saw the tiny heap splayed on the bed presenting a gargantuan abdomen he changed his mind. "Prepare the operating theatre I am going to carry out a caesarean section. If *you* don't know why she needed to be here," he snapped, "at least someone with some sense did."

Washing his hands in water and carbolic as he prepared for the operation, he wiped away any lingering thoughts of the thrills of the previous night. He was ready and prepared as the tiny woman, ravaged by rickets was put under the ether by his medical student and washed with more carbolic by his assistant. "Knife," was all he said before the operation was under way.

John had already performed several similar operations and was perfecting his technique each time. He had only lost one of his caesarean patients up to now. This had been due, he felt, to the fact that the woman had already lost too much blood before she had been brought to him. Due to her condition of placenta praevia she had haemorrhaged when her labour started and consequently died from the shock of losing too much blood. If only his technique had been swifter, if only he had known about her sooner; he had watched the life slip out of her and been powerless; as powerless as when his wife had passed away.

Haunted by these images he had been prompted to improve the approach to pregnancy and help eradicate the dreadful suffering that many women endured to give birth, costing some their lives, and many of them their child's. Even from his limited experience he could see that tragedies might be averted if the women could be followed during the antenatal period of their pregnancies. Pregnancy toxaemia, placenta praevia, twins; all and more would be diagnosed and treatment plans made. He was in favour, unlike others of his craft, of raising up the new profession of a trained and registered midwife. She would be a practitioner in her own right, who would monitor pregnant women by running clinics and going into their homes to teach basic hygiene and nutrition. He wanted to abolish all handy women, or at least have them properly trained, if they were able. He was already using a few of his beds for antenatal purposes. Women had been turning up at the hospital to see him, for he was rapidly gaining a reputation, and he had been admitting them for rest and recuperation, particularly those who were weak having undergone many pregnancies in quick succession.

Unfortunately, however good his popularity was with the women, his fellow professionals were mostly opposed to his ideas. They had tolerated what they thought were whims up to now only because his father George Brown, an eminent physician in the town, had been highly thought of. They assumed that as there was no money to be made in midwifery, he would soon come to his senses and shut down his fanciful clinics and return to real medical matters. However, his displeasing behaviour this particular morning which the other doctors soon heard about, had stretched their patience.

"Why did you not call for me sooner?" asked John. He was angry with the nurses but had waited until after the operation to address them.

"But the night staff said to give her a few hours as nothing was progressing."

"Of course nothing was progressing. Did you not look at her condition? How would anything get through a pelvis like that? How long have you worked here? Haven't you learnt anything? Her uterus was so thin it was on the verge of rupturing, I was just in time. Words fail me. Where's Sister Thompson?" He stormed down the long Nightingale ward leaving the poorly trained nurses to raise their eyebrows at each other and wonder why he was making such a fuss as everything had turned out all right in the end. The wrath of Sister Thompson was however another matter. It had been her afternoon off the day before and she was not yet back from visiting her mother. They hoped the good doctor may have cooled down by the time she returned and not mention his fury to her.

John was far from cool. He had gone straight from the ward and into a difficult meeting to which he had been summoned by his fellows to explain his reasons for performing the operation. He knew none of them would have done so; none of them would want to do something which might damage their precious reputations. He paced up and down the corridor until called and entered the large heavily panelled room. He took some pleasure in its imposing grandeur as it helped dwarf the daunting physicians. From a distance they looked like small children in their oversized leather chairs, most of their bodies hidden by a long table. He was gestured to join them but all the chairs around the table were occupied. John could see a collection of smaller wooden chairs at the back of the room. He walked down the length of the room to take one, his footsteps noisy on the wooden floor. Finally seated, the proceedings began as if already in conclusion.

"A caesarean operation is still far too dangerous," Professor Wilson's voice trumpeted out pompously. John's senior, who liked to preside on all matters concerning obstetrics and midwifery, offered his condescending guidance. "Far better to get out the Simpson's perforator my dear chap. After all," he snorted, "it's only one infant and the wretches always come back for more."

Chortling followed from the others and John felt his blood boil inside him; he hated that medical men were capable of slighting others less fortunate than themselves. Surely they knew better than that? He did his best to keep himself in check but could not help but retort; "That particular wretch and others like her are incapable of delivering an infant through the birth canal as you well know and if I were able to follow Radford or Sinclair in Manchester and prepare those women with ricket-torn bones for elective caesarean section antenatally, the operations could be conducted in a calm and controlled manner."

"How on earth would that change matters? It sounds like a waste of everyone's time to me." The chortles changed into raucous laughter.

"Where do I start?" said John exasperated. "Firstly it would eliminate the continual repetition of pelvic digital examinations and manipulations which cause much distress and possibly introduce infections. Secondly it would prevent the exhaustion of the mother so she is in better condition at the start of the operation." He looked around them all trying to look at each individual in the eye. "And thirdly there would be plenty of time to arrange for those who cared to further their knowledge and develop their technique to come and observe the operation." He stopped there and waited for their reaction, panting slightly with the emotion of speaking his mind. There was silence from the group. One of them lit a cigar and the match struck as if wordlessly voicing their contempt. He drew in the vanilla smoke, lay back in his chair and blew it out leisurely clearly aiming it straight at John.

"Well, let us all hope she survives and then we will not need to say any more on the matter." As the professor spoke John's shoulders tightened but he had no more to say. It was no use; he could get nowhere with them, they would not change their old ways, that had been a foregone conclusion. Frustrated with their lack of vision, he rose from his seat so abruptly that he knocked it over. He picked it up; almost throwing it back in place and stomped down the lengthy room, the echo of his hammering feet pounding in his ear drums. The voice of Professor Wilson penetrated his rage and John's advance to the door faltered. "Of course there is the, ahem, small matter of payment for use of the theatre." An assault of patronising eyes pierced his very being as he reached for the door handle.

John was tired of the ongoing war with his seniors and they had won yet another battle as they knew exactly where his weak spot lay; money. Once outside, the doctor bent forward massaging his brow completely beaten, his shoulders slumped against the heavy polished mahogany door. The guffaws came again loud and clear from the other side yet he was determined to find a way around his opinionated elders. Some of them were very near to retirement so the obstacles would disappear naturally, given enough time. This was unfortunately not the biggest challenge for John. Up to now he had managed to fund his midwifery through his other medical practices. These days however, in an attempt to make a difference, he was spending so much of his time in his chosen speciality that as a result less money was available. Some other sources for financial support were desperately needed. It was unthinkable for him to use the inheritance from his father as it would be self limiting, and now he had a wedding to think of...

"My little star." Estelle crept back into his mind. He stood away from the door took a deep breath and squared his shoulders. It would not be easy. He knew he still had some authority at the hospital thanks to his father's name and had the drive and conviction to make it work. He checked his pocket watch and marched back to the ward shouting for Sister Thompson to begin his morning rounds.

Chapter Five

John wanted Estelle to move back into the blue room which was next door to his; three years of celibacy was long enough for any man. Estelle, however, insisted on sleeping in the nursery after the announcement of the engagement. She argued that little Georgie had grown close to her and it would be too upsetting for him if she were to leave him by himself. But this had been an excuse; so taken aback by the intensity of emotion from their one intimate encounter, she was afraid. She had only ever loved one man and she was not ready to admit to anyone, least of all herself, that she might find pleasure with another. Troubled by her feelings she used the excuse of pregnancy to keep her distance and with John's honourable nature he obliged and adhered to the more respectable arrangement. Even so, he relished spending the larger part of his evenings in the nursery however innocent his assignation, and little Georgie was delighted to see so much of his father.

It had not gone unnoticed that he had stayed all night in the nursery and his bed was left untouched even though it happened only once. Even Cookie had something to say. "I shan't be able to look him in the face again. How could he? Madam barely cold in her grave, what is he thinking of?"

Charlie grinned, "I don't think that's too difficult to work out."

"Well if he couldn't wait, he could at least be more discreet. He's straight up to that nursery and with all the excuses not to need a chaperone and as for her, the jumped up little trollop that she is." Fay and Polly exchanged glances. Cookie had never said anything like that before having always come to Estelle's defence. They both put their hands to their mouths as if in disbelief.

"Well I reckon he deserves a bit of fun after all this time," said Charlie, still with a grin on his face.

"Well you would, seeing as you're a man," Polly chipped in.

"A bit of fun? E's going to marry that bit of fun." Cookie's voice was getting higher and more animated.

"Only 'cos he has to," whispered Polly to Fay with her hand covering her mouth.

"Er, hello everyone, I was just wondering if there was any honey. Georgie's throat is a little sore and it may help him." A pin could have been heard to tinkle on the stone floor if there had been one falling. Cookie was quick in motioning Fay to get the honey jar down and searched hastily for Georgie's silver spoon in the table drawer herself, but nobody could think of anything to say to break the awkward silence. "Thank you," Estelle proffered, leaving as quietly as she had come in.

"Do you think she heard us," whispered Fay eventually.

"Well you never said anything so you're all in the clear," replied Polly. Anyway, she knows what she's doing, the manipulating little bitch."

"That's enough!" Cookie shouted, her voice returning to its usual trumpet.

"Well it's no more than what you were saying. Anyway, you'll see what I mean when a premature baby arrives all chubby and big, if you get my meaning."

"Really?" asked Fay, the penny dropping slowly.

"Really," replied Polly with a wink.

Estelle arrived back in the nursery trying to be brave. She had heard every word, and she did feel like a manipulating bitch but it had only been to survive. She could not think of any other way. With John it had been so easy. He had begun to make arrangements for a marriage immediately but when Estelle announced she might be expecting a baby, he hurriedly erased all ideas of a summer wedding, the sooner the better would be more preferable, all things considered, he thought. By the end of April she would be about ten weeks by his calculations. Estelle thought otherwise but she kept that to herself. She would be more like seventeen weeks. She could feel herself expanding already. Polly was right, this baby was going to be a very good size considering it would be so premature but she would have to cross that particular bridge when she came to it. For now she would just have to tighten that wretched corset. She smiled at the big brown eyes of her charge. "Now then Georgie, this is my magic medicine."

When John came home from evening surgery Charlie met him in the front hall and helped him out of his outer clothes, taking care not to shake off too much of the rain water that had soaked them.

"Nasty weather doctor, hasn't let up all day."

"Indeed, thank you."

"Er, Polly asked me to enquire if you wanted the fire lit in your room tonight."

"Ah! well, er, no thank you Charles, not tonight." John gave a small cough then added "Er, I think I shall brave the cold and damp just now, there are many others who have not got that choice." He gave another cough and headed up the stairs to the nursery. He paused half way up, "Could you say to Polly that I will eat in the nursery tonight?"

"Very good doctor," Charlie replied, barely able to stifle a grin. John held his gaze at Charlie for a moment then carried on up the stairs.

"Daddy I've got a frog in my throat!" shouted Georgie as he saw his father opening the nursery door. John checked in his son's mouth and then, satisfied it was nothing serious, patted him on the head and went over to Estelle.

"How's my best girl?" he asked attempting to place a kiss on her cheek. He missed as she leant away, she didn't dare to reciprocate; she still felt the bond with her first love; it wasn't right to... "Is something wrong?"

"Oh it's that lot downstairs," Estelle replied, looking away.

"You mean the staff?" he chuckled. "You do have an amusing way of describing them. Yes, I do believe they suspect something. Does it matter? They are only staff, after all."

"Well it matters to me. I'm not used to being spoken about from where I come from."

"And where is that? Have you remembered something?" John asked hopefully.

"No, not really, nothing new anyway."

"Give it time, maybe after the child comes you can relax and things may return then."

"Relax after a baby? Aren't they a full time job?"

"Well yes, I suppose so," laughed John. "Speaking of which, we must get Nanny organised."

"Nanny? I'm the nanny," Estelle retorted.

"But dearest girl," said John; his second attempt to embrace her failing as she feigned business. A little bewildered and very frustrated; Estelle had held him off since... since he had asked her to marry him. Did he now have to wait until they were married? His temper was frayed. "You are very soon to become my wife, you cannot be Nanny as well."

"Have I not proved I can do the job?"

"Yes, of course! However we still need a nanny, whoever heard of not having one? Anyway I have already put things in motion. George's previous nanny is free to return at a moment's notice; she is no longer tied by family commitments. You will need to move out, and soon." Estelle knew his decision was sounding final and may have to live with it. She would have to work out how to change his mind but for now said no more on the subject. Meanwhile, she busied herself on thoughts of where she was to sleep when the 'real' nanny returned and studied the various rooms carefully.

Including three attic rooms, the house had seven bedrooms and the nursery suite. There was one room at the back of the house next to the nursery, and three at the front. The second and blue bedroom, the one where Estelle had first slept, had a connecting door to the master bedroom; John's room. The bedroom at the back appeared to be the third, and similar in size to the blue room. Vicky had slept there on the few occasions she had stayed the night; it had been her room when growing up. The fourth room, the smallest but the one Estelle most favoured, was next to the master bedroom and closest to the bathroom. Estelle liked the opulence of the bathroom. The wash basin was set in carrera marble and rather grand, with a glass shelf and brass soap dishes. The kitchen range's back boiler brought hot running water to it and the white-enamelled, claw-footed cast-iron bath. She enjoyed nothing more than to relax in it and wash her cares away and admire the magnificent stained-glass window above her. However, she knew it would be anticipated that she move back into the blue room with the connecting door into John's. It wasn't that she didn't like the room, it was that John would be so close... it would be so easy for him to... she wasn't ready, not yet; not until they were married at least, and even then? How could she when her heart still lay with... Yet John was so...it was getting harder to turn away from him; and the blue room was near to the nursery; it would be expected she take it.

In the small amount of spare time he had, John had continued to try to solve the mystery of who Estelle really was and where she had come from. The wedding banns had started to be read out at the local church and he did not want to go through the complication of a special marriage licence. Her intriguing birthmark held the key. The very same birthmark that was depicted in his father's newspaper cuttings, the ones he had pulled out the night Estelle arrived.

John and Vicky's father had been killed eight years ago in an unfortunate rail accident. He had been up to Edinburgh combining a visit to see John who was in the middle of his medical training there, and to attend some lectures which had ended late. He had taken the night sleeper back home to Yorkshire. The train had gone as far as Thirsk but the signalman there failed to prevent it from running into a goods train. The exhausted railwayman, having recently lost a child, had fallen into a devastating sleep resulting in the death of seven of the passengers and injury to a further thirty nine. On account of his rigorous training, John was only able to make very brief excursions back for the funeral and for arrangements for his mother and younger sister.

On one such occasion, when going through his father's papers, he found a few old newspaper cuttings of medical reports that his father had enjoyed collecting. Amongst them was a clipping that was more intrigue than medical, collected, John supposed because it happened locally. It was a report of a baby that had gone missing in a nearby road. What caught his eye at the time was an artist's drawing depicting a birthmark on the baby's buttock. This would be a clear mark in any identification and was a perfectly symmetrical 'Star of David'. He had a vague memory of some such incident when he was a small boy, but had long ago forgotten about it. He read on to discover that the child had been but a few hours old and the third daughter to Lord Peters who had taken temporary residence in the area. According to the press cutting, the fault had lain with a nursery maid and a transcript of her statement had been printed. Apparently she had been tending the child when a caller came to the side door of the residence. As she was by the door, she took it upon herself to open it. Her statement continued to say she placed the child temporarily on the floor as she needed two hands to operate the locks and by the time it was done, an errand boy whom she realised had been the caller was cycling off carrying a large package. Presuming the package to be of importance, she ran after him momentarily forgetting her charge. After successfully relieving him of the package, she returned to the side door but the baby was no longer there. The report went on to print that no ransom note had been forthcoming and enquiries were continuing.

As far as John recalled, the baby had never been found. He needed to make some very discreet enquiries. This was why he had made an initial decision not to mention Estelle's birthmark in the newspapers when asking for anyone who knew her, too many old scars might be brutally opened. If she really was the long lost daughter of Lord Peters, he had to tread carefully. If Estelle had been kidnapped all those years ago and been brought up by some gruesome fiends then it was no wonder she would prefer not to remember. How wonderful if she might be reunited with her rightful family. He penned a letter and had Polly send it out; he already had the address, he had sought it out immediately. It was what to put in the letter that he had been reticent about and had finally taken Vicky into his confidence. "How would the family feel after twenty eight years of nothing?" Vicky wondered. "Or worse, supposing they'd had regular ransom notes which they'd refused to pay and in the end the kidnappers had given up and thrown her out onto the streets?"

"Now you're being too fanciful," snapped her brother, "You're being no help whatsoever.

"I'm just attempting to cover all the possible circumstances that's all," Vicky replied and stood up as if to leave, rather hurt at his attitude.

"I suppose you are right. Anyway I think I know what I shall write." John was contrite, he realised he had been abrupt and decided to change the subject. "I hope you are being of some help to Estelle? I mean with the preparations for the forthcoming event?" He felt he had to clarify the subject as Vicky was looking very quizzical.

"I am presuming you mean your wedding. Of course I am who else is there that could help? Anyway, I have recently been through it myself; I know what has to be done."

"And how is it going?" Vicky put her hand to her heart as if trying to protect herself and held herself steady while the other one reached out for a nearby chair.

"Oh, er, I er, I'd rather not say," she answered hesitantly.

"Why ever not?" It was John's turn to be puzzled, but then remembered how his sister's mind worked. "I meant the wedding plans, not your marriage." He put his hand on his chin and began to rub it. He saw that she was agitated by his question but still came back at her in his usual abrupt style. "Look Vicky, I'd rather not be the one to say I told you so but, I told you so."

"Oh John, I know you did, but I was in such a mess when Mother passed away and he was just, well, he was just there. I think he caught me when I was at my most vulnerable." The words tumbled out from her mouth so unexpectedly that she sat down in surprise as if she had no control over what she said. John seized on the opportunity.

"What's the problem, am I allowed to ask?" He spoke more gently now, he never liked it when his sister was upset.

"Oh John, I don't know, I just don't know why but I'm so unhappy." Vicky burst into tears and let her brother dab her cheeks with his handkerchief. When she had composed herself she continued. "I get up in the morning and he has already left at some beastly hour. I go about my day not knowing which direction to take as he has left no instruction. He comes home at night having missed the evening meal saying he has eaten at his club and then goes up to bed in the guest room. I don't know what I'm doing wrong. Am I a bore to him already? I'm sure married life isn't supposed to be like this. I just don't know what to do." She started crying again.

"Dearest sister, no it isn't. You poor thing, please don't upset yourself. I thought something was amiss but did not realise how bad it had been for you, no wonder you jumped at the invitation of something to do, maybe you need an occupation, something to fill your day that you can chatter about in the evening."

Vicky thought for a while. John always knew what to do.

"You are absolutely right, I do need an occupation, I've even gone to some of the women's suffrage meetings to fill in some time. I actually feel as if I'm becoming like an old maid." John looked enquiringly at her. An old maid? What on earth did she mean? He slowly put two and two together.

"You mean he hasn't even, you mean the, er, the marriage is not consummated?"

"Oh John, now you embarrass me but, no, it is not." She started to cry again.

John moved toward the window of the library and back again to the oak desk in the middle of the book lined room then over to the door then back to the window, his movements mimicking his angry thoughts. "My God! How could he?" The words boiled out as if from a steaming kettle left unattended to splutter furiously. Despite her despair, Vicky was amused; her brother always looked a little ridiculous when he was angry. His nostrils flared out, he strutted about, and he looked like something between a cockerel and a bull about to charge.

"I think you mean how could he not?" Vicky replied, managing to alter an embarrassing giggle to a fit of coughing. She had finished crying and felt the better for it.

John felt sorry for his young sister. She had married in haste after the death of their mother. Their dear mother's heart had never been strong after she had contracted rheumatic fever as a child but had got noticeably worse after losing her beloved husband in such tragic circumstances. She soldiered on as best she was able for many years, her health deteriorating little by little. In the end she was unable even to get out of bed before her breathlessness overcame her. Even though Vicky had lovingly cared for her every need, three weeks later she was dead. If only Vicky had waited for her grief to abate and not said yes to the first man who appeared, but she was so headstrong. Any decent suitor would have been sensitive enough to give her space to mourn. He had his own misgivings about the gushing and exuberant Jason but could not understand why. However he now wished he had not let him ask for her hand but he had been too wrapped up in his own life at the time and assumed she would have refused him. He now felt guilty and remorseful for not taking more care of his little sister and wanted to make amends. "Come and stay here for a while, see if he notices," said John.

"Thank you, I think I will when the child arrives, but it's not the answer."

"No, but it might cause some changes." He stopped suddenly. Child? What do you know of any child?"

Dear brother, did you think I didn't know?

"But I expressly asked Estelle not to speak of it until after our marriage." John's nostrils began to flare. Vicky started giggling again.

"She didn't have to. Just because you're a doctor doesn't mean you have the monopoly on the diagnosis of a pregnant woman. Good grief John, it's not exactly difficult. Anyway thank you for the invitation. Meanwhile, my dressmaker is already busy sewing and I have engaged caterers to work with Mrs Cook, she is preparing menu suggestions as we speak. I must get on, Estelle will be wondering where I have got to, I promised I would take her to town, she does not feel ready to be on her own." John's usual pomposity turned to abashment as he watched his sister flounce out of the room. It had never entered his mind that anyone else would know his fiancée was pregnant and wondered how many others knew or may suspect. He shuddered at such thoughts and put them to the back of his mind, and kept his thoughts on his sister.

She and John had always known Jason, there was some vague family connection and their respective fathers had become close friends following Mr. Brown senior's marriage. Jason's grandfather, the late Mr. P. J. Bartram, had been very successful in the clothing manufacturing business, and being something of an entrepreneur, had acquired the land surrounding Meadowsring believing that the growing town would have need of it for housing stock. The house that John had been brought up in and now owned was originally an old farmhouse on the land. Mr. P. J. Bartram had sold the house for a token sum to John's father when he had wedded Mr. Bartram's favourite niece.

It was due to these family connections that John had not considered more about Vicky's decision and he was now infuriated mainly with himself. Not having had to consider matters of being a 'full blooded male,' his supposition that Jason was the same as himself was automatic. As young boys they had romped around together easily enough exacting adventure out of every opportunity. Later though, on reflection, Jason had tended to prefer to pair up with Vicky rather than him in their childhood games and there had been some form of distance between him and Jason that he never fully understood. However it had never caused him any dislike of the fellow. On the contrary, his liveliness and vivid way of thinking had coloured his youth and sparked his own imaginations. He assumed Jason had favoured Vicky because he was sweet on her. So why now had he married her but failed to do his duty? What on earth was wrong with him? His nature could not allow him to understand, but being a fair minded man, he did try to see it from Jason's point of view. Maybe although Jason loved her, he had known her for so long it was like a brotherly devotion to a sister? Yes, that must be it! That he could understand. Satisfied with his explanation he was reassured that the situation would change in due course; no man could hold out forever, he knew that from his own experience. As for her disclosure of attending those dreadful meetings with those alarming suffragette women, he could only hope she would come to her senses.

Chapter Six

John and Estelle's wedding went as all well-planned weddings should. The bride was beautiful, the groom gallant, the day rushing by far too quickly for those who had invested many hours in its planning. It was a small assembly but some remarkable names had appeared on the guest list. There had been much correspondence between John and Lord Peters and it was agreed that he and Lady Peters would attend the service in order to see Estelle without her raising her suspicion. John had said nothing to his fiancée on the subject and Lord Peters was also being very cautious. The idea that their long lost daughter may have been found alive and well after so many years had been difficult for him to digest and he was naturally concerned how Lady Peters would take the news. So worried in fact that he had not explained in full to his wife why they were to attend the marriage ceremony. He had managed to convince her with a story that he had once had connections with the groom's father and felt honour bound to attend.

The guests shivered in the chill of the church as they waited expectantly for Estelle to walk down the Gothic nave. They were not disappointed, her beauty struck them all and warmed the most frozen of hearts. It was almost too much for Lady Peters who could not help but stare at the stunning vision. Clasping her hands to her breast she almost fainted as the contours of Estelle's profile, framed by ostrich plumes from her overly large headdress, brushed past. It was not from the marvel or the emotion of the occasion that she felt so overcome for she had attended many weddings. No, there was something else about this bride that had caused her heart to leap. She recognised something but could not, at first, comprehend what.

Twenty eight years had gone by since Lord Peters had been required to sort out the estate of his wife's deceased uncle and needed to be in the locality. Against all advice, as she had been near to her confinement, Lady Peters insisted that she be by his side. She had been particularly close to her uncle and wanted to make sure his affairs were in order. The lovely park where she and Lord Peters took a stroll the previous day had not then been created, and the house they had temporarily occupied still looked out onto meadowland.

They, like everyone else, had been intrigued by the discovery of the standing stones, but had never had an opportunity to see them, until now. They were fascinated and even more so as the ancient circle had been so close to their residence; on the doorstep, as it were. While standing in the middle of the stones, Lady Peters had a thought. They could see the door where their baby daughter had disappeared from, it was the side entrance of the house and directly faced the park. Immediately, her mind travelled back to that time; she could remember staring down from that very door at the large and uneven stone step that served as the threshold. She hadn't been able to tear herself away from it at the time in the hope her daughter might be returned. She now wondered if it might too, have been a standing stone; innocently unearthed by builders oblivious of it's true nature who, expeditiously, put it to good use. She and her husband moved nearer to the house and the door step but found it impossible to tell; they could only see the one façade, they could not be sure. They moved on to take tea.

After the disappearance of the Peter's third child, life had not been allowed to stop, yet it had felt as though a great rock had wedged itself inside them. Their family life continued with their two other daughters, two years apart in age and very much alike. They had taken most of their features from their mother, her long Roman nose, prominent chin, hazel eyes, curling blond, but now greying hair. One was taller, like her father's family but that was the only difference. While they were growing up their mother thought constantly about their lost sister; did she look the same as them or had she taken more from their father whose devilish eyes flashed when in mischievous mood? Quite the reason why she had accepted his proposal of marriage all those years ago. She was tortured because she did not know if she would recognise her child if they were ever to meet again or if she would be able to love her as much as she had yearned for her all through the years. Today, watching this bride, she slowly understood that she was seeing something long wished for, something she had hoped and dreamed about for much of her adult life. So similar in shape was this girl's face to that of her own daughters' that her heart lurched and beat at such a pace that she had to sit down and gather herself. The stone that had been lodged in her chest began to crumble away.

Seeing his wife's reactions coupled with his own, was just the verification that Lord Peters needed. Estelle was indeed their missing child! After all this time, this was surely her. He helped his wife back to her feet and supported her with his arm and watched in fascination as the wedding ceremony took place.

Lord and Lady Peters were the last of the guests to leave the church as the little party moved outside. Lady Peters was having a little difficulty in composing herself. Her emotions had gone from elation to disbelief to anger to fear and back again, she did not know what to think or believe. Had her husband known of her whereabouts all the time and only now chosen to tell her? Was it really her? Had he spent all this time looking and only now found her? Is it fate that brought them there today? Is her imagination toying with reality? After all this time would she really be sure to recognise her? There was no real doubt, not this time. In the beginning she had looked at every passing child in the hope of finding her baby. Every town she visited was a place of renewed hope; every year that went by she tried to imagine how her child might look. Even today she had wondered how she would have looked like as a bride, just as she had when before their other two daughters had married. She had not felt such elation since giving birth that third time; the moment when she had been handed another perfect infant to cherish by the physician, when the pain and doings of childbirth were washed away by the attendees and she had been made ready to receive her husband, Austen. That same joy was in her now as she had stood in the pews during the service. She wanted to embrace the girl and hold her close; she wanted to shout out to each and every one that she had found her long lost daughter, but she could only tremble inside as a lifetime of discipline of rank and title restrained her. During the service she dared not speak to Austen. He would not know what she had been thinking, her belief that this dazzling vision standing before her God repeating her vows was their lost child. She looked across at him for the first time as they prepared to leave their seats. He was already looking at her intently. "Well Sybil?" he asked as if he had been expecting her to say something. She could contain herself no longer.

"That's our child. Oh Austen, she's our baby girl. We've found her!"

"Yes my dear, I really think we have." He replied, uncharacteristically taking her hands in his own.

"Oh Austen, did you know? Why didn't you tell me before about her?"

"I didn't know."

"You didn't? Then how have we come to be at this wedding?"

"I will elaborate; I did not know for sure, I wanted to be able for us to see her without her knowledge. The plain fact is that I have been in correspondence with the good Doctor John Brown, for the last few weeks. I received a letter out of the blue from him stating that he thought he had found our missing child. Of course I was wary of such a letter but at the same time curious. I vaguely remember reading about his father's death in the paper and so knew he was of good standing."

"His father's death reported in the paper makes him of good standing?"

"I mean, by way of complete coincidence, it was his father who was the physician in attendance when you gave birth here in this town so unexpectedly. If you remember, our child had a curious birthmark on her buttock shaped like a star."

"Of course I remember, it's imprinted onto my heart."

"Well, this fellow Brown sent me a drawing of the very birthmark that he claims is on the buttock of the girl outside this church as we speak. Before I saw her I did not know how I would be able to verify this for myself but now having seen her face and seen your own reaction, I believe that the birthmark is not the only necessary proof of identity."

"Where has she been? Who took her?"

"Unfortunately, this we have been unable to ascertain. She has suffered a lapse in her memory following a recent accident. Brown found her lying in the road and being a 'Good Samaritan' as well as a good doctor, he took her into his care. Destiny appeared to strike and he fell in love." He looked at his wife, his eyes glinting faintly. "All highly romantic, just the sort of thing you ladies love to gossip about," he added.

"Indeed!" retorted Lady Peters.

Lord Peters continued, "My dearest Sybil, however delighted we are feeling, I do believe we will need to proceed with caution in this matter. We are strangers as far as she is concerned and will mean nothing to her. Wherever she has been and whatever she remembers or doesn't remember, she will have no recollection of the day she was taken from us; she was only a few hours old. We barely had time to get to know her ourselves."

"I have always known her; I have never forgotten her, not for one moment of my life since. She has been in every shadow, every sunset, every gust of wind, each time the girls cried, I heard her cry too, each time they laughed I imagined that was the way she laughed, I could go on and on."

'And you do,' thought Lord Peters to himself. "Come," he said aloud, "let's go outside and meet our beautiful child and wish her well." They took their place in the line of the unassuming guests and waited to offer their congratulations. Lady Peters gulped at the chilly air barely able to contain herself. It was almost too much; her heart began its recognizable but indecipherable skipping of beats again.

"Of course Estelle isn't your real name is it? You must have another name, do you know what it is?" was all she could manage to say as her turn came. Of all the things one might or might not say to a daughter one had not seen for twenty-eight years. There were so many things she might have said, so many things indeed she should have said and that was all she could utter. The bride looked at her quizzically before answering. She had noticed this fine lady whilst in church but only now could she see her more closely. There was something about her, she did not understand it but there was something she identified, some sort of connection. It unnerved her slightly but she replied brightly.

"Have we met before? Please forgive me but I have been introduced to so many people recently I have found myself to be in such a muddle as to who might be who." Her answer made Lady Peters smile. Despite the uncultured accent, her voice sounded so familiar that she laughed in the pleasure of hearing it which fortunately put her heart back to normal rhythm. She felt more in control of her emotions.

"Yes, we have met before, but it was many years ago and you were rather small."

Sceptically, Estelle replied "Oh really? "I am sure that cannot be the case."

"Well I am very sure of it; however it was an unbearably brief meeting and a long time ago but it remains deeply embedded in my mind. Please, may I kiss the bride?"

"Of course." answered Estelle, confused. Feeling the need to underline the fact that this was definitely their first meeting, continued, "I am sure that it is quite impossible that you have met me when I was small." Lady Peters stroked Estelle's cheek with her fingers wishing she had first removed her glove.

"How beautiful you are," she said as she placed a kiss on it and then before she could help herself she found she was whispering into her ear. "I know your true name, whatever you call yourself now." The bewildered bride was left speechless. There was absolutely no way this woman could possibly know who she was.

"What did you whisper in her ear my dear?" asked Lord Peters when the queue had moved on.

"Nothing, just how lovely she looked." She could not meet his stare, she kept her eyes lowered but she was glad that she had said it all the same.

"Good! Well I think that went well. A good formal introduction was all that was needed. No need to hurry these things. We will invite them to take some tea at a suitable time after their honeymoon."

"How did you find Lord and Lady Peters?" John asked his bride as they mulled over the day. Estelle was not entirely sure how to reply but did her best.

"Intriguing." She thought for a little while. "Are they family friends? I haven't heard you mention them before?"

"Not exactly, I have been corresponding with Lord Peters over the matter of your birthmark."

"My birthmark, whatever has my birthmark got to do with anything?" John grinned as his hand began to search for it; he had had enough of talking and had other more pressing things in mind. Slowly moving her skirts out of the way with accomplished hands he located her little brown star.

"It has everything to do with who you are and how I feel about you." He knelt down as he turned her half around and began kissing it. "....and precisely why I fell in love with you. May I?" he asked on tenterhooks. Now they were married he could not let excuses of being pregnant get in the way of his eagerness any longer and, when he thought about it, there were very safe ways of going about things. His excitement was getting the better of him, he did not wait for an answer and moved her final petticoat out of the way. He started under her navel and Estelle, nervous about the inevitable, yielded as he gently worked his way down. Surrendering to his advances she could only gasp with irrepressible joy as her mouth accepted his explosive pleasure and, as he languidly tasted her delight, she came blissfully to rest. Her heart, normally in another place, another time, where she could have never imagined what was happening to her now, was beating wildly with abandon. The guilt did not set in till later.

March 1900.

My love,

I write this letter as I once promised I would, and I will write again trusting that one day you will hold my letters in your hands and learn something of my life after I left you.

I am so sorry; I know you will have no answers. Please forgive me, but I can never come back to you even though I think of you all the time. I do not think I had a choice, the circumstances were too great and I had no control over them. Even though I cannot be with you I will never stop loving you.

Please try to understand.
All my love and always yours. X.

Chapter Seven

John had always been very unforthcoming about his first wife Eleanor but it was plain to see that Polly had been devoted to her. Even now, the first Mrs. Brown's hair brushes kept reappearing on the dressing table no matter how many times she stuffed them in the drawer. Clearly Polly could not entertain the fact that Estelle was now Dr. Brown's *significant other*, she really was so infuriating. Estelle had to get rid of the brushes somehow but she couldn't just throw them away. She had an idea. She pulled out a dress that she had never had the opportunity of wearing from the wardrobe. It was rather low cut and far too tight for her. She wrapped it into a bundle with the brushes inside. After locating some brown paper she made a parcel of it and placed the bundle under a loose floorboard, killing two birds with one stone; she hadn't wanted John to know about the dress. It was very elegant with its bodice adorned with beautiful lace but had been a wasteful expense. Her figure would never be like it had been, her baby, when it came, would put an end to that! The dress could stay there for now, out of sight along with the brushes. She picked up her favourite book and sat down to read quietly, any activity, these days, tired her out.

Estelle, naturally curious, had wanted to know all about her predecessor and had tried to glean information soon after she arrived. She wondered what kind of woman Eleanor was, how she had looked, what she had been interested in. Trying to be as sensitive as she could, Estelle had asked John about her after finding a photograph of him with a noticeably striking female in the drawer of his desk. She had replaced it carefully and respectfully but it concerned her that she felt a little uneasy that John had been married before. All John would say on the matter was that his first wife had been tall with chestnut hair and then changed the subject. Vicky eventually furnished her with all the details making her wish she had never asked. It was evident that the Browns had been a devoted couple; Estelle had not liked the jealous pangs that engulfed her every time she thought of it.

Purely by chance one day in the library Estelle came across 'Mrs. Beeton's Book of Household Management' when searching for something to read. Inscribed on the front page in impressive script was 'To our darling daughter Eleanor on your wedding day. Let us hope that this little offering *goes a long way in keeping you in holy wedlock. God be with you.'* Unlike the brushes, she had no intention of throwing it away and was reassured that she felt a small bond with the late Mrs. Brown in that they had both had had to delve into the unknown. Poor Eleanor, she hadn't come through whereas Estelle was still here and able to struggle her way along.

Estelle snapped the pages of Mrs. Beeton's expertise shut and wondered how she could put into practice the advice about dealing with employees from such an authority. It all seemed so easy; if she showed her spirit and was diligent in her tasks, her domestic staff would follow. It was easier said than done! She got up awkwardly from the blue velvet upholstered chair which was not quite the correct shade when matched with the wallpaper, and waddled over to the window. Not much was happening in the street below, the bustle of early morning was long past. She could never manage to get up in time to see the world of the early risers. The steady flow of figures on the early turn stoically heading towards the factory had long since dried out. The dogs chasing the delivery boys on their bicycles and barking at the legs of those pulling their barrows, had returned to their back yards to doze in the quiet. Even the taxis had finished collecting and delivering those with business in town. It would soon be the time for the nannies to fill the streets with prams and small children on their way to the park. Yes, she was glad she was Mummy now and did not have to be up with the rest of the early risers like Nanny. Little Georgie loved calling her Mummy too and did so over and again when she cuddled him to sleep.

She watched Mr. Walkpast, so named by her, because he walked past the house several times every day. She could not think of why he needed all those trips backwards and forwards; there was something curious about him, she could not put her finger on it. His faltering step in the otherwise deserted street broke her reverie. Maybe, as Mrs. Beeton says, if she were to have the essential quality of an early riser then it would be certain she would have an orderly and well-managed house. Estelle pondered this for a while but came to the conclusion that she wanted to be herself, and an early riser she was not. No, she would have to find her own way of dealing with things. She wanted and needed things to change. After all she was the mistress of this house; it was *her* house and soon to be her baby's. She would not let them get the better of her.

A thought struck her; had she missed a trick? Mrs. Beeton's name went hand in hand with food! She sank heavily down on the chair again and rubbed her swollen tummy.

"Not long to wait now." She was savouring growing a baby inside her. Its active kicks were a pleasure, a wonder, a marvel, a little miracle; she could not decide which. She felt so proud of herself and hated having to try to hide it. She wanted to show it off; say to the world 'look at me, I'm having a baby, isn't it wonderful!' At least Vicky shared her exuberance and had helped to gather together the layette joyfully, as if she were expecting a baby herself. Poor Vicky, no hint of a pregnancy and how long had she been married? Estelle felt she would have to do something about that, something wasn't right, not right at all.

By the time the baby arrived, Estelle had asserted some authority over the staff and contrary to what Mrs. Beeton said, she decided to start with changes to the food menu. Although delicious, it was heavy on the waistline and Estelle knew that hers had become larger than it ought. Yorkshire pudding, pies, pastries and treacle sponges had to be stopped. Her pregnancy was the perfect excuse as it allowed her to be fussy.

Uncharacteristically, Mrs. Cook turned out to be very compliant with the amended menus, seemingly relishing the experience of experimentation. The different combinations of ingredients Estelle had stipulated had turned what was a frenetic, kitchen with Cookie at the noisy helm, into a calm haven. Fay had full responsibility of wrapping and labelling all the newly acquired herbs and spices and placing them alphabetically in the recently commissioned spice drawer. She delighted in her responsibility and studied the usage of each; information that procured surprising respect from Cookie. Fay, for probably the first time in her life, glowed with pleasure and little by little, as her confidence and knowledge grew, her body unfurled; the hunched frame of a frightened creature slowly vanished. Everyone downstairs thought she had suddenly grown but Fay's fresh countenance was noted in a different way by Estelle. She had been much troubled by the gaunt-looking tweeny maid who had lurked in the corners, unnoticed by most of the household.

Providing Fay with books on herbs and spices and their culinary usage and the introduction of a more cosmopolitan menu had been a brainwave. Little Georgie began to follow Fay everywhere hoping to catch a glimpse of her beautiful feathers that she surely concealed under her skirts. He compared her to the story of the ugly duckling, one of his favourites and insisted that Fay was going to turn into a swan very very soon.

Polly of course proved more difficult. Referring again to the oracle Mrs. Beeton, who wrote that all servants should be expressly told of their duties they were expected to perform, Estelle duly called for her and stated plainly every position of work she expected from her just as Mrs. Beeton stipulated. Strangely, she got the impression that Polly looked down her nose at her every time they met. She always did what was asked of her, but so disdainfully that it would often reduce Estelle to tears. She did not know what to do; if she went to John she would feel as if she were a failure. Knowing she could never bring herself to dismiss her, she simply put up with the situation in the end.

Charles, in contrast, had never caused her any worry; he seemed to be as accepting of her as John himself had always been. In any case he was John's responsibility and Estelle had little to do with him. He always had a smile on his face and made one feel happy just by being around him.

The baby's cries brought her back to the present. She placed her hand on the crib, looked in and smiled. A warmth crept into her heart. Ever since she had given birth she had felt a sense of permanence, that she really did belong in the house and it was not just temporary. She felt settled now as if the umbilical cord that had connected her to her baby had also connected her to this house, to this place for ever. She thought back to nearly a year ago and remembered everything she had tried to put to the back of her mind. 'No I must never forget. How could I ever forget?' she berated herself. How could she, when there was little baby Rose, lying there, so beautiful, so perfect? Estelle would tell Rose everything one day when she was older. She knew that she would have to tell her the truth. One day when the time was right, Rose would be told who her father was and where she had come from.

"Now now, there's no need for all that whimpering and carrying on." Nanny marched into the room and picked Rose out of her crib with the firmness that all nannies employed. "Are you hungry?" she murmured a little more gently, and handed Rose over to Estelle. Rose began suckling earnestly and Nanny carried on bustling about satisfied that Estelle was producing adequate amounts of milk for the baby to thrive.

Nanny had returned to the house soon after the wedding though Estelle had been very indignant about it. She could not see John's point of view at all in taking Nanny back and they had argued repeatedly about her reinstatement. Estelle felt perfectly capable of taking care of little Georgie even after she had had the baby. John who thought she was being ridiculous was quick to say so. This hurt and upset Estelle, imagining that the marriage was over before it had barely begun. It was Vicky who helped change her mind. Nanny had been with them ever since Vicky had been quite small and was almost part of the family. She and John loved her dearly; she had been the one who had bathed them, put them to bed, tended their grazed knees, and above all had been there for them when their parents had died. How could they not love her? Considering this different perspective, Estelle understood that she would never have her way and resignedly admitted defeat.

She surprised herself however by taking a certain liking to Nanny. There was something about her mannerisms, her strait-laced ways. She was always in her uniform, even on her afternoons off. Her dark hair was scraped back in a plain style, she did not seem to care about matters of fashion. Yes she was not young, but older women still cared about their appearance didn't they? Maybe she did in so far as her collar and apron were always crisply starched and clean, her shoes always polished, but that was about it. "Have you never wanted to get married and have children?" Estelle asked her one day. Nanny stopped abruptly what she was doing, folding little Georgie's vests in precisely the same way in order to produce a neat stack to put in the drawer. She put her hand briefly to her heart and looked wistfully into the air before carrying on as before.

"Certainly not," she replied and then excused herself and started coughing and needed to find her handkerchief. Vicky later told Estelle what she had learned about Nanny. Apparently when she was eighteen and about to be married, her betrothed had succumbed to a fever and died within a week. She had been so terribly distraught and resolved to remain a spinster and in mourning for the rest of her life. She could not face such a loss again.

"She must have been deeply in love," Estelle said to Vicky.

"I suppose so." Vicky replied with a shrug of her shoulders not knowing quite how she must have felt.

When Rose had suckled until almost bursting, Nanny cleaned and changed her. Perhaps John had been right after all, having Nanny was a good thing. She had certainly jumped to Estelle's defence when John wanted her to have the baby in hospital. Nanny was not reticent in speaking her mind to John and was horrified at the thought. "In that place of death and pain, over my dead body," she had put it.

"But she will be in the right place if things are not straightforward." squeaked John, feeling as if he were twelve years old. It was hard to talk Nanny down; she had a way of winning arguments.

"Look at her John, what in God's name could go wrong?"

"Anything and everything, at any moment. You could never understand."

"John," she said more gently, "I understand why you might be worried, but confinement at home where she will feel safe is the best place. I know of a good midwife as I am sure you do, and you of course will be here if needs be, so there's no need for any concern."

"John please listen to what Nanny has to say, she is usually right, isn't she?" pleaded Estelle. The idea of some interfering old handywoman messing with his wife was too ludicrous to contemplate but he had had a long day, his temper was short and he did not have the strength to argue.

"Just in case anyone has forgotten, I do know a bit about childbirth," he grunted in defeat as he stalked out. He never won with Nanny. The two women grinned in allegiance.

Yes, having Nanny around had definitely been a good thing Estelle thought as she picked up Mrs. Beeton to see what she said about child raising. Afterwards, when she was alone and Nanny had taken Rose out, Estelle began to write on some paper taken from her desk.

September 21st 1900

My Love,

Last time I wrote I could not bring myself to tell you something but now it is time. It will be a shock for you. Here goes! We have a daughter, Rose! And she looks so like you. I remember the time of her conception, can you? Oh my dearest love, can you remember the last ever time we made love? It was then. Feeling her alive inside made me feel so close to you, your baby inside me telling me she was there, linking us together. When labour began all I felt was joy, each pain bringing us nearer. As the pains grew in their urgency, I went to bed early; I did not want to tell anyone that my labour was starting as I did not want any interference. By the time John discovered me I was only just managing to stay in control but I just had to do it on my own and in my own way. She arrived boisterously into our world later than she should have and all was well! The world felt good on that day. I wish for the time you might meet her, for I am sure that time will come, one day. For now, I will give her enough love for the both of us and when the time is right, tell her all about you, about us.

John is a good man but he can never replace you. Please do not ever be jealous of him, I had to stage-manage things so he would believe Rose belongs to him. I shall never tell him that you are her true father as he looks after me well and I could never hurt him. You are my true love and you always will be for the rest of my life, I miss you so.

All my love, always yours, X.

Chapter Eight

Everything was taken care of; cooking, cleaning, looking after the children. She supposed that if Nanny had not been around her time would have been fully occupied, but she was, and really did seem to have everything in hand. Estelle did in fact spend a lot of her time with Georgie and Rose, but had the freedom to leave whenever she liked, or whenever Nanny said so, which was perhaps a more accurate description. Consequently, Estelle found she had nothing much to do except wait for John to come home in the evenings. Alas, his nightly thrusts of frenzied, self-indulgent pounding may have helped him unburden his anger towards the rigidity of hospital policies, but only added to her frustrations. She could understand up to a point and was willing to placate him, but it left her dampened and suppressed.

One afternoon while chatting with Vicky, who had come to stay after the confinement but had since returned to her own home, Estelle found herself discussing her feelings. She wanted to do more than just sit around and take tea; surely her life had more value? She would love to be more of a help to John with his work. She had plenty of time on her hands and she was very interested in all aspects of childbirth, especially now as she had become a mother. There must be something she could do as John was always so occupied but seemed to be getting nowhere.

Vicky listened attentively, she was no stranger to tedium and voiced her sympathies. She put down her cup and took Estelle's hand in hers as she reached out across the table. Part of her was incredulous as to what her friend and sister-in-law was saying. How could someone who had everything be so bored and unfulfilled while she, who had every reason to be unhappy, was trying to keep a brave face. But she had a big heart and was always ready to help. "We could go shopping if you like, or there is a new art exhibition at the gallery if you would prefer," she added hastily sensing the shortcomings of shopping. There was no point in buying a new dress if one's husband wasn't appreciative.

"Actually Vicky I was thinking more on the lines of seeing if I could help women during their confinements, but you have just given me an idea."

"Good grief Estelle, you have one baby and now you think yourself as an expert."

"What I mean is trying to help John with his work. You know how desperate he is for reform and is trying his best to train the local midwives to be more efficient and set up clinics but he lacks the funds and backing to do so. The idea I have is that maybe we could organise our own exhibition, or some such thing which would raise some money to help him. By the way, I have been delving into his midwifery books and he always answers my questions without ever patronising me. It's something I very much respect about him." Estelle almost surprised herself when she added the last sentence; she had never thought that she might have more feelings for John than for Rose's father and it made her blush.

"What about a sale of work?" Vicky interjected enthusiastically. "While they are there on the doorstep so to speak, they can have instruction on proper feeding for their babies and the importance of keeping them warm and prevent things like cold feet!"

"Brilliant idea, but we have to find a way of organising it."

"Not as problematic as you would imagine. I could gather a host of women who would be more than pleased to be engaged in charitable works. I will get on to it right away. It feels good to have a purpose, something to be occupied with. Vicky drained her cup and jumped up but Estelle motioned her to sit down.

Vicky is everything all right at home, I mean with you and Jason?"

"Quite all right thank you." She gave a cough and hurriedly changed the subject. "We must think of a name for ourselves. I must go, things to do you know." She left the drawing room and Estelle finished her tea reflecting on the afternoon's discussion. How marvellous if she could be part of John's efforts in being a vanguard for midwifery advancement. It all sounded very grand and, she mused, might put an end to his appalling short temper and even better than that, his heaving haste in the bedroom. That might certainly alleviate her own dissatisfactions. Her pondering led her on to thoughts about Vicky's marriage. John had inadvertently disclosed the issue of Jason's failings. 'But,' she thought, 'Jason *had* to consummate the marriage. And he will.' She was sure of it.

Estelle had held assumptions about Vicky and Jason's relationship ever since she had first met Jason. At the time she had tried not to show it but her surprise had not gone unnoticed even by John who had quizzed her later about her reaction. "Why did your jaw drop when you were introduced to Jason, do you know him?" Estelle had looked at Jason and immediately realised something about him saying 'of course you are' as they had shaken hands.

"Not really, just his kind." Estelle had answered after a long pause while thinking what to say.

"His kind?"

"Oh you know what I mean, but I'm not sure Vicky does. Why on earth did they get married?" she asked.

"She was in a vulnerable state and he was in the right place at the right time and swept her off her feet as they say." Estelle chuckled at that last remark.

"I hardly think he would do that. Does she know?"

"Know what in God's name?" John was becoming exasperated.

"John don't you know either? Isn't it obvious? He likes men!" John breathed quickly and deeply. Of course, that was what was strange about him; that was what had raised his suspicions. How on earth had he not figured it out? No wonder the marriage had not been consummated, Jason had used the marriage to hide behind.

"Poor Vicky," he said out loud without realising but inside he was fuming. Estelle, however, when she had thought more deeply about it, refused to believe that women were completely off-limits, it didn't fit at all. There was something about Jason, she had felt such an affinity with him from the moment she had met him; a familiarity, as if she had always known him. She was sure that he would be capable of providing offspring, somehow, he just needed to be pointed in the right direction. She needed to find a way.

John was impassive about Estelle and Vicky's charitable ideas. "It's all very well raising a few pounds but my dear girl, we would need thousands! Look, if you would really like an occupation, why don't you think of some changes around this house? You are mistress now and it is right for you to have it as you would prefer. I will engage Jones again if you would like; he is very good, very reasonable rates."

Estelle looked about her. The hall in which they stood was already impressive with a beautiful mahogany staircase and deeply wainscoted walls and the black and white checked floor tiles reflected the light from the stained glass window up to the landing. The library was completely panelled in mahogany, nothing to be done in there; the parlour, it wasn't used enough to warrant changes; maybe rearrange some of the furniture; she hated that the kitchen was in the basement but at least it kept the staff out of her way; the bedrooms, when she thought of them, well, what was the point really? They were perfectly fine as they were. What difference would there be if the wallpaper was changed? She was resolute, as usual.

"No, there is absolutely no need in changing anything at all."

"Good," said John, markedly relieved. "Anyway, to other matters, please come into the library, it's time to tell you something." She had to be told where she came from, although he had as yet no clue where to start. Their conversations had not touched on the Peters since their wedding night and considering Rose was almost three months old now, John felt confident he wasn't going to lose another wife from childbirth, he felt the time was right.

"No no no! You have got to be kidding! I don't believe for one moment that she could possibly be my mother nor he my father, not for one minute." His thunderstruck wife banged the library door behind her, grabbed her hat and coat from the hall stand and rushed outside trying to catch her breath. She leant against the front door and bent forward clutching her knees and gasped at the biting December air in panic. She needed to run away, she did not care where. Just as she thought her world was settling down, it was crumbling apart yet again and she needed some respite. Her hat and coat still in her arms, she began running as best she could, even though her long petticoats and skirts caught at her legs and her stupid corset was too tight. Her hair came loose and got in her eyes but she carried on. She reached the lake in the park and stopped abruptly. Realisation dawned. That place where she had feared to tread, that place where she felt nausea and trepidation, without a thought as to what she was doing she had just, as it were, spirited herself through the east gate and found everything was still normal! Estelle sat on the bench at the lakeside and looked around, waiting to catch her breath. It was truly a beautiful place; she had forgotten how healing it had been for her back in January, its timeless presence such a comfort and it was here that she had drawn strength. She watched a moor-hen swoop and land delicately on the water, she saw the uniformed nannies with their charges and prams parading down the main path towards the north gate, she noticed the old man, Mr. Walkpast using a stick to keep an eager dog at bay, she smelt the bronzed leaves in the late autumnal air, and she heard the birdsong change as a rain shower threatened. She felt a resonance with the whole world.

She thought about what John had told her in the study. He had begun by saying they had been invited by Lord and Lady Peters to visit but she had soon coaxed out the truth as to the reason behind the invitation. Could it really be true they were her parents? In her wildest dreams she would never have thought she could be a daughter of nobility. She laughed out loud, amused by the very idea, but then life had already dealt her the strangest set of circumstances and maybe this was the next fanciful episode. She tried to think about her childhood and if she could glean anything from her memories, but she of course could not think as far back as being a newborn baby, when she was supposedly abducted from an open door. Estelle tried to piece together the snippets of information her own mother had passed on to her about her coming into the world. Something was in the back of her mind, something about how she came to be named. It suddenly became the key to information that had been locked away for such a long time. A story her mother once told her when she had questioned why she was called 'such a stupid name' as she once exclaimed when feeling bored and and in the mood for goading someone.

There it was; the answer to a mysterious kidnapping stared her in the face. She realised something that her own mother would never have considered, nor imagine that her supposed daughter may work out. Her mother had never given birth to her; she was not her real mother after all, not one jot. She had already been given her name by the Peters and her mother had unwittingly kept it. In that moment she was fully awake, fully present, fully aware. She was returned, and in her rightful place.

Drenched by the cloudburst that eventually unleashed, she made her way back through the east gate and let the waves of understanding of what had happened after her birth flood through her body. Dripping all over the freshly-mopped tiles in the hall as she entered the house, she thrust her hat and coat to Polly and ignored the unambiguous tutting as she clattered upstairs in her muddy shoes. She showed no fear; neither her mother nor anyone else could hold her back.

Estelle's meeting with her 'apparent parents', as she liked to call them, went rather well. Lady Peters had written constantly beforehand, informing her of family history and accounts of her two sisters. Two of them! Surely one was more than enough to fill requirements. She would have been more pleased if one had been a boy; she would have liked the idea of having a brother. However Lily and Violet, her 'apparent sisters', were both married with two children each, both with one boy and one girl. "Violet has stayed in society but Lily was unfortunate enough to lose her heart to a mere businessman. What can one do in this day and age?" Lady Peters entreated hoping Estelle would have the answer. She, John and the children had accepted an invitation to the Peter's estate at Tiplin Hall to join the Christmas festivities for a few days. As the wine flowed, so did the conversation. It did not seem to matter to her alleged sisters that she had been absent most of their lives and Lily had even remembered the event of the stolen baby. They chatted endlessly about children and husbands and fashion and how ghastly it must have been to be abducted. Estelle simply agreed, not knowing what else to say about the matter, but more importantly she felt accepted. The family had immediately welcomed her and all had shed tears including herself; there was no mistake that she was one of them; she looked so much like them. "It's as if half of her is Lily and the other half Violet. It's so uncanny." Lady Peters repeated over and again.

"That's incredible my dear. It's almost as if they were related," replied her husband facetiously. Estelle was quite taken with her 'apparent' father. His dry sense of humour, usually unnoticed by the rest of his family, amused her. He was also prepared to discuss broader topics of conversation than dresses and who was doing what with whom. They spent an entire afternoon in conversation sitting together in a shuttered window seat in the north hall looking out onto a long border to the right and a topiary yew to the left. The large and very ornate Jacobean fireplace sported a huge fire which warmed the whole rear of the house including the back stairs and first floor. By the time tea was served he had gleaned her opinion on various matters from the women's rights movement to the plight of the poor and learned a little of her character. She had lifted his spirits, not only by being returned, but with her lively conversation. Finally he could talk about important issues that really mattered with a member of his own family. She must be invited again, soon. Little Georgie and his new step-cousins had been sent to find the adults and the five children charged down the large passageway towards them shouting boisterously. Lord Peters let them clamber all over him; he loved to have his grandchildren around. Their happy voices, bright and pure, resonated through the aged rambling halls; just what was needed to bring the old place back to life.

My love,

     I have been given some news that has been hard for me to get my head round and I think it will be the same for you. I have been told that I was abducted soon after I was born. My mother and father, who I have known and loved all my life, are not my flesh and blood. My real parents are Lord and Lady Peters (Austen and Sybil; look them up) and I am the third of three daughters. Apparently I simply vanished while being in the care of a maid. That is all I know and I am still trying to understand. I thought I should let you know.

All my love, always yours. xx

Chapter Nine

The occasions when Estelle had been in Jason's company were few; he hardly ever came to family gatherings, always with the excuse of a busy work schedule in his family's textile company, conveyed by the over-compensating Vicky. When he had graced them with his presence, his friendly manner was a welcome stimulant compared to John's stuffy colleagues. There was a fine line between making polite topical conversation with them at their tedious dinner parties and not upsetting their weighty notions of self-importance. Estelle had to bite her tongue many times; she had to keep them sweet for John's sake.

Estelle had tried many times to see Jason on his own but it was proving very difficult to arrange; he was never home alone when she called. In the end she decided to write to him saying she wished to speak to him "on a matter delicate in nature." Estelle hadn't known how else to put it and hoped Jason would be too intrigued to ignore it. She still wasn't sure how she was going to approach the subject of the marital bed; hopefully she would be inspired.

Inevitably, curiosity had got the better of Jason and they arranged to meet in the tea rooms on the way to town on the other side of the park. A convivial atmosphere greeted Estelle as she stepped inside, provided mainly by the warmth from the huge oil burner. She looked about for Jason and spotted him in the far corner beyond the large serving counter gesturing for her to come over. Although quite a well-made man on account of his love of food, with boyish looks framed by curling blond hair and eyes the most beautiful shade of blue, he did look pleasingly handsome. She walked towards him slowly, and perhaps somewhat apprehensively, avoiding the beautifully laid tables and the numerous identical curved-back beechwood chairs as best she could. He had already ordered, the tea tray and cake stand arrived just as she sat down. After some initial chatter, Estelle decided to begin the offensive. "Dear brother-in-law, I have to ask you something, the question has been burning on my lips for quite a while."

"Oh do go on, sister-in-law, I do like a bit of excitement. I take it that it's to do with the 'delicate matter' as you put it so thrillingly?" He pulled in his chair and leant forward in readiness. He took a sip of tea just as the words leapt out of her mouth.

"I would like to know why you married Vicky when you would manifestly prefer a man as your lover." She could not believe how she had come out with it so brazenly. The many ways of broaching the subject had made her brain swirl and her wakeful body toss and turn during the small hours of the recent nights. Her strength of character had grown in-spite of emotions jostled by motherhood, desires thwarted by a preoccupied husband, and finding out that her mother was not her real mother at all. She might not yet be aware of her rising strength but she was certainly demonstrating it now.

Tea sprayed in an explosive burst from Jason's mouth and peppered the crisp white table cloth as Estelle's statement shot through his ears like a bullet. A fit of coughing ensued and culminated by his face becoming such a shade of beetroot it caused people sitting at adjacent tables to ask if he was all right. "Yes thank you, I am perfectly well thank you." He answered standing up and adjusting his collar in a futile attempt to regain his composure. Estelle watched and waited uncomfortably. He hovered at the back of his chair wiping his mouth with his napkin and made as if to say something then touched his lips again, then coughed once more. Eventually he gained enough self-control to speak. "Not here; outside," he said cagily. He felt in his pockets for some change and thrust it towards Estelle while trying to propel his chair out of the way of his escape. He marched out obliging Estelle to pay the bill for the tea. Another step forward - Vicky had always managed the matter of payment when she and Estelle had been on their outings; she was getting better.

She rushed outside as soon as she could in time to see Jason entering the park by the main gate at the top of the street. She continued and found him on the way to the bandstand sitting under the weeping willow, head in hands. "How did you know?" His words were only just audible but Estelle knew he did not want anyone to hear, though no-one was around. It was far too much of a cold and damp January day to be sitting outside. Anyone who was about his business was walking too briskly to make any meaning from a snippet of conversation. Mr. Walkpast however was in the distance, almost running along. 'So, he's here again,' Estelle noted as she observed him almost lose his footing on the greasy wet earth.

"Let's just say I can tell. The point is what are you going to do about it? You cannot destroy Vicky like this, she deserves so much more."

"And you think I don't know that?" he hissed back at her. "Do you not understand how it tortures me to be like this, to be this way; abnormal?" He gave a deep sigh before continuing. "Look, Estelle, if you really want to know, I thought if I married Vicky it would be all all right, but I can't, I just can't."

"Can't what? Jason. We are talking frankly here aren't we?" It was a while before Jason replied. He had thought that Estelle wanted to ask for his help in persuading John to take some interest in her fund raising ideas. The topic now under discussion had come as a bolt but in a way, he was glad to have it in the open; it had been eating away at him and making him sick with worry. Maybe it was time.

"The fact is, Estelle, I do love Vicky, and I do, you know, want to be married in the true sense of the word, but, but..."

"But what Jason? Please, try and tell me. After all, a problem shared is a problem halved."

"All right, I'll tell you what I can't say to her although I'm quite shocked that I'm talking to someone about it, my affliction that is. It's about my sensitivity towards other males, it's so wrong."

"But lots of men have very strong bonds with each other," she encouraged.

"Not like this, like mine. Oh, it' all so ghastly." His whole body shivered at his thoughts. "It was at school," he elaborated, "I acted perversely, with other, other, with the seniors, they made me. It's in my mind all the time; it won't go away." She put her arm round him as he blew into his handkerchief, oblivious to the grey and dreary mizzle that echoed his state of being. "How can I give myself to her when I'm so defiled?" he continued, "How can I sully her when she is so fine?" Estelle managed to stifle a giggle, Jason was beginning to sound melodramatic. But what a relief! He had been vilified by a gang of bullies and now he believes he is homosexual. He might be a bit effeminate but that was all. He realised he did want Vicky and it was only his self-imposed shame that got in the way. Jason continued to pour out his heart while his sister-in-law tried to mend it, but in due course the rain got too heavy to ignore.

"Come on, let's get some shelter in my house," she said getting up. Jason followed like a puppy dog. "Before we arrive, I've got some things to say to you Jason. Firstly, it doesn't necessarily make you homosexual. Secondly, you and Vicky love each other and are married to each other and nothing ought to get in the way of that. Thirdly, you must understand those older boys instigated what happened and intimidated you because of the power they had over you. It wasn't your fault. You must understand that."

"It wasn't my fault," he repeated. Jason was quiet until they got to the front door, "It's a strange feeling, but I have an impression of being so much lighter. I never thought I could be free of my guilt, I will think further about what you have said."

"That's magnificent, it's a new beginning," Estelle replied, pleased she could help, but then recognized she had stayed out too long; her breasts were heavy and Rose would be hungry. "We must get inside."

"Yes," he said tentatively and then smiled. "But no thank you I won't come in, I've got things to do at home; I think I need to talk to Vicky. I'll hail a cab. Goodbye, and thank-you very much."

'Alleluia!' thought Estelle. Despite the depressing weather, life might be about to become somewhat brighter for Vicky and Jason.

They never spoke of it again, but a few weeks later, a large bouquet of flowers arrived for Estelle with a note from Jason that said simply 'Yes, Magnificent,' and when Vicky called the same afternoon she had a curious air of contentment.

Dearest love,

I write today to tell you that I am feeling better about the whole situation of my parentage. I spent Christmas with them and we all got on very well. However, that is not why I write this letter; I want to tell you about Jason. He is the husband of Vicky, John's sister no less. It's as if I have known him all my life and it's such a strange feeling. He is such a tonic and you and he would have got on so well. If you only knew of the conversation I've had with him recently, you'd be astonished by it all. Such intrigue! He had convinced himself that he was homosexual because of an incident in boyhood. We had a very long discussion about it, Vicky and a happy future depended on it, and now I think he's busy enabling her to produce some offspring!

All my love, always yours. x

Chapter Ten

John entered the parlour, a large glass of single malt in his hand. He hovered by the fire and took large draughts of the whisky. He had been in a meeting at The Royal arguing a case for providing the town with a lying-in hospital for pregnant women but felt he was on the losing side of a long-fought battle. Was it just he who felt the need of a proper training school for midwives and only he who cared about mother and child welfare? Was he the only one who understood how hundreds of babies' lives had been sacrificed and how hundreds more had gone blind or been otherwise afflicted through want of proper sanitation and attention at birth? Some infections could so easily be prevented if only things were kept clean. He had heard that nurses would bring sheets from their own homes into the houses of the poor and Sister Thompson had told him the story of a friend who had bathed babies in pie dishes as there was such a lack of equipment in some households. On top of that, he had received a letter from John Ballantyne, a contemporary of his father, an obstetrician in Edinburgh who had just had a book published 'Antenatal Pathology and Hygiene'. John had read the book and rejoiced; someone else shared his aspirations! They had corresponded regularly; this latest letter proving that even an eminent physician such as Ballantyne, was facing opposition; his ideas were deemed 'too impractical' by officialdom. He dropped the letter and sighed, wondering if the world had gone mad.

Estelle brought the children down from the nursery. She wanted to divert his mind; she had sensed his mood when he had gone straight towards the drinks cabinet in the library. "Bad day?" she asked as she kissed him on the cheek. "Is there anything I can do to help?"

John shunned her greeting, paced around the room and replied curtly. "Can you build me a hospital? Can you train enough nurses to staff it? I think not. No Estelle, there is nothing you nor I can do!" Instead of showing her how pleased he was to have her back he had acted unchivalrously. It wasn't his intention and ashamed at his behaviour towards her, he drained his glass and managed to swallow his anger down with the liquor. It helped bring him to his senses. Estelle had been away visiting her parents and his only company had been his darkening moods and they were clearly getting the better of him. He kissed her, sealing his apology on her lips "I'm sorry, I don't want to take it out on you." Little Georgie, seeing that his father had softened, appealed for attention and John gestured for him to sit on his lap as he sat back down. He and Georgie chattered away leaving Estelle deep in thought.

John was always busy at the hospital and Estelle had needed to occupy her idle hours. Her self-assurance had grown and she had confidently enjoyed several jaunts on the train taking the children to see their grandparents on her own, even Nanny had been left behind. While at Tiplin, the subject of John's wish for a maternity hospital had been discussed at length. It happened that Lady Peters was something of an expert when it came to fund raising. She had been on the committee during the building of their local cottage hospital. Estelle had found her to be a fountain of knowledge and had learnt so much from her. Her father also wished to give her his help in whatever way he could. "You have political clout and I'm sure that will prove to be very useful," Estelle had told him and her choice of phrase had caused much amusement. But he had an unexpected surprise for her. He and Sybil had discussed it and they both thought it the correct thing. However it took her completely by surprise; it was so generous a gift. He even apologised after he had shown her a painting of the property they wanted to donate as it was in a far worse condition than its image portrayed. He also begged to be excused for taking the liberty of engaging an architect to draft some outline drawings to extend the property. He thought it best to be fully prepared when they presented their plans to the authorities to change its use into a hospital.

Estelle could not thank either of them enough for being so benevolent and kind and over the months thoughts and ideas for a new maternity hospital had slowly developed. Nothing had been said to John as he never had time to listen to her 'blethering' as he put it and a complete arrangement had to be in place before she wanted to present it to him. It was taking a long time, but yes, maybe she could build him a hospital; at least she had to give it a jolly good try. Over a year had gone by and Rose was eighteen months old now. It felt like she had been born yesterday; she understood now what her 'apparent' mother had said, how the years would fly by.

Nanny came in to take Georgie and Rose up to bed leaving John and Estelle on their own. Rose was growing fast and was toddling everywhere giving Nanny such a hard time chasing after her. She should really have retired but when little Georgie came along she had not been able to refuse when asked to be re-employed. Then of course there was that new little bundle of joy, Rose. Yes, she was still very much needed so she decided not to retire quite yet. "I have some good news to tell you," said Estelle as soon as Nanny had shut the door.

"Do go on, I need something to lift my spirits."

"Your sister is expecting a baby this August." John looked at Estelle as if he did not understand what she had just said. It made her giggle. "I got it wrong about him, obviously!" she explained.

"Well, thank the Lord for that. Oh Estelle, that is good news, now that has cheered me up. I will go and see her tomorrow, make sure she is well."

"I'll go with you; it's been a while since I've been to call, she comes here so often I hardly feel the need."

With some difficulty, Charlie pull-started the Arrol-Johnston and drove it round to the front door listening to the engine noise. He was concerned about its sound and would have liked to drive it a little further as he thought there may be a problem. However John would not hear of it; he was keen on driving himself and dismissed Charlie, insisting it was fine. However, the car had coughed and spluttered along, eventually giving its last gasp half way up an unreasonably steep hill. Charlie had been right in his suspicions! John and Estelle had no choice but to get out and walk the final mile. "We'll go by the post office and send a boy to tell Charles so he can come and see to it. Damn, it had better get us to the theatre tonight." said John.

"Dirty petrol," claimed Estelle. "Charles will fix it." John did not even think the comment worth a reply and they ventured on chatting about 'The Importance of being Earnest,' the play they were going to see at the Grand that evening. Estelle vaguely knew where they were going but had not paid much attention until they turned a corner and walked onto the top end of Reid Street. She stopped in mid-sentence. She was explaining to John that Lady Queensberry, an acquaintance of her mother, had been the 'real' Lady Bracknell, having lived in Bracknell. "She's the mother of Bosie, you know, Oscar Wilde's..." She clutched John and stared wide-eyed at the large building in front of them. It was run down and dilapidated but there could be no mistake. It was exactly the same as the painting her father had shown her. "What is it, do you remember something?" asked John, ever hopeful for the disclosure that her memory had come back.

"No, no, it's not that." She sounded wistful, far away. "John," she continued altruistically, "what if I tell you that you are standing in front of your maternity hospital?" John laughed emptily. "No I mean it. I know you have dismissed my and Vicky's ideas, but listen now. This old building happens to belong to my supposed parents! It's part of an estate from my supposed," she stopped and revised what she was going to say, "from my mother's family. They both admire and respect you and see you as a pioneer in your field and their wish is to present it and its grounds as their way of helping you to achieve your ambitions. And that's not all, we have lots of plans to raise money to build extensions and kit it all out. It was all supposed to be a secret until we could sort out the legalities but now I've seen it, oh John, I think I'm going to cry. It's all slotting into place; I can see it now, a wing on this side, an extension on the back an entrance porch on the front." Her last sentence came out in sobs, she was quite overcome.

For once, John was lost for words and held his wife close saying nothing, his mind elsewhere. He was remembering her as that lost little soul in the street whom he had taken into his home and brought back to health and then fallen in love with. The same woman he was holding now; her strength and determination was shining through; she had come so far and he hadn't really noticed until now. He had been so engrossed in his own problems he had neglected her, shut her out, ignored her offers of help, separated himself from her; even used her when he needed gratification. What sort of a man was he to have done that? He had clearly lost sight of what really mattered and all the while she had been by his side, making plans to help the future of obstetrics in his town and all that he had ever dreamed of. He wanted to shout with joy, to lift her up off the ground and dance with elation and tell the whole world how much he loved her but his reserve forced him not to. "Thank you," was all he could say, "Thank you so much my little star." He really must, he thought, be more open with her.

When they returned from their visit by cab to congratulate Vicky, Charlie had already retrieved the car. "Dirt in the petrol," he explained when John asked what had been the problem. "Cleaned the carburettor, put some fresh petrol in and she was away." John supposed Estelle's diagnosis of the problem had been a lucky guess and thought no more about it with the understanding that women could not possibly have knowledge of the intricate goings on of a car's engine. In case it happened again it was decided they would stick to the original plan of Charles driving them.

The excitement of the play over, John was interested to find out how far the plans for a maternity hospital had advanced. They had touched on it only briefly at Vicky's house and he wanted to know more. Estelle told him about it at length after they looked in on the sleeping children. Their conversation drifted onto the subject of women dying during childbirth. It was an opportunity for Estelle to coax out information about his first wife. "The time you and Eleanor had together with little Georgie must be very valuable to you."

John realised he should have anticipated the question but it struck him as if he had been punched in the stomach. He lowered his head and took a deep breath; he needed a little time, but he had told himself not to be so closed, he knew he must start talking about Eleanor at some stage. Estelle waited patiently, her heart beating fast; he was going to open his heart; admittedly about someone else, but she had to know for her own peace of mind. He was looking straight at her and about to speak. She looked back bravely. "Estelle, you have to know that I loved Ellie with all my heart. To see her radiance as she held up my son in her arms to show him to me was a joy. Then to see her struck down and taken so quickly when not a thing could be done was a tragedy." Estelle listened, numbed by his words. He continued, poignantly delivering all the pent up emotions that he needed to be free of at last. Shifting his thoughts from Estelle to remembered times, his hand found one of hers as if in need of reassurance. She held it firmly. "Little Georgie was six days old and always hungry but Ellie felt well and had even come downstairs for a little that afternoon. We had been discussing the christening I recall, but she then thought the parlour too chilly and went back upstairs to lie down. I followed a little later." He paused. Estelle put her other hand out for him; he took it in his and kissed it. He continued, "It normally attacks on the third day; I thought she had been spared, but not so. I found her shaking violently in a rigor attack and very afraid. She did not understand what was happening. I did, I knew then I would lose her. The sweats came swiftly; she was burning up and moaning with pain. She started struggling for breath and then, then it began; delirium. I remember the daylight fading from the window from bright sunshine, to orange glow, to dusk and finally darkness and I failed to be of any use as her tormented body writhed in its own suffering. By the time

Georgie was howling and in need of milk she was calm enough to nurse him a little, her last act of love. I remember her lovely chestnut hair on the pillow. It was wet with perspiration and plastered around her beautiful face. She was completely exhausted as Georgie suckled. The end came soon after that, she slipped away peacefully, I am thankful for that."

They sat in the silence, their hands still held together and the stillness of those moments brought peaceful comfort for John. For once, Estelle was lost for words; she had not expected such a heart-rending description of Eleanor's last moments. She felt totally guilty. How could she have been so jealous of a poor woman who died because she had a baby? Finally she broke the silence. "It must have been a dreadfully bad time for you, how have you ever been able to get past that?" John came out of his reverie, looked and smiled at her.

"Simple, I met you."

"But you love her." Estelle could not help herself; insecurity getting the better of her. She withdrew her hand.

"No, I loved her, and that's the difference, the past tense. Estelle please, do not try to compete with Ellie, it serves no purpose." John observed Estelle as she digested his words. He had never considered she might feel unsure of their relationship; but then he remembered Ellie had apprehensions and moments of self doubt when their relationship was in the early stages. He came to the conclusion it was just a female peculiarity. He tried to explain. "Let me make a comparison. It's the same as asking me if I prefer Georgie to Rose. There is no answer. They are both individuals and as such I love them differently; neither one more than the other." Estelle listened quietly as she began to grasp his thoughts. Although Rose was her own flesh and blood, she had formed a strong bond with little Georgie and did love him very much. Poor John, he could have no idea that Rose wasn't his daughter. She felt guilty about how she had deceived him.

"I really am very sorry John, I should never have brought it up, it can't have been very pleasant for you, now I feel bad."

"But you mustn't. I'm glad we've spoken about it, I swallowed my grief for a long time and I don't think it did me any good; you have helped me by allowing me to talk about it. Anyway, I hadn't finished what I was trying to say earlier." He took hold of her hand again and kissed it. "What I wanted to say was that I think I loved you from the moment I saw you. The night I carried you home and put you to bed, Estelle, I couldn't take my eyes off you and it was all I could do to tear myself away."

Blushing with the picture he was painting of his passion for her, Estelle remembered something; she had woken that first morning dressed in his nightshirt. She asked coyly, "did you really undress me because my clothes were ruined or was it for other reasons?" He dropped her hand and clasped both of his in front of his mouth while pacing round the room wrestling with his thoughts.

"Estelle, I am not entirely comfortable with what I did but I set out with good intentions, I wanted to check your body for injuries and of course I needed to undress you. I had undressed you completely before I realised that you had no under garments. I should have called Polly but it was so late in the night. On reflection I did not want her present; I suppose I wanted the moment to be mine; it felt very special for some reason, as if I were unwrapping something so very precious."

"And were my clothes muddy and ruined?" She had wondered what had happened to the dress.

"Er, no! Well I'm not sure. There's a bag in the hospital for the poor, I put them in there, I don't know why." He paced some more. "Perhaps I thought I had sullied them in some way. Except for the cloak, I hung that somewhere or other. Are there any more questions or can we change the subject now? Is it bed time?" He asked hopefully.

At first, on her part, even though she liked and admired John, it had been simply a marriage of convenience. But things were changing, their relationship had deepened, especially since the birth of Rose and now the plans for the hospital were materialising they were partnered together in a professional sense as well. Estelle felt part of something new and exhilarating but her mounting feelings towards John were equal to her growing guilt and shame. She must not allow the expeditious nature of their almost nightly coupling to change; she dare not make more of a response, it would be such a betrayal. She took a deep reluctant breath before speaking.

"Actually, I think I want to be on my own tonight, would you mind staying in your own room?"

John was taken aback "Oh, yes very well, I shall see you at breakfast." She had not refused him since she had been indisposed with child. He uttered a terse goodnight and Estelle breathed a sigh of relief as he closed the door behind him. She remembered the thrill of their first time together and of other times. It could be breathtaking between them if she did not feel so culpable and he wasn't so full of stress to notice. Could she really love two men at the same time? But that was just the point; it wasn't at the same time. That was then and this is now and after all, the present moment is all she had. She reached for her writing materials; she must tell him about all that had been happening, she owed him that at least.

March 1902.

My love,

So much has happened since I wrote my last letter; Rose is growing in leaps and bounds and is learning to walk. She is hilarious to watch. I wish you could see her, she is so adorable. However, I have other exciting news to tell you and you'll never in a million years guess what! I'm going to build Reid Street Maternity Hospital! Of all the things I thought I might achieve in my life, this was never one of them. Unbelievable!

I have come to terms with the fact that I have had two sets of parents; one set for now and one set for when I grew up. My new parents, the Peters (did I mention they were Lord and Lady?) have donated an old empty house that stands on Reid Street. I can see it as the very heart of the maternity hospital. Can you imagine how I must feel as I look at it now? It needs plenty doing to it; it's far from looking like it should be. We have put together an initial working committee from local men who carry some clout when it comes to getting things moving. An appeal has already gone out to 'the many charitable and philanthropic people' as my new mother has put it to raise a sum of ten thousand pounds. We have engaged an architect to help in the design so it will pass the approval of the medical officer for health. I am so excited; I just wish you could see me now!

All my love and always yours. x

Chapter Eleven

The sun peeped over the eastern horizon bringing a brand new day a little sooner than the last to raise the people's spirits out of the gloom of winter. Spring was approaching. The needle-sharp morning air carried the light rays through the chinks in the bedroom curtains allowing them to land on Estelle's sleeping torso. Their enticing dance moved slowly over her face and crept under her closed eyes waking her up. Reaching her arms above her head as far as she could and then bending forward to touch her toes she stretched out of her sleepy quiescence and stepped over to the window to let the daylight burst in. It was one of those days when one could not help but feel the joys of the season and Estelle tripped lightly down the stairs and into the hall glad to be alive. Last night she had come to a decision to break free from the past. She had slept well but woke earlier than usual and wanted to make her peace with John. She'd had enough of imagining other times, other circumstances, her duty was here and now. She thought she might surprise John and bring him up some breakfast. Breakfast upstairs was far more private than the dining room with Polly or Charlie coming in and out at any given moment.

She found no one in the kitchen, the back door was swinging wide open and the fresh morning air snapped greedily at the heat from the stove. Estelle wrapped her arms around herself, shivered on the doorstep and looked out into the back yard. Fay appeared through the hedge, spade in one hand, scissors and greenery in the other. She stared open-eyed when she saw the unexpected figure in the doorway and the spade clattered to the ground. "Oh Miss, I mean Madame, I'm so sorry," she panted as she picked it up. Not sure quite what she had to be sorry about, Estelle ignored the comment and ushered her inside noticing her grubby hands and the dirt that had stuck to her shoes.

"What on earth have you been doing with that spade, digging for gold?"

"I, I'm so sorry, I shouldn't have."

Fay was looking frightfully flustered. "Buried someone then?"

"No, of c-course not. I, I've, I'm preparing the ground for s-some seeds."

"Well that sounds interesting. What seeds?"

"I'm so sorry M-Madame, I didn't mean no harm," Fay snivelled.

"Fay, please, I'm not cross. What seeds? Please, come and tell me all about it while I put the kettle on."

"Please no, that's my job." Fay reached for the kettle but Estelle pulled it out of reach.

"But it's my kettle," remarked Estelle "so I shall put it on the stove. Now sit down and tell me what's going on in my garden."

Later, Estelle took a tray full of buttered toast and marmalade and a pot of tea upstairs into John's room. He stirred as she entered but sat up eagerly when he saw her. She lay the tray on the bed and sat down carefully, not wanting to disturb the tea pot. "John, I'm sorry about last night, I was, I was feeling, I wasn't..."

"No need to apologise," he interrupted "of course there must be occasions when you are indisposed. I am the one who should be apologising, it's just that last night I thought we, we were, well, I was a little taken aback that's all." Estelle poured out some tea and handed him a cup imagining what to say.

"Sometimes, John, sometimes I haven't felt good about myself, as if I can't be with you properly."

"What on earth are you talking about?"

"It's as if there's been something keeping me apart from you. I can't explain it fully." She dared not tell him another man had always been between them. She could not say how she had kept her eyes firmly closed and tried desperately to think of something else through guilt of wanting him to have been someone else. Latterly though, the image of that other man was faded and sometimes she could barely remember how he looked. "I think it must be something to do with before I met you, you know, the bit I can't remember. What if I had been married?" Now that she had begun she started letting her imagination run loose. "What if I had children, lots of children even, what if they have been left without a mother? What if I had done something terrible and am being hunted down?" John could only laugh. She looked so endearing as she sat next to him creating idiotic notions.

"Yes, I'm sure you must be a dangerous criminal who needs to be put behind bars for the safety of the whole of mankind. Come on now, do you really think that is true? Besides, nobody has claimed you, apart of course from your parents which is a good thing, not a bad thing." They sat silently drinking tea before John spoke again. "Look, wherever you have been in those intervening years has made you what you are today, so rejoice and stop worrying. You must let go of it if it's upsetting you. What if there was another man? He hasn't come looking for you has he? And anyway you are married to me so that's that."

It was the way he had explained things that helped shift something inside her. He thought so differently from her, so matter-of-factly, everything in its place and ordered. What he had said the night before, about Eleanor; that he was still able to love her as she was in the past without interfering with his love for her, his present wife. She needed to do the same. Of course! She wasn't betraying that love at all, she could see it now. She snuggled up to John and placed some toast in his mouth. "Yes, here I am before you, the sum total of all that I am."

"And jolly nice that is."

The other slices of toast were thrown to the birds later by Polly with repulsion. "How could they at this time of the morning? Disgusting is all I can say." She was telling Charlie and Fay what she had witnessed earlier. She had opened the door of the good doctor's bedroom in order to start cleaning thinking he had long gone. He was like clockwork, always leaving by eight thirty and this was after nine! How could she have known he had not been down to breakfast, after all, it had been her late start and she had only just come down herself. There they were, large as life and plain as day stretched out on the floor, bare legs in every direction. "The brazen hussy that's what she is."

"Well it's good that somebody's enjoying themselves in this house is what I say," sneaked Charlie under his breath to Fay.

"I can't think why Polly doesn't like her," Fay remarked after Polly stalked off. "I think she's nice. She said only this morning I could grow as many herbs as I like and she would find some books for me on how to use them."

"Our Polly has a mind of her own," sighed Charlie. "She thinks she can better herself and she's got a bee in her bonnet 'cos that's exactly what our Estelle's done and she's really jealous."

"How can you dare call her that?"

"It's easy, she can't hear me! Don't get me wrong, I likes and respects her for who she is, 'specially now she really is high class but when push comes to shove, we're all the same on the inside. Take yours truly for instance." He stood up and did a twirl. "One day I'll be bettering myself I will." Fay giggled as she watched Charlie parade up and down the kitchen with his unsophisticated version of an upper class toff. "Only wish," he continued soulfully when his show was over, "that Polly would believe it too."

"But she enjoyed it when you took her to the variety club, she couldn't stop talking about all the acts that were on, me and Cookie were fair jealous."

"That's not the same as talking about me though is it? She might well enjoy the fun I give her but not who I am; in her eyes I'm only a simple servant after all. She'd far rather get taken out by that philandering shopkeeper to that new place, The Grand and be bored senseless by a play just because it's the fashionable spot to go." For the life of her Fay could not understand how Charlie had found out about the clandestine tryst Polly had had with the butcher's son only the previous night. Polly had made her cover for her and made her swear on her mother's grave that she would not tell a soul.

Chapter Twelve

Estelle arranged to be with Vicky as soon as she had word that her confinement had begun and met a hard-pressed Jason in the hallway. "Thank goodness you've come; I don't know what to do. She is refusing for me to call the doctor saying it's a necessary process; but she's crying out in such agony."

"It's all right, don't worry, it's the pain of childbirth, I'll go straight up." She found Vicky on her knees and panting in the grip of distress. "Just breathe long deep breaths till it's gone Vicky. How long have you been like this?"

"I didn't want it to be a false alarm," she blurted when she gained back the power of her body from the overwhelming muscular contraction. "I wanted to be sure it was really happening. Oh no, it's coming again. Please, no more," she pleaded as an unworldly spasm wracked her defenceless torso. Estelle called out to Jason to arrange for the doctor to come without delay as she listened to the anguished augmenting sounds of impending climax. This was no false alarm, anyone would know that.

"I think my waters have gone," grunted Vicky as she failed to control her body as it strove to expel its very innards. Estelle assisted her sister-in-law out of her restrictive clothing and helped her sit down on the chair but then froze in shock at what she could clearly see. It was unmistakable. The thick black tar of a stool that a baby first passes was oozing from between Vicky's legs. Instinctively Estelle knew something was wrong and encouraged Vicky to let her look. As Vicky's contractions drove her to push Estelle could see a very large scrotum appearing into view. She swallowed hard; she knew the doctor would not get there in time. A baby coming head first she could have hopefully managed, but bottom first? Even John had expounded the dangers and complications of a breech birth. What chance had she got? She took a long and very deep breath.

"Vicky, nature has determined your baby is coming with its bottom first rather than head first. We must trust that she knows best but I want you to go from the chair and lie on the bed now at the very end." Fortunately or unfortunately, Vicky was beyond caring which way her baby was coming as her whole bearing was overturned. As the powerful force pushed, a scrotum gave way to buttocks; then legs freed themselves and dangled inactively as if in suspended animation. Estelle watched in wonder as nature worked its miracle and more and more of the tiny body was born. She heard her voice calling for Vicky to push and she saw her own hands easing out miniature arms by twisting the baby by the hips from side to side. As if life was in the balance, the baby dangled inertly as a doll, towards the floor; its head yet unborn. What now, what was she to do next? The minutes passed like epochs on the ticking clock as they waited silently for another contraction. One started and Estelle saw the nape of the baby's neck appearing and knew it was time. Talking to herself as much as to Vicky she grasped the tiny feet and lifted them away from the floor until the baby became upside down. She could see its face appearing. "Don't push any more, the baby is coming on its own, just breathe slowly, let the baby's head come slowly, that's it."

The baby dangled limp and still upside down as Estelle held tightly to its feet. With her other hand she cradled its head and laid it gently to the floor and started to rub at the blue flaccid body with a towel. The silence lasted too long for its poor mother. "Is it dead?" she asked, desperate to be brave. Estelle put her hand on the tiny chest and felt a slow but definite thump of a beating heart. She covered a miniature nose and mouth with her lips and blew in a tiny breath, and another, and another. She could feel the heart quicken, she blew in some more, and as if realising it was born, the baby breathed for itself and cried out, almost in protest at having been put through such an ordeal.

"No he's very much alive, here take him, he's very handsome and he's yours." She placed the now beautifully pink-coloured baby into Vicky's grateful arms. At the same time the doctor burst through the door.

"Get out of my way, out of my way. Wait outside, you're no use here," he added as he eyed Estelle with reproach. Estelle left the room as bidden and leant against the wall outside bending forward to grasp her knees and then up again drawing breath in and blowing it out in quick succession as though there had been a shortage. The hovering Jason could not contain himself any longer.

"Estelle, tell me, tell me," he gasped. "Please tell me everything is all right." Estelle almost looked through him as she had only just noticed he was there and was so euphoric she could barely speak. She had helped to bring a baby into the world and there were no words to describe how she felt at that moment, but Jason's pleading eyes, brought her attention back. She grasped both of his hands and stared at his face laughing elatedly.

"It's a boy," she exclaimed. "You have a son Jason, a son. Congratulations!"

"Oh my, that is wonderful news, and Vicky?"

"I think Vicky is the happiest girl in the world at the moment. You can see her as soon as the doctor says you can, I'm sure." Still hanging on to his hands she kissed his cheek and then jumped up and down. It was infectious; Jason found he was jumping too, then skipping and leaping and by the time the pretentious Dr. Pearson appeared they were well into a dance reminiscent of a polka. It took a loud cough from him to realise they were not alone and to slow down. With a look of revulsion he informed Jason that he may now go in and see his wife and child and that all was perfectly well. He left shortly afterwards giving Estelle such a scornful look it unnerved her; she could not imagine why he appeared so disapproving of her.

"Well that's simple to comprehend," explained John later after Estelle related how she had helped to bring his nephew into the world. "He is of the opinion that women lack the ability to make any decisions of importance and therefore should not be anywhere near a hospital committee even if they might be the daughter of the benefactor. Believe me, he made no bones about it at our last meeting at The Royal. Unfortunately he does not stand alone, his bigoted sentiments are shared by others who are against women being placed in any position of power. Let me assure you that anything, and I mean anything that's not within their immediate control meets with controversy." So that's all it was! Estelle, satisfied by his explanation, stopped worrying. There was nothing the overblown Dr. Pearson and his contemptuous attitude could do, he was powerless to change her role within the maternity hospital and he obviously knew it but what a shame he and the others felt that way. Thank goodness there were good and forward thinking men like John and her father who thought better than those who believed women were there to focus only on child rearing and maybe a few charitable good deeds. Presumably the Dr. Pearsons of the world believed women were completely incapable of managing the birth of a hospital as they were far too inferior to men. Or maybe his disdain was because of what he thought he had seen; she and Jason may have given the wrong impression to the old 'fuddy duddy' as they had danced around outside the bedroom. Estelle laughed, had he thought they were lovers? 'The very idea!' she thought.

Chapter Thirteen

The sun came out at last and Rose and George were keen to go out to the park when Nanny suggested it. Estelle thought it a good idea as they had been stuck inside for days with the continual rain. She also wanted to get out for a while and told Nanny she would take them herself. Even though employer and employee got on very well, the suggestion did not go down at all well. Nanny had suggested the park as she had in mind to chat to the other nannies who would be doing exactly the same thing, and catch up on the gossip they had missed due to the poor weather. After much tactical discussion on Estelle's part, in the end, Nanny got the morning off and Estelle took the children on her own, pleased at being able to do something with them by herself. She tried to be with the children as much as she could but Nanny was always taking charge. Nanny was not a bad influence, nor did she do things that she did not approve of; on the contrary, she was an absolute treasure but Estelle simply felt inhibited by her constant presence; as if somehow she were superfluous. Nanny however, wasn't getting any younger, and wasn't in the best of health. Estelle could not visualise her ever picking up her skirts and being able to chase after either of the children if they ran off. "I cannot imagine ever daring to run away from Nanny," John surmised when Estelle asked his opinion and Vicky echoed his feelings. She held vivid memories of the 'no running' and 'no shouting' laws that came into play on Nanny's excursions.

"It seemed a pointless endeavour, taking us out for our enjoyment," Vicky explained. "Playing was out of the question. We had to walk, or rather march in single file behind her and 'woe betide us' if we couldn't keep up! Good exercise it might have been, but fun? I think not." It had been these comments that had prompted Estelle to take the children on her own in the first place.

The children loved going to the park. George ran around freely, honing his skills with the hoop and Rose pottered about picking daisies. Estelle sat on a bench and kept an eye on both. "Don't go too far away," Estelle called out to Rose as she ventured further and further towards the stone circle.

"But Mummy I want to jump off all the big one stones," replied Rose. Even after all this time Estelle was still wary about that area of the park near to the east gate. Rose reached the circle and defied her mother by clambering over the nearest stone. Resignedly Estelle moved to a nearer bench. "This is a magic circle," declared Rose with great authority as she danced about. "Do you know Mummy that all the fairies come here to have a big big party?"

"Do they now," replied Estelle, cautious with Rose's fantasy.

"Yes they do. The fairy queen sits here on this one stone and all the others dance about to the drums coming out of the ground, and then they all have something to eat." She arranged her daisies one on top of each stone.

"Lovely!" replied her mother.

"They are getting ready to go to work now."

"What do they do?"

"Mummee! Don't you know what fairies do?" Rose exclaimed with incredulity. "Well, what they do, is, well, they have to go and um, they go and look for all the fallen out teeth under all the pillows."

"Of course they do," said Estelle standing up and observing the clouds in the sky. "Oh dear, I think it's going to start to rain. Come on now let's catch up with that brother of yours and find an ice-cream. Look, I think he's made a friend."

"But I want to stay here," said Rose, her mouth turning down.

"Maybe we'll come back this way."

Rose gave out a big sigh, jumped over two more stones and caught up with her mother who was moving away tactically. The rain was too heavy when they made their way back and Rose's second visit to the stones was thwarted. She was appeased by the thought of getting her paints out at home after tea and painting all the fairies she had seen.

Nanny had returned in a somewhat better mood than she had been in when she had left. She had spent the time with her sister who lived a short walk away and had been laden with family gossip. She was happy to provide both children with their paint-pots, carefully encasing them in old smocks to save their clothes. Nanny fussed about tidying shelves and tutting at the mess the children were making with their paints.

"They are only young once," said Estelle bravely in their defence.

"Mm," was Nanny's only reply.

"Daddy Daddy!" they both shouted as John entered the nursery, dropping their brushes and running towards him.

"Don't touch me!" he ordered. "You are covered in paint!" he added by way of explanation. Instead of jumping all over him as they usually did on his return from work, they condescended to grab hold of his hands and led him to their easels, showing him their art. "Very good, very good," he said obligingly.

"That's me with my hoop," said Georgie.

"Indeed it is, I recognise your blue breeches but why are there two of you?"

"I haven't drawn myself twice, that's Francis, my friend from the park."

"Ah! I see," said his father.

"And that's me and the fairies at the park."

"Beautiful," said John encouragingly.

"Finish off now you two," said Nanny, "It's almost tea time."

Family life had kept John sane while his efforts to change maternity care at the Royal had proved fruitless. However, that would soon be behind him when the new hospital was ready; assuming he would be considered for a post. Perish the thought that he would not, but Estelle would surely see to that. She and John left Nanny and went into the parlour to discuss arrangements for a trip John had been organising for himself. He was going up to Glasgow to work alongside his mentor, the illustrious Dr. Cameron. John had been his student many years before and so knew and appreciated his great knowledge and expertise in obstetrics and midwifery. It would be such a valuable experience for John to work alongside him but meant him being apart from Estelle and the children for several weeks. He would miss them, he thought.

"We are going to miss you too," replied Estelle. "Perhaps we could visit you at some point? The children would enjoy such an adventure."

"I would prefer you here, I think, out of harm's way. Glasgow isn't the place to bring the children. Best enjoy the sunshine here rather than the uncertainties of impoverished tenements and shady slums there. The park is at its best at this time of year don't you think? You must write to me about all its blooms and blossoms, I will be in need of some colour up there."

"Yes, whatever," sighed Estelle.

March 1905

I spent yesterday morning in the park with the children. How pretty it looks now the crocuses are out in their colourful swathes over the grass. Rose insisted on playing around the standing stones and even though more than five years have gone by since my accident nearby they still make me uneasy. She says she likes to be with the fairies that live there; she has such a vivid imagination! Even Vicky thinks the circles are surrounded in mystery and declares she has heard tales about mists lurking like Will-o'-the-wisp ready to draw her into danger. Stories like that give me the shivers.

Five whole years! Such a long long time, I wonder, is it the same for you? Have you waited five whole years in the hope I would return?

John said it was a coach and horse that knocked me over but I don't know much about that. All I know is that I was in the wrong place at the wrong time and because of what happened I was given a whole new existence. Even if you wanted me to come back I can't now, purely and simply. What I am trying to say is that I am settled and happy. It does not mean I don't still love you, I do, but it is so difficult with all this separation.

I feel we are still connected through our darling daughter, Rose. I see your eyes, your cheeky charm and your smile, the way you cock your head to one side when you are thinking; I see you all the time and it is impossible for me to forget you, ever.

All my love and always yours. X.

PS. The painting with this letter is Rose's interpretation of the standing stones. I think it is remarkable in its accuracy. She is quite the budding artist!

Chapter Fourteen

John spent many months away from home over the next years learning as much as he could from his contemporaries. He even went to Germany to learn from the gynaecologist Ludwig Fraenkel who, like John, believed social living conditions an important factor in gynaecological illnesses. But he did not go for lessons in social science; he had been fascinated by Fraenkel's work concerning female reproduction. It was ground-breaking research and John wanted to learn more.

In his absence Estelle buried herself in the affairs of hospital planning. It took the passing of several years before the maternity hospital was formally opened despite the tremendously successful efforts of the fund-raisers. Money had come from many unexpected places including the local choral society and the brass band who gave concerts in aid of the 'hospital building fund.' Promised subscriptions had been received so rapidly and so generously that a trust fund was instigated to realise an annual income for running expenses. Lord Peters made it his business to employ Estelle in as many aspects of the planning and design as she was able. She was fully immersed in plans for ward layouts, canteens, offices and staff accommodation becoming quite the expert; she had a gift of knowing what would work well and what to discard.

There had been a frustrating delay before finding a good contractor. A whole year passed before a tender was submitted that everyone was in agreement with. The first contractor had withdrawn over arguments about the central hot water system. His tender had not included this expense and he wanted to omit the whole apparatus. This seemed incomprehensible to the committee members and trustees who wished to be completely up to date; they opposed him unanimously and also insisted, with Estelle's prompting, that electricity be installed as well. However, the diagrams of pipes that would carry hot water from the gas fuelled basement boilers to every corner of the building proved to be her match, she left that to the architect and the plumbers to argue over and the unfathomable wiring configurations to other specialists. Eventually, when all the complications were smoothed over the new tender was accepted unconditionally. The building work could begin.

It happened that almost every member of the general committee for the hospital was a woman. There had been no particular plan, even the management board was staffed entirely by women, and a barely concealed smile came over Estelle's face when a job application for a certain Dr. Pearson was unanimously turned down. The consensus of opinion was that he would be far too set in his ways. The board had been intending for the hospital to become a training school for midwives and Dr. Pearson's prejudices had peppered his application so abundantly that he did not even qualify for interview. John's hand had practically been bitten off when he applied. Even though it was a foregone conclusion as, in a way, the hospital had been built for him, he still needed to go through the normal administrative channels. His periods away in Glasgow and Germany gaining more experience had impressed, and coupled with his sincere commitment to the education of midwives to a proper standard, he was the ideal candidate and just what the board was looking for.

"It wasn't just your handsome face then," Estelle remarked after John told her of his successful interview and how his plans for a training school for midwives had been well received. John looked at his wife quizzically. "I see the way they can flutter their eyelashes at you, other women I mean. Just a joke, I meant you got the job on your merit not your looks. Oh never mind," she added as 'Humph!' was John's only response. He had no time or inclination to notice any flirtatious emanations from females he came into contact with. As far as he was concerned the women he worked with were treated with the respect they merited as colleagues, no less for being of the fairer sex and he had been well trained in social graces and manners all thanks to Nanny. "Do you actually have a sense of humour?" Estelle teased as she tried to tickle him inside his jacket.

"Only on special occasions," he teased back. "Talking of special occasions, has Vicky set the date for the christening? I may need to go to London to meet with the Central Midwives Board."

"To approve your school? My goodness things are suddenly moving quickly. I am really proud of you, more than you could ever know." She hugged her husband as if he were leaving that moment. Although she did not enjoy it, she dealt with his frequent absences in the knowledge that it was necessary. She thought about the little training school that John wanted to set up and imagined how many midwives might complete their training there with John at the helm, a guiding light in the path of midwifery.

ЧАЧА8

"Incredible," she uttered out loud and kissed him affectionately before elaborating on the preparations for the christening of Jason and Vicky's new daughter. Another breech baby; delivered this time by the local midwife; Jason had wasted no time in summoning her after Vicky's first pangs of labour, dismissing any ideas of employing the services of Dr. Pearson.

"Bicornuate uterus," was John's short response to the news of being made an uncle again.

Estelle walked through the long nightingale wards soulfully. They were already stamped with individual character even though they were similarly designed. Two tidy lines of beds with impeccable hospital cornered sheets waiting with patient expectation on paired sides. The windows above them so bright and tall, they touched the lofty ceilings above. It was a pity they were just a little too high to see out. Still, the staff would be too busy to dawdle at windows and the new mothers would only have eyes for their babies. The double doors of each ward opened out onto corridors with treatment rooms and utility areas leading off on either side. There were other rooms for office use, bathrooms, small kitchens and of course, nurseries with cots ready to be filled with new life. Each ward was named after the greater benefactors to the hospital and each bed had a brass plaque with the name of its sponsor above its head. Downstairs in the hospital's bowels, the kitchen ovens were waiting to be lit and the staff dining room had newly-delivered tables and chairs.

It was ready, she could do no more. Tomorrow the doors would open and the women would come to deliver their babies within these walls. Five years had passed since she and John had walked past that old and derelict building. Five years since she had envisaged her life's purpose; how she would help instigate John's career and intertwine their relationship beyond husband and wife. She made her way outside and looked back at the front gates glancing at the iron- wrought letters arching over it. Over the years she had poured her heart and soul into this beautiful building facing her and now understood why she had felt so connected to it even from the first moments of knowing it, it was the future, her 'raison d'être'. One day someone would pull it all down, for nothing lasts forever, but that time was surely a long way off. For the present this love would sustain her through the years to come whatever they may bring for she had achieved something great, something truly wonderful! This was her hospital.

The next day brought expectant women on a visit to an antenatal clinic that John had organised. They had been enticed by an open invitation to look around and see what the hospital had to offer them. It wasn't until much later, after the hospital had seen a thousand births, that the building had its formal opening.

'The British Journal of Nursing Supplement' had described well the scene that opening day. There was a blue sky overhead, and even smoke from the town's industry did not ascend up the hill toward the hospital. The dirty fumes, like the political crisis generated by all the social reforms, knew to keep clear and not to mar the day. The day had to go according to plan: it had been years of work; it was crucial for Estelle, she felt almost as if she were being judged.

Estelle helped everyone find their places for the ceremony. The kindly 'friends of the hospital' were seated on the balcony at the side of the hospital. In the centre a group of nurses in their neat out-door uniform provided by Jason waited patiently. The newly-appointed matron, dressed in navy and a becoming white cap sat down, nodding to her staff to do the same.

A man of enterprise, Jason had long ago seen an opportunity of procuring business from the hospital. Bed linen, uniforms for nurses, cooks, cleaners, porters, nightdresses for the patients, baby clothes; all of these were required and his factory was precisely placed for the provision of such articles. He had wasted no time offering his services; his cloth was of the very best quality for each necessity; it would boil wash with no shrinkage and could be dyed to any colour required. He bewitched the committee with his suave charm and his rivals could not better his prices. He won the contract which set him up successfully and moved his family into a newly built villa, further away from his factory in town, but much nearer to John and Estelle.

It had been of some concern that the death of the King might cause the grand occasion to be postponed as it had occurred so recently. However, on this most perfect day, all was to go ahead as planned. The Lord Mayor occupied the chair as the Service of Dedication was conducted by the Lord Bishop of Ripon and Vicar of Leeds. The whole assembly joined to sing 'Now Thank We All Our God'. Estelle sat proudly, but felt ill with the apprehensiveness of having to make a speech. Lord Peters was first, with an address referring to all the good work done thanking the honorary members who had visited all cases and collected funds, the expert medical staff for their skill and kindness, and the nursing staff for their efficient services. Estelle's concentration drifted, she was feeling too nervous to listen intently, anxious about what she was going to have to say. The characterful Miss March from the board had written her speech for her, but she found it difficult to learn as it wasn't at all what she would have written. "But this is what we, the members of the committee want. We can contrive to use the fact that the whole world is in mourning to our advantage. If we drum up a bit of patriotic fervour in the speeches, we might induce increased popularity for the hospital and that will bring in more revenue," Miss March had argued.

"Whatever!" Estelle had replied. One did not argue with the Miss Marches of this world, it wasn't worth the trauma. She had practised and would be word perfect but in case she did slip, she had it all written down with large markers and would not get lost. Her old anxieties were at play, her heart was racing, her hands sweating and the wretched corset that Polly insisted she wore made it impossible to breathe.

Polly, the bane of her life. There was no love lost between them despite the years of service, if there was ever meant to be between employer and employee. 'Of course there was,' she reprimanded herself. On the other hand she was so very proud of what Fay had accomplished with very little help from her. Fay had advanced out of all recognition from her early days as an unkempt scullery and tweeny maid. The success of her little herb garden had developed into an interest in herbs for medicinal use. She had spent all of her spare time pestering the local pharmacist in his little shop in her search for knowledge. Taken with her enthusiasm, he had let her borrow many of his cherished books and would have employed her on as his apprentice had it not been for his son who wanted to follow in his footsteps. Fortunately for Fay, the pharmacist's son was clearly sweet on her and the future of the chemist shop was clear; the son would follow the father into the business and marry a girl who knew her medications. They would live over the premises and she could help him serve in the shop. She was the loveliest of brides. "You see, she really has changed into a swan," whispered Georgie to his mother when he watched Fay walk down the aisle.

"To save life and preserve health; these are its twofold aims," she heard from her father's lips. He was still talking, it was not yet her turn and the mayor was next. Her mind wandered back to Polly. She wondered why she still kept her on but then she did not have a plausible excuse to get rid of her. If Polly hated her that much she would leave of her own volition. Then there was the love sick Charles who clearly doted on the condescending housemaid; he obviously had masochistic tendencies to endure her unshakable reproofs. He was going places too; his little side line in car maintenance had grown steadily; so many people had cars now and they all needed looking after. Why Polly continued to dote on that porker of a butcher's son when Charles had remained loyal over all these years she could not imagine.

"I now call upon Mrs. Brown to open the hospital," she heard the mayor say from somewhere in the middle of her head.

'Cripes, Its me' she thought and stood up trying to pretend to herself she wasn't really there.

"Just pretend they're a load of cabbages," she remembered her other father used to say to her when as a child she had needed her nerves quelling in order to read out in class successfully. It had worked then, perhaps she should try it now. Indeed the assistant matron's face did resemble a cabbage of the savoy variety. She had seen her earlier when she looked around to see where John was standing, across from where she was placed. She stifled a giggle which came out as a cough, took a deep breath, looked round at the cabbages and walked towards the entrance.

"I formally announce The Reid Street Maternity Hospital to be now open." Everyone clapped politely as she cut the ribbon. When the applause subsided she began her prepared speech quite forgetting to get out her crib sheet. "Welcome to you all. How pleased I am to be here today and how delighted I am to have been at the beginning of such an institution started by those who could see a bright future for those who were still in the shade. I know that all you mothers have much appreciation for the skill and kindness that has been shown you when you needed it most and I am sure that all the babies who first see the light in this hospital will grow up healthily."

Estelle went on to say how glad she was that the opening ceremony had not been postponed and was sure that its object was one which would appeal to the Queen Mother even in the midst of her sorrow. Pausing quickly to breath she continued on the royal theme by telling of Queen Mary's sympathy for the little ones and of her numerous visits to the East Lambeth slums. She then presented the hospital with two large framed pictures of the

Queen Mother and of Queen Mary to adorn the walls of the new hospital. The pictures had been provided by her mother. Sybil had insisted there was absolutely no wall space to do them justice at Tiplin and - thank goodness - the hospital would be the ideal place for their permanent display. She donated them gladly. They fitted in perfectly with the speech Miss March had written. She and her mother had obviously collaborated.

Estelle finished by describing herself as a working woman and her contribution to the hospital was her little gift. Another committee member got up and thanked Estelle warmly "for her services and charming speech," and moved a vote of thanks to the Lord Mayor and Lady Mayoress, dwelt on the educational value of such an institution to the poor mothers and on the privilege of supporting such a charity. She then ended with a call for three cheers for Queen Mary. The National Anthem then brought the morning's programme to a close.

As soon as they were able, Estelle, John, Vicky and Jason repaired to John's office and made appreciable progress through a single malt in celebration of a successful opening ceremony. Estelle was relieved it was over. Like all events, it had taken very careful political planning in order to go smoothly. "Here's to new times," said Jason, taking the liberty of refilling everyone's glass from John's liquor supply. Estelle, intoxicated by the warm glow of strong drink, was for the moment at least, glad she was party to it all even though she hoped that all women, not just the poor, would come to make use of it in time. Unable to stomach any food that morning, the alcohol was going straight to her head and she needed to eat something. Fortunately Jason had organised a lunch at The Granby for the V.I.P.s and had them all chauffeured into town by his newly acquired fleet of taxicabs. He enjoyed his food and had already indulged, as usual, in a hearty breakfast of porridge, bacon and eggs, kidney and steak washed down with beer, but was still able to consume a heavy lunch. It had not gone beyond Estelle's notice that his waistcoat was looking rather tight. She thought he ought to watch himself; she would have a word with Vicky.

Entrepreneurial by nature, Jason's many business endeavours were going from strength to strength and he would exhibit his wealth seeking social respect. In contrast, Lord Peters being part of the landed gentry, had seen his family fortunes slowly dwindle. The agricultural depression that had started in the 1870s had forced his father to sell and then the huge death duties that were paid out when he died had taken their toll. With the political climate changing the old order, he was having a challenging time. As a member in The House of Lords he would have none of Lloyd George's demands to increase taxes from the rich. But he was all for improvement, he had spent his life doing what he could for 'poor unfortunates' but could not see how he could sustain his gifts if his money and estates had a super tax imposed on them. "He's the son of a duke, he should know better. What is he thinking? What is the world coming to? Does he want us all to lose?" But change was coming, and there was nothing he could do.

Estelle had grown to love the family seat herself. The house, of many architectural styles as each generation added its mark, held hundreds of years of history within its stones. Time always seemed to stand still there and the echoes of memories from the generations of Peters that had lived and loved there spread from the grand rooms to every little nook and fancy carving. The grounds, or rather the woods in which it stood, for there was little by way of formal planting, held their own enchantment. It had been opened to the public for entertainment, families came to take meandering walks under the trees and picnic by the stream where the ground dipped to the water, dashing down and splashing into a pool, inviting young and old to paddle. Her father now believed he might be the Peters that would let it all slip away and he felt an ache in his heart.

Chapter Fifteen

Charlie was on his back on the garage floor grappling with the steering arm when he heard Polly's cries. The spanner clanked on the ground as he lost his grip, and cursing, he pulled himself from underneath the car declaring it a day. He wasn't sure if he had been using expletives because he had failed to undo the rusted nut or that Polly was still hankering after that pork pie of a butcher. Years before he thought that she had won the lecher's heart but now he knew the degenerate had only one intention in mind. Charlie had seen him many times with various young misses keen to grow fat as a butcher's wife. Finally one of them must have managed to pin him down; Charlie had heard he was to be wed. Polly's lamentations must mean she had found out. Oh dear, poor Polly! Oh well, he would be there for her, if she would let him, to pick up the pieces.

Charlie wiped his greasy hands on a rag and followed the noise into the kitchen toward the love of his life. She sat wretchedly, her face puffed and the colour of beetroot. Fay was sitting beside her, failing miserably to bring any comfort and most likely the harbinger of the news. He stopped at the threshold in his oil-soaked overalls looking as if he were about to step out from a picture. His masculine frame was silhouetted by the low March sun as its light shafted through the back door, down the back passage and into the door frame. The love-torn man smouldered dejectedly. He knew what he wanted to do; he wanted to take her, and shake all memory of that pot-bellied pork chop out of her so he could not sully her any more. He wanted to take her into his arms and show her how much better a suitor he would be. He wanted to.... for years he had craved her but he would never have dared say. Instead he had watched her snub-nosed haughty face gradually change from its youthful bloom to lacklustre and become more and more down-trodden thanks to her so-called admirer. Charlie's love for her had never wavered and he was still so full of desire.

Polly made no attempt to hide her distress and she rushed at Charlie with such force she took him off balance and clung to him. His heart pumped deliriously as she held herself unrestrainedly against him; his strong arms around her. "What am I going to do? What am I going to do? Oh

Charlie, what will I do now?" Over and again she sobbed out the words and Charlie breathed in her hair, her neck, her essence.

'Never mind her, what am I going to do?' he thought. He had to let go of her soon, his arousal was becoming unacceptable.

Fay, who had her youngest sitting on her knee coughed. The heat in the air was a little stifling and she needed to take control. She cleared her throat. "Lets all cool off and have a cup of tea. Its always desirable when conditions are beyond our control. Charlie will you please leave and get out of your oily garb while we boil the kettle. Polly will you take Maggie while I draw some water." Polly, disinclined to let go of the warm body that had surrounded her in comfort, scooped the tiny child onto her lap reluctantly and sat back at the table. Suitably shamed by Fay, Charlie stuffed a hand in his pocket and almost limped back to the garage.

Charlie lived above the garage in a small attic which had been modified when the old coach house was converted into a garage. Being the only male in service in the house, it maintained a proper distance between him and the attic rooms of the female servants. It suited Charlie well; his own living room furnished respectably with a stove for warmth and making pots of tea (he had never cooked a meal, preferring to eat at the house where he could be near to Polly) and a separate small bedroom. He had the old outside privy and washhouse at the back of the garage to himself. Perfect! His little domain; his personal residence on a fine street so near to the lovely park. What more could he ask for? Only that Polly would come to her senses and realise that he was the man for her? He sighed and stripped off in the washhouse, chilling himself down with the freezing water. He tried to make some plans. She would need distraction for her tortured mind. Maybe he should ask the good doctor if he might borrow the car? He could take her out on a drive, surely that would impress her? Maybe take her in it to the theatre where she used to go with that oaf, and without a chaperone. She had gone with Charlie once, and had a lovely time, even though they had been with a group of friends. She had hung onto his arm as if they were a couple. Pleasant times, years ago; youthful frolics, behind them now. It was time now to be serious; he would woo her somehow. He could take her to the tea-room in the park to start with, the windows had a lovely view of the young copper beech trees that flanked the sides of the main walkway. He had noticed them coming into bud that very morning when he had gone, as usual, for his walk. Oh dear, maybe he did after all, come across as a little boring, he thought.

Charlie went back into the house but stopped in the back passage to listen to the conversation that, unknowingly the speakers let float from the kitchen window just like Polly's despairing wails had done before. He was horrified. Phrases such as 'he must never know it's his' and 'you must disappear for a while' made his ears prick up. He listened, repulsed by what he heard.

So, the butcher's boy had seduced her! He was even more rotten than his meat! She was ruined, he had seen to that; destroyed any decent future for her. Charlie could save her though, Charlie would rescue her. They would marry and he would recognise the child as his own and no one needed to know the truth.

He moved into the kitchen to put his proposal to Polly, very politely as they drank their tea, with Fay across the table pretending to attend to Maggie.

A few weeks later Charlie caught Estelle in the hall looking for Polly when no one had answered the servant's bell. He tried to explain to her that Polly had left and was not coming back. "What do you mean she's left? Where has she gone to?"

"Its written in the note she left me Madam, to America, she is off to America Madam." Part of Estelle wanted to say 'well good riddance' but she would not say so out loud, especially to Charles.

"America? Why on earth would she want to go there?" Why did she not tell me of her plans?" Estelle was incensed. How could she leave without any notice? Well, of course, it was Polly and just like her to do something like that! "Well Charles? You look as though you have got something else to say!" Charlie was shifting about furtively from one foot to the other as if he was not quite ready to leave.

"Oh Madam, I really don't know if I am wrong or right in telling you this. I'm really not."

"Why not tell me anyway and then we can decide about ethics." Estelle was intrigued, there was certainly more to this. Charlie took a large breath to calm himself, he did not know if he was betraying Polly or helping her.

"She's got herself into trouble like; in the family way Madam, so she had to leave, see?"

"Oh, I see," Estelle replied calmly but her stomach churned, understanding completely how Polly felt. She also believed that Polly knew that John wasn't Rose's father but had never betrayed her; maybe she had been more loyal to her than she thought. "Charles, why are you doing this to her? She isn't the only one to blame, you have to take your share, you have to marry her for goodness sake.

"Its not that simple. Its not mine and I *have* asked her to marry me but she has refused me."

"Oh Charles, I'm sorry, I just assumed that... how gallant to accept another man's child." She was so full of admiration for Charles she could have wept. There were such good people all around her, surely there was something she could do to help. Estelle paced about the chequered floor but then stopped suddenly, as though an imaginary wall stopped her progress. There was a look of horror on her face. Charlie didn't know where to look; at the floor to hide his shame at betraying Polly, or follow Madam's gaze, for she had surely seen some phantom; she had taken such a sharp intake of breath and not let go of it for some time. He felt relieved as she continued to talk; he liked her voice, it soothed him, like his mother's used to after his father beat him.

"Wait a minute, when did she leave, are you telling me she is already on a ship?"

"No Madam, not yet, I think her ticket is for the tenth." He saw relief on her face; he was mildly surprised that she was showing so much concern.

"Then we've got two days to change her mind. Where is she now?" Charlie was hesitant to tell her. "Charles you must tell me, who is helping her?"

"She's going to Southampton tomorrow with Mr. Peach's son, you know, Fay's husband," Charlie mumbled, but then with growing confidence that Madam might actually stop his beloved Polly from leaving, he related all he knew of the plans. Fay's husband's brother and his wife had left for America hoping for a different kind of life following their marriage five years before. They had hoped for children but it had never happened. The arrangements were to look after Polly until she had the baby and then adopt the child as their own. Polly would have to make provision for herself afterwards.

"They are going to keep her baby then kick her out onto the streets? How does she think she would cope in such a strange new world; it's preposterous! I can't let that happen. She must stay here, we must sort something out."

"I've tried and tried to help her Madam, but you know Polly, no one can change her mind once its made up, but if you think you can change it I would be so grateful."

"May I enquire, do you know whose child it is?" she asked tentatively, not wanting to cause Charles any embarrassment.

"Mr. Eckler junior, the butcher." He mumbled the name as if it caused pain to say it out loud.

"That slimy piece of lard, what on earth does she still see in him?"

"Couldn't have put it better myself Madam." Charlie grinned at her retort, it matched his feelings exactly.

Estelle felt that what ever happened, she must not let Polly get on that boat. She marched along to the chemist's shop with the full intention of changing her headstrong maid's mind. There was too much was at stake, whole lives had to be considered. A baby was to be born, was that so dreadful?

It wasn't far to the shop, through the park and on into town, but when she arrived Estelle was not sure how to get to the living quarters. She went straight into the store itself where she found Mr. Peach, Fay's husband. He was occupied with dispensing something brown into a medicine bottle and giving it to a disgruntled elderly gentleman at the head of a long queue of customers. Nonetheless, Mr. Peach took time to show Estelle the back stairs and gestured her up to the room at the top of them. She found Polly there sorting through some clothes. Polly stopped what she was doing as soon as she saw who had come up the stairs. "Madam," was all she said quietly, but looking surprised to see her mistress.

"I think we need to sit down," said Estelle looking round for some space; there were clothes everywhere.

"Yes Madam," Polly replied in her usual mechanical fashion. She cleared her clothes from two chairs to make some space.

"Polly," began Estelle, "I know what has happened and I do not want you to go away. We must find a way for you to stay here and nurture your own child. Charles has already told me he wants to marry you. Why don't you stay and let him keep you?"

"But America is meant to be full of opportunity and any ways, I can't palm another man's child onto Charlie, he is too good for that." Estelle thought for a minute about what Polly had said. She, herself had not thought twice about saving herself from probable ruin when she had been unexpectedly pregnant. Polly on the other hand, who was clearly of a much higher moral standing, had no similar underhanded designs. If Charles is too good for that then surely so was John. For the first time she saw good in Polly and felt ashamed of herself. She hung her head before she spoke.

"You know that's exactly what I did don't you Polly, and Charles wants marriage, he always has."

"But the ticket is all paid for by Mr. Peach's brother, Mr. Peach." Polly's phrasing might have caused some amusement on another occasion, but the seriousness of the meeting prevented it. Estelle smoothed out her skirts as if making room for her speech before continuing, at last finding a way to reach an understanding in their relationship.

"Oh Polly, there is so much I need to tell you I don't really know how to start, but here goes. I'm trusting you with this knowledge because I know that despite my barging in like a usurper twelve years ago, you have kept it a secret from my husband that I was already pregnant. You could so easily have said something. You see when I arrived here," Estelle continued, "I was really messed up and confused. One minute I was happy and the next...I had moved from a place so different and finding I was expecting a baby, well, I don't know how else to explain it, my disorientation was total. As far as I knew at the time there was no going back to who I was. I didn't think I had much choice, I had nowhere else to go. It felt the only way was to stay."

Polly chewed over Estelle's disclosures. She had never known for sure if Dr. John had fathered Rose, but had kept her mouth shut in case she was wrong. Finally she knew the truth; what she could have done with that bit of information! However, they were bound together now, both guilty of the same transgression; she understood why Madam felt safe in revealing all and how it would remain secret between the two of them. She sat spellbound at what her employer was revealing; never in a million years would she have guessed that she would say the things that she did.

Estelle ended by warning her that whatever the enticements of the land of the free may promote, the inequalities of the class system would leave her nowhere to run. "...So you see if you go, well, God only knows what will happen to you, I shudder to think. I was very lucky, how much luck do you think you will have? Even if you make it through and give the child up;

then what? It will be so hard, there could be terrible consequences, stay here, the place that you know and love."

Finally Polly managed to ask a question. "So you hadn't lost your memory at all?"

"Not really, although I was very confused for quite some time after. Can you understand now how desperate I was Polly? Can you now see how determined I was for my child to have a father?"

"Maybe, but Rose must have a real father. Oh!" Polly pondered, "was he married too?" Estelle wondered how far she was going to go with her revelations.

She answered poignantly. "Yes, he was married." Her mind pictured the scene from all those years ago. Estelle had begun to wonder just how strong the marriage had been. She thought he had loved her so much; but when she saw them together, "Then I saw him with her," Estelle continued. "And I just walked away. I didn't think much about it at first but then I got myself into such a fog, I was so confused. Then when I came here I just couldn't go back, then I realised I was pregnant and, well, you know the rest."

"So he never knew?"

"No, he never knew, but one day I hope he will. That's not all though, when I was growing up, I had no idea that I had been kidnapped from Lord and Lady Peters and it came as more of a shock to me than to anyone else. It was as if I had vanished into thin air, there were no witnesses, and then twelve years ago, for whatever reason, it was time for me to come back, as if it were all meant to be. Anyway, what I am trying to say is you belong here too, you belong with Charles, he is more than willing to take care of you. Please, you must not get aboard that ship, do you really think you have a future if you do?"

"You sound like Cookie, she didn't want me to either."

"Well listen to her then if you won't listen to me. I wish you well Polly whatever you do." She got up to go but before she did, felt the need to embrace her bewildered ex-maid.

Estelle asked Mrs. Cook as soon as she got back why she had not informed her about Polly's plans considering she knew of her intentions. Cookie shrugged off any responsibility and complained that Polly had accused her of being as mad as a hatter. "Said I'd scared her half to death just because I dreamt of a ship disappearing below the water." Estelle closed her eyes in anguish. To her way of thinking, when people started to have premonitions, everyone ought to take heed.

It was nearly a week later and Charlie was shouting from the hall demanding everyone's attention. "What in God's name is all the shouting about?" asked John annoyed at being dragged from his ablutions.

"It's Polly, I mean it's the Titanic, it's sunk! Here look, in the paper." John rushed downstairs and grabbed the paper out of his hands while Charlie continued, more in sobs than yells. "I waved her off just the other day when she left with Mr. Peach, she was so excited. I can't believe it, surely it can't be true!"

"Good grief! Estelle, come and read at this! The unsinkable ship has sunk! Look, don't worry Charlie, it says no lives were lost, Polly will be fine I am sure, no need to worry."

"I thought you always said not to believe what was written in the papers," Estelle remonstrated. She was coming down the stairs clutching onto the bannister for support with no attempt to conceal her tears. The tension over the last few days had ruptured, she had hoped against hope that Polly would change her mind, and now it was too late.

Conflicting reports about the tragedy came in dribs and drabs over the next few days, but it eventually became clear to everyone that an inconceivable disaster of catastrophic proportions had taken place. No-one could see how a newly-built ship could go down taking with it most of its passengers and crew. Charlie was inconsolable. Estelle's guilt worsened; she had not done enough to persuade Polly to stay. They all took to wearing black as a mark of respect.

Chapter Sixteen

Estelle was brooding, but it wasn't just because of Polly, that she would now never have the experience of being a mother; something no woman should miss; no it wasn't that.

Estelle had never conceived another child and although she thought it a little odd, she had not spent too long considering the matter. In fact she was rather glad; Rose was so special to her and she feared that another child might steal her place. Vicky had succeeded in pushing out a further three children, she was quite the little mother, she enjoyed every minute of her contented and busy existence. Jason was able to indulge her accordingly as his businesses continued to expand. She always dressed in the very latest designs from Paris, and like Lily and Violet, had tried to encourage Estelle to come to Paris with her so she would have enough clothes to carry her through the Season. According to Vicky, if she were ever invited to an event in a great house, she would need several changes of dress for just one day alone. Estelle didn't think she had ever noticed if her mother changed her clothes several times a day when she had visited Tiplin; well, perhaps maybe once a day. "But that was because she wasn't entertaining," explained Vicky. "And anyway, when you come to stay in our London house you are going to need plenty of ball-gowns. I will bring you my catalogue and you can choose. Oh, and then there's Ascot." Estelle could barely keep up with Vicky's social calendar. If not London, then it was Cowes, then on to the south of France for the winter; children and nanny in tow and a small army of staff.

Georgie and his good friend Francis blasted through the front door kicking a football and Estelle was brought back into the present.

No, her brooding wasn't for the lack of more children either. She hadn't realised how the disaster of the Titanic would affect her so personally, and what else was there to come?

The two boys raced around the hallway until Estelle felt that something was bound to be broken unless they calmed down. She suggested they go down to the kitchen to find some cake. Time had passed quickly, they were growing up so fast. It wouldn't be long before Georgie, or rather George, which he now insisted on being called, would be eighteen. She kept trying to keep it from her mind but it welled up nonetheless. She knew that nothing could be changed, it would happen whether she liked it or not and she would have to find her own way of dealing with it. She had been spending her days trying to pretend that all was normal; but it wasn't. Never in a million years had she thought she would mourn for Polly; that had come as a big surprise.

The following week brought a knock at the back door, very soft. Cookie was annoyed; she was in the middle of making pastry; they needed something to eat; the remains of the Easter fare had been given to the poor as the household had lost any appetite for rich food. Most callers knocked and walked straight in announcing who they were. Clearly this caller was not of the same intention and now she would have to stop what she was doing and mess everything up with her floury hands. She wiped them as best she could on her cloth and took it with her to protect the handle of the door as she tugged it open. Her voice sounded curt, "Yes?" but then everything changed. She took the caller into her ample arms in such a tight embrace they almost suffocated. At length the poor soul was ushered inside, not into the kitchen but straight up the back steps and pushed into the hall where Cookie started shouting "Look, quickly everyone, look who's 'ere." Charlie was first, he had been tending to a sash cord in the dining room and couldn't help but rush towards Cookie's charge with an embrace that lifted her clean off her feet.

"For pity's sake put me down or you'll be squeezing the life out of me!" He replaced Polly's feet back on the floor but continued a strong hold on her upper arms just to reassure him that she was real.

"How can this be, how can this be? Its a miracle that's what it is, a miracle. Drowned, that's what they said. You were supposed to be drowned." Estelle, who had been in her bedroom came out on the landing with tears of relief. They had searched through the lists of survivors every day; it was indeed a miracle.

It turned out that Polly had had cold feet about all the arrangements. Once the Titanic had set out, Polly thought a lot about what her mistress had said. She had certainly been right about the class distinctions; the different social classes never mixed. Polly, being a third class passenger, found she only had access to certain areas of the ship, namely the dining room and what was called a general room which, depending on the time of day, was also a lounge, a nursery or a recreational room. It was crowded and noisy; there was nowhere to go; she was alone and scared and the dismal prospects of what lay ahead had unnerved her. She soon realised that marrying Charlie had been the better option and when, after six torturous hours, the ship stopped off at Cherbourg, she disembarked. When she heard the news of its sinking Polly at once knew "that God has rescued me and forgiven me for my sins. He was trying to warn me with that dream Cookie had and everything Madam said. I didn't listen, I didn't believe, but everything came true. I'm saved, that's what I am."

The wedding was a quiet affair; the fewer persons present meant the fewer to see Polly's expanding waistline. Afterwards, the old Miss Polly Wilson became almost unrecognisable as the new Mrs. Charles Todd, obliging to all, who could never do enough. Estelle relished the meek and mild mannered woman who asked very gently if she might, if Madam would consider, to re-employ her. The whole situation needed to be re-considered. Polly, who had been staying with Fay, moved in with Charlie above the garage after their marriage so naturally she was near at hand for duties; it would be ludicrous not to utilise her knowledge and expertise. Yet she was soon to have a child; but had that ever stopped Estelle in what she had wanted to do? These things could surely be sorted out and besides, she needed to rethink the running of the household. Mrs Cook was near to retiring age and she had never replaced Fay preferring to hire help on an occasional basis. Yes, she was sure Polly could be redeployed, they could work something out together.

The household settled down again, but Estelle's sense of foreboding had not diminished. The hospital was up and running like an enormous machine and, apart from the occasional meeting, did not take up much of her time. She was wise enough now to realise that she felt better when she had a diversion; something that would let her feel the freshness of the day and the wind in her face. For the moment, she took herself off to the park. They would be busy planting out the annuals now the risk of frost had gone, she would enjoy watching the coming and going of the seasons from a groundsman's point of view. She put on her outdoor clothes and went as briskly as she dare, trying to clear her head. It didn't help, however. The tidy rows of fledgling flowers, midget gems, little promises of greater glory to come that would give hope and joy to most, were not enough for her. Estelle remained troubled, and she did not know what to do about it.

John inadvertently came to her rescue later in the day. He liked to please his wife and when he arrived home earlier that evening, he had been formulating an idea. Since he began his work at the new hospital his humour had changed entirely. His black moods were gone and thankfully the heavy atmosphere that previously accompanied them. In their place was the John she had known when they first met. Estelle loved to hear him telling tales of exciting events and skilful endeavour. In his turn John liked Estelle to question his every decision, he definitely thought it prompted him to improve his practice where necessary.

On the surface married life looked very peaceful for John, although he sometimes found it hard to comprehend his wife. On the one hand she had the countenance and tenacity to create a hospital and on the other she was worrying over life's trifles such as what to have for breakfast. Had her accident been really so bad that it had impaired her in some way? He was not convinced and he put it down to whatever had happened before they met. There was one such vexation as he settled down that evening, but this time his reaction was total amusement. Estelle was apprehensive that George was growing up fast and it wouldn't be long before he reached adulthood. He knew of course that it was every mother's anxiety how their children would fare in the 'big bad world'. But she need not have worried over George's future. He was guaranteed to follow in his father's footsteps and study medicine, just as he had done. Either Glasgow or Edinburgh, that was the plan. A new hospital building was going up in Glasgow and would be finished by the time George's training began. He would leave the choice to his son of course.

"He's got quite a way to go before he has the key of the door. Stop worrying about him, he has a fine head on his shoulders, mark my words, he will be absolutely fine."

"Oh John, I do hope so, I do hope so." He patted his wife on her shoulder hoping that would make everything all right and changed the subject. He hated his wife to be upset.

"By the way, I saw something on the way home that got me thinking. I'd like to purchase a bicycle for you." John had been momentarily halted in the motorcar by several bicycles cutting across his path as he had set off from Reid Street. He saw the joyful smiles on the riders' faces as the small party pedalled by, waving an apology. One of the ladies had her hand on her escort's shoulder as they rode together. Two others raced along in competition with each other and laughing all the way. What an enjoyable little scene. He had not thought of riding a bicycle as a leisure activity. Delivery boys used bicycles, workers commuted into town on them instead of relying on horses, but now come to think of it, he had seen a growing number of women about on bicycles. He remembered an article he had read once about female emancipation and how a bicycle gave women a feeling of self-reliance and independence. Just the thing for Estelle, he thought, she likes to be free and out in the fresh air.

It was Estelle's turn to laugh. "But John, I haven't ridden a bike for..." she stopped herself before correcting what she was going to say, "I mean I wouldn't know if I could ride, I might never have ridden one."

"Would you like to learn?" She contemplated the suggestion. Pumping pedals hard up bottom-gear slopes; lungs bursting, forcing out each breath, determined thighs pushing, aching for repose, onward, upward. Then the apex; elation, easing breath and free-wheeling down and down.

"Yes yes, I would love to learn."

"Jolly good. I knew my feeling was correct. I shall order one straight away."

Alas, there was shortly to be a new concern for the household. Estelle came across Polly leaning over the landing bannisters rubbing her forehead.

"Polly, what's the matter? Please tell me you aren't still working today."

"My head, it's banging, I can't see properly."

"Polly, I'm going to put you straight to bed in the back bedroom."

"It's just a headache Madam, I'll be all right." Estelle, worried for her maid who was now heavy with child, ignored her and ushered her into bed and drew the curtains.

"The light will make your head worse," she explained. Polly soaked up the unexpected role reversal and let herself be tucked into the luxurious bed by her concerned employer. "I am going to call my husband immediately. Close your eyes and get some rest."

"There is no need for all this, I shall be fine in a bit, it's only a headache."

"Have you forgotten you are expecting a baby? You need rest, it's very important."

A few days before Estelle had caught sight of Polly's ankles and had noticed how swollen they looked, and wondered when Polly had last been to the ante-natal clinic. She must ask John to have a look at her, she ought to be slowing down, the extra hours; it was too much just before her confinement. But Polly insisted on carrying on as normal saying her legs would be fine when she put her feet up. Now Estelle was angry with herself for not pushing Polly more forcefully.

Estelle's insistent phone-call to her husband prompted John to give instructions not to move Polly, to give her a teaspoon of Epsom salts and not allow anything other than milk to pass her lips. He said he would attend her as quickly as he could. Estelle did as he had asked, thankful he recognised the urgency, and waited impatiently for his return. She didn't have to wait long; he had hailed a cab from outside the hospital entrance, and arrived within fifteen minutes. He bounded up the stairs and began his examination by checking her blood pressure.

"How is it?" asked Estelle.

"Too high to move her. She'll need one teaspoon of the Epsom salts every hour for six hours. I will give her morphia to keep her respirations down; she needs to perspire. Measure any urine she is able to pass."

Admiration for her husband washed over Estelle's body as she watched him attend to his patient. He was so clever, he knew exactly what to do. "When her bowels are moving freely I think we will be able to take her to hospital and induce her labour." The last sentence surprised her. She started to procrastinate.

"Bowels?"

"Yes, what else do you expect Epsom salts to do?" She brought the commode without further fuss and had cleaned and emptied it several times over by the time John decided it would be safe to move Polly to hospital. Charlie was ready to take them. The car had been checked and ready for hours - he knew about engines; childbirth was the mystery. Polly had ignored his pleas to do as the midwife said and attend the clinic regularly. She claimed she knew better and it was a waste of time, and now, according to Dr John, she was gravely ill.

"It would not have stopped her blood pressure going up, but we would have known about it and encouraged her to rest more and try to manage it that way," the good doctor explained. He was angry with himself; Polly practically lived in his house and he had been unaware of her developing a pre-eclamptic condition, something that was potentially life-threatening if not kept under control. If he hadn't noticed, then how could he expect anybody else to bear the responsibility of her welfare? John understood how helpless Charles was feeling and how much it now fell on him to provide a happy outcome for the couple.

He would need to examine Polly as soon as she was settled at the hospital. It wouldn't be too difficult to induce the labour as she was so close to her confinement date. Labour was usually very swift in a true pre-eclamptic. He would use a dilator if she wasn't ripe and pull on a Voorhees bag for a few hours to dilate the cervix; this would be his penance for not keeping a closer eye on her. He would have to use ether as an anaesthetic as chloroform might bring on a fit. He was hopeful that if her blood pressure stayed sufficiently low and any albumen in her urine kept at a low measurement he would not have to proceed to caesarian section.

A bump in the road brought John back from his reverie and he put out a hand to steady the sedated Polly who was slumped against him. They had wrapped her up well, the night was cool; fortunately there was no rain, he hated motoring in the open-topped car when it was raining, particularly with a sick patient.

Much as he wanted to get his wife to the hospital as quickly as he possibly could, Charlie slowed down to maintain a smooth ride. John went over his thoughts and views on the newly favoured vaginal caesarian section. Although he acknowledged it cut down the risk of further contamination in an already infective patient, he was not keen on the procedure; perhaps he just needed more practice. He wondered if he were becoming too set in his ways, but he soon banished that thought.

Charlie had chauffeured them comfortably to the main door of the hospital and John instructed him to bring a wheelchair and a nurse which he managed admirably, before collapsing like a quivering wreck. John dismissed him as the party reached the door urging him to go home and help himself to some whisky in the drinks cabinet as it was going to be a long night.

Like an automaton, Charlie drove the car back home and into the garage, closed it up and cleaned himself down before entering through the back door of the house. He found Estelle in the hall, pacing up and down. She looked at him expectantly but he just shrugged his shoulders saying he had dropped them off and come straight back and had been instructed to drink whisky. "Of course, how remiss of me, come into the library I will get you some. Have you eaten? No of course not. Let me get something, you must eat even if you think you can't." Estelle had seen him shaking his head. Food was the last thing on his mind. She poured out a large whisky and made him take a seat while she went for some nourishment. "I will bring something for us both, I need to eat even if you don't and, Rose has been baking tarts today."

Charlie managed an omelette and some treacle tart and snacked later on bread and cold chicken after they heard the hall clock strike two. Staying up late was always a hungry business even under normal circumstances. As three o'clock chimed Estelle poured more whisky for Charlie who, like her, paced continually around the room. Four o'clock sounded and a solitary bird chirruped; a lonely herald before the dawn chorus would announce the new day. That particular miracle, in all its glory, went unnoticed in the library for its occupants had at last managed to shut their eyes.

The shrill sound of the telephone got them both to their feet and they rushed towards it almost colliding in their semi stupor of sleep. "Yes, yes, I understand. Yes, yes. We will. Yes, yes, goodbye," was all Charlie could glean from the side of the conversation that he could hear, but it made no sense to him and he hopped about from one foot to the other trying to be patient but failing miserably. Estelle hung up. Charlie held his breath, his sleep deprived eyes staring wildly at her, his hands clutching hard at his cap. Estelle put a hand over them to calm him and smiled. "It's a girl Charles, a girl."

"Polly, how's Polly?" His voice was small and high-pitched, he was finding it hard to get the words out.

"John says she is no worse, which is good news, and now that she has had the baby she will begin to improve. Naturally though, she will be very tired and will need rest." Charlie paced up and down in pent-up frustration trying to say something, all the time his temper was rising.

"Good news, is it really good news? That rat, Eckler has got a lot to answer for that's all I can say, causing my missus all this grief." He continued to pace muttering to himself then stopped, looked over at the door and made for it purposefully, his head down like a bull charging at a target.

"Charles you're tired and overwrought, you don't know what you are saying. I am sure Polly is going to be fine, she just needs a little time to recover. Please, don't do anything you might regret."

"Regret? I'll not regret it, I'll, I'll..." but Estelle did not get to hear the rest. As quickly as she could she raced for the door and stood in front of it blocking the way. "

"You will have to get past me first Charles and I am not going to let you, I'm sorry. Polly is going to need your help and support and she won't get it if you're in jail charged with assault." Charlie turned away when Estelle looked him straight in the eye, he could not face her, he knew she was right. Polly would be horrified if he went round and punched him and anyway, the fathead would know then he was the father and he must never find that out, never. Charles' fervour dissolved and his tired frame wilted. He was exhausted, it had indeed been a long night. Estelle put her hand to his shoulder and congratulated him on having a daughter. "She will be yours Charles. Who will rock her to sleep, who will read her bedtime stories, who will she come to with scuffed knees? You will be the very best Daddy she could ever have. Go and get some sleep, we shall go and visit this afternoon." She removed her hand and Charlie nodded in agreement as he sidled away, but not before he was able to conceal the tears that had formed in his eyes.

Estelle waited for John to come home. She wasn't ready for sleep yet, she was thinking about her sensational and impressive husband. What a man! Brave, heroic, single-handedly saving the day and conquering all adversity. Her mind raced around in a similar vein until the bedroom door opened with her champion in its frame. She held her arms out and welcomed him into her bed.

Chapter Seventeen

"...Of course Jason had little choice but to sell all the taxicabs in the end. The enterprise never recovered after the drivers' industrial action the other year and then there was all that business over the fuel." Vicky stopped briefly to take a breath and continued, "Anyway, he said he got a good price so all's well that ends well. Never mind about taxicabs, has your bicycle arrived yet?"

"No, and I feel like a child looking forward to birthday presents." explained Estelle.

"You will have to do Daddy's happy dance then," said Algie, Vicky's eldest who had been listening intently to his mother and aunt's conversation. It was a lovely early summer's day, the sun warm and full of promise. Vicky had brought the children over for the day, spending the afternoon in the park along with Rose who had shepherded them around. George said he was far too old to play with his young cousins and didn't want to be seen with his sister anyway. He had conveniently absented himself saying Francis was expecting him.

"Daddy's happy what?" Estelle said with intrigue.

"Don't you know it? Daddy has a special dance for when he's feeling happy and we call it his happy dance. Do it with me Mummy and show Auntie Estelle." Vicky sighed but duly obliged and danced with her son. Estelle laughed so much it brought tears to her eyes as she realised she had been the inventor of the happy dance.

"Well now Algie. Yes I do know your Daddy's happy dance and I know when he danced it for the very first time because it was with me. When you were first born your Daddy was so very very happy that you had arrived safely, he danced and danced outside your room until the doctor allowed him to see you.

"He danced it for me?"

"Yes he danced it just for you and now please may I dance it with you because you have made me feel very happy."

Estelle's bicycle arrived at last. She loved it and rode it everywhere, her way of escaping the hurly-burly of life. She could pedal her cares away and breathe away the knot in her stomach that was becoming a constant reminder that she was in a state of anxiety. As the months went by and autumn came, then winter, which went into spring, there was nothing she could do. Like everyone else, she could only watch and wait for what approached.

Throughout the summer the weather was beautiful and might have been celebrated forever had not the demise of the Archduke superseded its glory. To take their minds off current affairs, for the bank holiday, Estelle, John, George and Rose joined Vicky and Jason and children for a picnic in the park. It seemed as if the whole town had the same idea. Table cloths and travelling blankets made the greens into chessboards and folk had disgorged their hampers and themselves upon them. Children's marching feet forced paths through the dainty fabric squares, their arms sporting imaginary trumpets and trombones for their fingers to play on in response to the rousing sounds of the music blasting from the bandstand.

"Lemonade or claret?" Vicky organised the beverages while Estelle put out the food.

"Don't ask silly questions," retorted Jason, helping himself. He had provided the most scrumptious pork pie from a recipe in an old cookbook found amongst his late mother's effects. He remembered from his youth the delicious home-made pies and had instructed a local bakery to make them according to the old recipe. Ever aiming to please, he believed it would be far more impressive than the usual 'squashed up sandwiches' and said so just as Estelle produced some.

"Well, someone had to. A picnic's not a picnic without them," she countered quickly. She noted later that squashed or not, they had all been eaten and remarked on it.

"Yes, the ducks loved the spicy chicken ones," retorted Jason. Estelle pushed at his arm, saying nothing.

Children playing happily, the lively bandstand loud with colour and music as golden sunshine reflected in its burnished brass, the mellowing wine; the atmosphere sparkled. It was like a dream. They drew solace from the park and savoured it but beneath it lay a deep sense of foreboding of what was coming.

Then it began. The newspaper headlines had captured Estelle's feelings of doom, doom, doom exactly. She went from confusion to panic to despair. John had a sense of stoic necessity about the whole affair. George was at first subdued about the prospect, then thoroughly excited, declaring he would enlist at the first opportunity. "After all," he declared, "Francis joined the Terriers on his seventeenth birthday and trains every weekend."

"You will do no such thing," said his father. "First of all you are not old enough and second you will be of far more help to your fellow man, when trained as a doctor. We shall hear no more about the matter." Estelle was thankful she and John were of the same mind over George. She could not imagine how she would feel about him as a soldier and would have him sullen and disrespectful rather than dead. She had no idea of how or what the war was going to do to her little family but she at last could give her fears and anxieties a focus; it was almost a relief..

"Don't worry too much, it won't last long," John told her in measured tones but he had his own reservations. His understanding of Germans was that they were ordered, thorough, hard-working, masters of organisation and had no sense of humour. Add their loyalty and comradeship into the mix and their characteristics, like precisely cut jigsaw pieces fitting together, did not make a pretty picture. As an enemy they may well be unbeatable. This he chose to keep to himself.

"It was a good idea to grow so many vegetables in the garden," Estelle said, popping her head over the morning paper. "It says here that everyone has started hoarding and food prices have gone up. Good grief, it's only the first week!"

"We all have to rally and do what we must," John replied. He hadn't really been listening, preoccupied by normal activities such as getting to work on time. "Well, war won't stop babies arriving, must be off, Pilkington enlisted on Friday, that makes us three down."

"Don't you think with so many men overseas there may not be as many babies? Estelle questioned.

"Now there's a thought."

Apart from the threat of food shortages, life carried on as usual for Estelle and she grew accustomed to the feeling of being at war. Cookie no longer worked every day, though she would not think of retiring. She came in for three mornings during the week, but realistically that was all she was able to do. Estelle assured her she and Rose could manage. Despite her age, her temperament never changed. "Them Germans 'ave been amongst us all the time. I've got no sympathy for them 'specially what they did to our Polly." Cookie had gone straight to her favourite pastime of tittle-tattle. "And don't think I don't know about that what shouldn't be mentioned."

Estelle gave her a sidelong glance as if she did not follow her meaning and Cookie continued. "Haven't you heard? they're arresting all the Germans still 'ere in England and those Ecklers are up next I'll be bound."

"You mean the butchers?" asked Estelle.

"I've just seen their shop sign been changed to Eckles. Do they think no-one'll notice? They've 'ad it coming for a long time. And what do you feel about Charlie? He keeps saying he's going to sign up whether Polly lets him or not. I said to Polly she's goin' to find it difficult when the baby arrives and 'im gone. Never seen a man so devoted to 'is first, well, not *his* as such, referring to what shouldn't be mentioned."

"No need to mention anything." said Estelle.

The first Christmas came and went and the first winter passed without too many changes. There was a sharpness to the March air as Estelle sat by the kitchen range, warmed by it in the preparation of the Sunday dinner. Usually Estelle tried to keep her distance from news of the war, it was her way of keeping sane. The government's media campaigns helped to some extent, as they were successful in censoring the slaughter; the constant rallies for men to enlist were the only clue to the truth. Twenty thousand volunteered every day, not realising they would fulfil their patriotic duty in swamp-like holes where they would eat, sleep, pray and probably die.

"Its not so bad as I'd thought," Estelle said chatting to Rose as they prepared the meal together. She allowed herself now to think about the war and was voicing her opinion, but as she was tasting her daughter's pudding mixture, Rose assumed she was criticising her dish and pulled a long face. Her mother misinterpreted her look. "At least Francis is safe in England, his battalion hasn't been mobilised," she encouraged and changed Rose's look to one of confusion.

"Oh, I thought you were talking about the pudding. Anyway what do I care about Francis? He probably won't even remember me when he gets back, I'm only George's little sister as far as he's concerned."

"I think you might be surprised, he's always had a soft spot for you."

"Well," Rose retorted, "if he thinks I'm at all bothered about him he can go jump. Pass me that knife will you, I'll start chopping these carrots." She began an angered attack on the innocent vegetables, her heart burning for her sweetheart. Her mother sighed - young love - how well she remembered.

It was to be a special meal, not only was it George's birthday but he had found out he had successfully gained a place at medical school in

Edinburgh. He had honoured his father's wishes of carrying on the family medical tradition. John had arranged it with his father's contemporary and mentor William Ballantyne who said that although it would be difficult for him to be responsible for him, as he looked after the female students, he would keep an eye on him. "It's such a good place to learn," John said over Rose's pudding. "You'll meet Haig Ferguson, he's about to open an out-patient clinic and further the cause of preventive medicine. Routine antenatal supervision, joy of joys."

"Are you liking my pudding?"

"Delicious Rose, delicious as always. Now then George, you must have a mind to study hard, it's far too easy to get distracted."

"Do you think the war might just be a teeny weeny bit of a distraction, Dad?"

"Not at all, so long as you remain conscientious."

"Do you think you will be an obstetrician George, like Dad?"

"No idea Rose, but be sure it'll be something exciting like cutting up dead bodies."

"That's enough!" said his mother.

"You've put me off eating now you horrible brother."

"I thought you wanted to be a nurse, you'll have to get used to that sort of thing," replied George.

"Since when did you want to be a nurse?" asked John.

"Since forever, I thought you knew."

"First I've heard of it," said her father. "Are you sure? It would be very hard work and..."

"There's plenty of time for Rose to want to do all manner of occupations before she grows up," interrupted Estelle. "Have we all finished? Good, then Rose, you and I will clear up and let your father and George talk about what they need to." Rose waited until they were in the kitchen before she tackled her mother about changing the subject. Estelle reminded Rose that her father might not be terribly keen that she wanted to have a salaried occupation.

"But Dad's all for women going out to work; he lets *you* go out and he works with women all the time."

"I don't earn any money, I just sit at committee meetings, there is a difference and when he says he is all for women working I don't think that he has extended the privilege to his daughter."

"It's not fair," grumbled Rose. "He's practically shoving George out of the door."

"He's going to university to study, which is a little different."

"Yes, so he can work as a doctor. What about me?"

"Oh Rose, you are so young yet, there's plenty of time, please try not to worry." Estelle felt for her daughter; it *was* all about George at the moment but then the fact that he was leaving home was a big event. She hoped things would settle down, it was too much for her to imagine Rose leaving as well. That was a few years away yet, she hoped.

Chapter Eighteen

Rose could not find her hairbrush anywhere. She was always looking for it, she could never remember where she had put it down, normally tossing it out of her hand for it to land where it might. Eventually giving up she went to her mother's room to borrow hers. She sat at her mother's chest of drawers and happily brushed her hair in front of the mirror that was perched on top. She liked that mirror; it was divided into three, the outer two panels flapping on hinges so that various angles of hairstyle could be easily viewed. Rose sat there for several minutes playing with the angles until satisfied that her hair was presentable. Her eyes wandered down to the Georgian bowing drawers. One of the top drawers was slightly open but try as she might, she could not shut it properly. She took the drawer completely out to see its problem and looked inside the opening. She saw something right at the back and pulled it out. There were several papers all hand written. Letters, lots of letters. Inquisitive by nature, Rose examined them. She sat and read them all thoroughly one by one, making sure she understood their content, putting them back carefully just as she had found them, in their secret hiding place.

"That girl is becoming more morose and reclusive every day," remarked John as he was welcomed with just a grunt in response when bidding her good morning. "And she hardly touched any of her breakfast. Lord knows what the matter is; I shall have to have words with her. Such a pity Nanny retired, she would have known what to do."

"I hardly think so; Nanny was losing her influence long before she decided to retire. It's just her age, I shall speak to her, it's hard to grow up, have you forgotten?" John had amused his wife by his ostensible ignorance of the painful change from childhood into young adult. Nevertheless, Rose had changed rather suddenly from a happy, outward going young girl into a dark brooding presence; skulking around in the shadows by the day, barely coming out before it was bedtime. Maybe there was something troubling her; Estelle resolved to investigate.

That time came sooner than she thought. A telegram arrived from Lady Peters that very day summoning her to come and speak on a matter 'of great family concern' that had come to light. Any telegram at that point in time was unnerving as so many of them started with the words 'We regret to inform you.' Estelle did not have immediate family serving in the war but she still felt uneasy when receiving a telegram. She packed a bag and waited at the railway station for the next available train. By then she had worried herself into such a state of anxiety she could barely catch her breath. The train arrived with quiet grace and had pulled to a standstill before she rose anxiously from her seat in the waiting room. She took a deep breath, trying to rid herself of apprehension and ventured bravely onto the steam-engulfed platform. She couldn't see a thing. The jostling pack of disgorging travellers; the strange muffled sounds; the disorientation; the foggy atmosphere, it was becoming too much, she could not keep her balance and she was falling.

"Here, let me help you." She felt somebody's arm around her waist pulling her back up. "Are you trying to get on or off?"

"On," she answered automatically.

"Just stay still; they'll all be gone in a jiffy. It's much better to wait till they leave the platform before trying to get on you know. Always in such a hurry to remember any manners so they are." She looked round and saw her saviour.

"Why, Francis, it's you!" Her fears melted into oblivion, the immediacy of the situation taking their place. She looked the young man up and down. How gallant he looked in his uniform. How sad that so many young men, boys really, would never come back; it was such a waste. But there was nothing to be done about it; she would have to detach herself from the whole débâcle as best she could. Estelle separated her torso from his strong arms and dusted down her coat. "How has it been?"

"Oh you know, drills, drills and more drills," he replied dismissively. Just got a bit of leave so I'm on my way home. Er, how is Rose?" he asked tentatively.

Ah Rose, of course! No wonder she has been the way she is. Francis has been away. She felt better immediately as she supposed she had put two and two together. "I think Rose will be just fine if you would care to pay us all a visit. George is away at present, he wanted to go and see what was in store for him when he starts at Edinburgh."

"Yes, I got a letter from him a few days ago. Thank you, I would love to call, I will let you know when my mother lets me out! There, I think its safe enough to board now."

"Yes, I think it might be. Goodbye and thanks for your help."

"Any time," he replied and shut the cabin door for her. Estelle found a seat and made herself comfortable and ruminated over the chance meeting. 'What a lovely boy, what a charming boy.' It kept her mind off the matter 'of great family concern.'

The Peters' chauffeur picked her up at the station but the reception from her mother on arrival at the house was rather cool. Estelle was anxious to know the reason for her mother's concern. "Come into the library, we will not be disturbed in there," was the reply. They sat down by the fireplace, the fire was as yet unlit and Estelle listened intently to her mother. "I have received a very disturbing letter from Rose. What she has kept as a closely guarded secret; or rather what you have kept secret has deeply troubled me. The fact that she felt able to confide in me at all is remarkable and thank God she has. It's no wonder the poor girl has been distressed. How could you deceive us for so long? It beggars belief." Estelle wondered what on earth she was talking about but was very soon to apprehend precisely its nature. She cringed at what she might hear next. "I received the letter yesterday and have spent all night deciding what to do. What I *should* do is to tell your poor innocent husband but instead I have decided to give you the benefit of the doubt. So, go on, I'm all ears as they say." She sat erect in her chair with arms folded, waiting.

Estelle felt like a naughty school child about to get the strap. "Please could you tell me the content of Rose's letter to you so that I may be sure of what you want to know?" She needed to know precisely what she was facing in order to give a sound answer.

"Rose says in her letter to me that she has discovered some letters in your hand that span many years addressed to some other, shall we say, person, telling him that he is her father."

'Oh dear, so it was nothing to do with Francis. How am I going to get out of this?' She needed a few minutes to think what to say. She had always intended to tell Rose about her real father but did not know how to begin and never meant her to find out in this dreadful manner. How could she ever speak about such events and how could her mother ever understand? "I am so sorry," she said. "Rose must be in a terrible state of confusion." She did not know what else to say.

"Well wouldn't you be so, if you found out such a truth?" Lady Peters was incensed; she had, since yesterday, worried over the torrid content of Rose's letter. How could her lost and found most beloved daughter do this to her? Such deception! What betrayal! Hysteria was rising within her and she was not liking it, not at all. She tried to remain calm, hoping Estelle had a viable explanation. "What I cannot understand," she continued before Estelle had managed to formulate anything, "is why you have lied to us all about your loss of memory, when quite clearly you have had no such failure."

'Ah! So that was it; it was the fact she had lied and not that she loved someone else and had become pregnant.'

"Mother, if I told you I don't think for one minute you would believe me."

"Let me be the judge of that."

Estelle found that either her mother coaxed it out of her or, after all this time, she couldn't hold it in any more. As her story unfolded, Sybil learnt much about her third daughter and those missing years. An ordinary life with an ordinary family; with parents innocent of any crime. They had waited a long time for a baby, and then she had arrived unexpectedly; it was like a gift from God. But they had never really known where their supposed daughter had come from originally. They were gone from her now, however. And the man in her life, Rose's real father? what of him? The poor girl; Sybil understood completely how helpless she must have felt. The twists and turns of life could never be fully explained in this bizarre and complicated world.

Sybil wondered what she would have done given the same set of circumstances. She had after all, her own secrets; although her daughter looked just like her siblings, and it was obvious that Lord Peters was her father. She had always imagined that her daughter's disappearance had been a form of punishment for a certain indiscretion in which she had partaken. Indeed, Lady Peters was not in any position to judge. Her feelings were unchanged towards her lovely daughter; an overwhelming sense of love and protection remained no matter the circumstances. She wanted, no, needed to help. How could she have managed to walk away, lost, if she had not found herself so uncannily in the very place where she could fit in so easily, but where it meant fabricating her past in order to stay there?

Lady Peters was feeling her years; her joints were stiff and her eyesight was not as sharp as it was, but her mind was still as quick when she needed it to be. She did remember what it felt like to be in love. The memory of him with another woman in his arms causing a great rift between them and their relationship. Estelle must have felt desolate. However, one has to be practical about these things; and Estelle had survived her ordeal. She loved another, but so what?

" 'I hold it true, whate'er befall; I feel it, when I sorrow most; 'tis better to have loved and lost than never to have loved at all' to quote Tennyson."

Estelle looked at her mother. "But I love John too!" she cried out. The words hung in the room as Estelle connected to them. She had never said so out loud; always imagining she held just a fondness for her husband rather than a full blown love affair. How much time had she wasted?

During those two hours together they cried and laughed, and laughed and cried, both understanding each other, both having known love and loss. Exhausted and with the chill of the evening around them, they sat quietly together warmed by the love in their hearts. Eventually the younger woman stirred and asked cautiously "Do you really believe me?" She could certainly understand how her explanation might sound.

"Extraordinary as it may seem, yes I do, and it clarifies why it was in your interest to pretend you had lost your memory. So much about your strength of character, your resourcefulness and determination has been expressed in what you have done and impressed upon me further that you are indeed my daughter."

"I've lived with this for so long, I'm glad I've shared it with you."

"Come now, enough. Let us warm ourselves in the dining room; it is surely time for something to eat, and for your own sake and for that of your husband, you must give up this silly nonsense of letter writing to someone who has gone from your life. You owe John that; he has saved your life entirely."

"I know that and you are right, I have to tell Rose everything and more, for there is something that I have not told you, it's something specifically for her to know about her father."

"Then I will trust you to tell her."

Once home again Estelle knocked tentatively on Rose's bedroom door before entering. She found her staring out of the window where she was sitting clutching hold of a book that she did not appear to be reading. "I hope I'm not disturbing you Rose but I wanted to come and have a little chat."

"If it's about the birds and the bees again then you don't need to tell me any more thank you very much," began Rose "I know all about it."

"I expect you do. No it's not about that; It's something else. May I sit down?" Rose gestured for her mother to sit and she did so on the dressing table stool nearby. "I need to tell you about something that happened to me a long time ago but it involves you and it is time for you to know." She cleared her throat, faced her daughter and gently unfolded her saga. Its substance was so unexpected that Rose would spend most of her life trying to comprehend it. Least of all when her mother told her she may meet her father when the time was right. "But he won't know who you are, he never knew about you."

"How will I know him then?" asked Rose.

"You will," was all Estelle said in reply. A knock at the door interrupted them. It was Polly holding a card for Rose.

"He's downstairs in the hall, I wasn't sure where to put him." Rose flushed and put her hand to her mouth as she stared at the calling card.

"Francis has called for me! He wants to see me!"

"Well go and show him into the parlour," said Estelle, highly amused by the incredulous look on her daughter's face. Rose sprang over to her dressing table to look in the mirror.

"Where's my hair brush? quick Mum, do my hair."

"Your hair looks lovely. Just go, he might not have long; his mother will want him back soon I'm sure." Estelle watched Rose leave the room, delighted for her daughter. But there was also a deep sorrow hidden behind her pleasure. If only she knew what might happen to him in this dreadful war; but she didn't and could only hope that Francis would be kept safe from harm.

Francis wasn't home for very long but he spent as much time with Rose as he was able and Rose drank in the sweet elixir of their love just like any other young girl.

It was much later when they heard from Francis' family that he had been posted from York to Gainsborough and then to France. On the fifteenth of April, his battalion joined the one hundred and forty sixth brigade. Rose speculated that an awful lot of brigades came before his so hopefully there would be plenty of soldiers in front of him going into battle. He had promised to write, and every day she keenly waited for the post to arrive. "Nice to see you up and about and ready for school early," said her father one morning. Estelle had not dared mention that she was being courted by an older boy, even though it was Francis. Rose was not yet fifteen, and fathers weren't always understanding about such matters, least of all John, especially as she was so young. Estelle had always known that Rose and Francis were meant for each other and was not surprised that they had realised it now; the war had simply escalated things.

Rose received a steady stream of letters from Francis. Amongst his romantic prose were also details of "a little skirmish with the enemy, my first encounter," in which he mostly described what the weather had been like. "Heavy rain fell all day on the sixth followed by dense mist on the seventh and then the eighth brought winds. All in all I think the conditions put a delay on the plans. However, that evening brought a fine sunset and on the ninth, when we made our attack, it was bright and sunny. Our job was to use our artillery to support the East Lancs as they went over the top, poor fellows. "

Estelle discovered later that he had been describing the Battle of Aubers Ridge. Eleven thousand British troops had been mown down by German machine guns in one day. Survivors were pegged down unable to get back to their trenches, and in all that carnage no significant progress had been made. "A total failure then. No wonder Haig called off the offensive, it's all so futile," she was talking to herself, upset by everything she was learning. "And Charles," she continued aloud "well at least I don't have to worry about him for a while."

Charlie's war was over almost before it had begun. He had enlisted with The Pals as soon as Polly had given birth to her second child. John had watched over her pregnancy so closely this time Polly swore she had bruises on her arm from the amount of times he wanted to check her blood pressure. However, he had no need to worry as everything had gone smoothly and she was safely delivered of a son, Freddy. Cookie had been correct in that Charlie looked as though he were the proudest man on earth; he couldn't do enough for his darling wife.

"He's used to service," claimed Cookie. "And now all 'e wants to do is wait on Polly. Well, she'd better not get used to it, now 'e's joining up.

On the morning of the first of July 1916, two thousand volunteers of the 16th and 18th Battalions of The Prince of Wales's Own West Yorkshire Regiment left their trenches in Northern France and advanced across No Man's Land straight into a baptism of fire. It was the first day of the Battle of the Somme and for Charlie and most of the Pals of ninety three brigade, their last. One thousand seven hundred and seventy men were either killed or injured. In the weeks following, as more and more window blinds stayed drawn and the newspapers were filled with photographs of the killed or wounded, they could only hope Charlie was 'just missing.' Polly spent much of her time praying and listening to the tolls of the church bell announcing the dead.

Polly was finding the separation hard to manage, especially with the baby; always crying, never sleeping. She went to the chemist shop to ask Fay for some laudanum soothing mixture to help Freddy stay calm, but Fay would only give her short shrift and referred her to Estelle in the hope she might help. Estelle could have described John's response before she told him of the matter but she knew she had to. She had seen that Polly had become withdrawn after Charles went missing.

"No mother should ever be tempted to use such a drug on their child to keep them quiet. It is poison, two drops of laudanum would be fatal. There have been far too many inquests on children where an opiate has been the cause of death. A child who is always crying and sleepless cannot be well. Where is the child? Bring it to me at once," demanded an exasperated John.

Estelle reminded herself that Polly was alone in a tiny flat with a small child and a new baby so soon after her confinement. She had already tried to tell Polly that maybe she should let little Freddy feed for longer but she would have none of it claiming that he would have to get into a routine quickly. She ignored Estelle's pleas for him to be weighed at the clinic and now, the poor little thing was looking half starved. If they didn't act soon his cries would tail off; he wouldn't have the energy for even a whimper.

John was furious. "Yet again Polly thinks she knows better than the rest of us. Why does she think we set up these clinics? Is it not to help educate those who obviously have no clue as to what they are supposed to be doing?" Fortunately Estelle had brought Freddy herself and left Polly in the flat with Rose and so was unable to hear John's anger vented towards her. Estelle tried to come to Polly's defence.

"No John, please calm down, I don't think it's her fault. Go and examine her and see what you diagnose but I think the real cause is that Polly is worrying so much about Charles, that she's confused in her mind and forgotten the baby's needs."

"Polly will be looked after by us," Estelle announced to Cookie. "Rose is going to look after the children after school and Polly can do some chores and be in our company. It's all arranged; and don't look so surprised, it's the war, we all have to do our bit and Rose is looking forward to it; she's quite used to little ones with all the cousins she has. It will be nice to put the nursery to good use again anyway." Cookie, for once, was speechless. Servant's children in the nursery? What was the world coming to!

John had been in total agreement with his wife about diagnosing Polly's condition and that of little Freddy. "Post-natal depression exacerbated by news of her husband missing at war before a full recovery from childbirth and the infant's failure to thrive as a direct consequence." He blotted the ink, shut the file and thought proudly of his wife for recognising the problem. He had not, he had to admit to himself. He was so busy with work; but then, this *was* his work and now he was unable to see the wood for the trees.

News came; Charlie was in a field hospital. Polly fainted, her prayers were answered and Freddy began to thrive. John insisted that when able enough to be moved Charles was to be brought back home and John would take over any treatment necessary. Polly quickly recovered, became even more devout and attended as many church services as she could.

"Shrapnel got me in the leg and I got pulled down and it broke in the process. Others fell over the top of me and gave me protection from the gunfire. I could hear them screaming in their own agonies but there was nowt I could do. I held a young lad's hand as he went, fell right next to me; most likely acted as my shield. His innards were spilling out of him, and the blood; it didn't take long bless his poor soul. Don't know how I managed, but I crawled back through our wire out of No Man's Land careful as I could. I got back to our lines and someone pulled me into the trench. I lay there for ages feeling gradually weaker; bleeding a bit, think I passed out. Woke up in a tent with me leg all strapped up. Saw some sights in there, I can tell you."

"Best not say much to the women, don't want them to get upset more than necessary," replied John. "Don't think you'll be going back just yet with that leg. As it was broken in two places, and with that shrapnel still left in, you'll be left with a bit of a limp."

"Better a limp than what the others got. Never forget that for as long as I live."

No, Charles was safe back in the fold thank heaven; one less worry for Estelle. But how many more battles before they can all come home? She could hardly bear it and started living in dread of it all.

Vicky saw how her dear friend and sister-in-law was suffering and, just as she had helped when they had first met, attempted to do so again. "You've got to get a grip," said Vicky. "Its the same for us all. We have to keep on going, worrying about things won't make them go away, you have to make the best of it." All she got back from Estelle was a glare as if to say she didn't know what she was talking about. Vicky tried again, in a different way this time; she wouldn't give up on Estelle. "You just have to take deep breaths and you will feel better. Deep breaths, long and slow." Vicky's words made Estelle stop what she was doing and listen. She remembered saying the same thing; so long ago, she barely remembered about that time now.

"How do you know about breathing?" she replied. Vicky laughed at the ridiculous question and Estelle, realising what she had just said, began to laugh too. She felt better; laughter was forever the best medicine.

"Well I have always known that breathing well helps all sorts of situations. You may have forgotten that I helped you with your breathing when you first came here. Do you remember our little walks up and down the paths? But then you helped me as well. You taught me; not to breathe, but how to breathe. You know, when I had Algie. You made me breathe long and slow and it made everything bearable." Estelle sighed, contemplating what Vicky had said and it made her think of something else.

"Do you realise 'inspire' has two meanings? One is to take a breath, and the other, to fill someone with the urge or ability to do something creative. So when a baby is born and takes his or her first breath, they are inspired to live. Conversely, when someone dies or expires, their last breath is expired from them."

"Goodness me Estelle, I had never thought of it like that before, it is literally the breath of life isn't it?" She could see a slight change in Estelle and wanted to strike while the iron was hot. "Why don't you go and help at Tiplin?"

Lord and Lady Peters had given their home over to help the war effort and allowed Georgievna, a Russian Grand Duchess to found a hospital there to treat injured soldiers. Lady Peters had met her while visiting the spa in Harrogate and they had struck up a friendship. Georgievna had founded several recuperative hospitals in the area already and Sybil thought that Tiplin would be very suitable. Estelle decided she was needed at home and couldn't go immediately but what Vicky had said was just what she had needed to hear. Worrying was making her feel negative about everything. She needed to be positive or she would suffocate with stress. She had been in this state many times before and had always pulled through; she could do it again. Somehow Estelle pulled herself together; she needed to for Rose's sake.

Cookie stopped to catch her breath near the house where Francis lived with his mother. She stood puffing and blowing with her hand clutching a fence post looking at the rest of the hill she had to climb. "And that's when I saw the window blinds all drawn. It could only mean that Francis was dead; he was the only boy in that family."

"Oh no! However can I tell Rose?" said Estelle.

"She was sweet on 'im wasn't she poor lass. Well she'll 'ave to know, can't pussy foot when there's war." said Cookie.

"I'll go round first, just to make sure, and give my condolences. Oh dear, poor Rose, she'll be devastated. Francis was such a nice boy."

"They're all nice boys till they're dead then they're poor brave boys, God 'elp them. Got two grandbairns over there since last month myself, lovely boys they are too."

Estelle got the confirmation from Francis' mother who had received the dreaded telegram from the post boy who was later heard to say he wanted to give up his job because he made people cry as soon as he knocked at their doors. "I could see by her stony face how she was suffering. What can one do? There is nothing anyone can do," wailed Estelle to John. John raged through the hall to rid himself of excess energy. He had no answer, coming to the conclusion that war was war and men would die.

Despite some criticism, there was no strategic alternative that the generals could realistically take. It didn't stop John wanting to help, especially when tragedy was brought so close to home with Charles' injury and now Francis. "Don't you think your skills are better placed here?" said Estelle. There was no way she would let her husband enlist. "You are already running every other doctor's clinics in general practice. Anyway, how many babies do you think are going to be born on a battle field? With Pilkington, your house-officer reported missing and the others not due any leave, you are needed here. Besides, how fast do you think you can run on a charge at your age?"

"It won't be long until they extend conscription to all ages and that will include me and I will have to go. Anyway, if I enrol as willing then I will not get called up, just maybe work elsewhere."

"It will be me." They both turned towards the voice on the stairs. "I'll be the one to avenge his death." George had heard them talking and come out of his room when he realised they were talking about Francis. He was on leave from university. Following conscription at the beginning of the year, he had joined his university's training corps and had just received a commission into a medical unit. Estelle had been horrified but he flouted her protestations. "Well what did you expect Mum, I'm no conchie. I knew I would have to join up sooner or later, I had to do something, I couldn't sit and watch the rest of my generation go into battle and be left back here." John had understood entirely. He had full admiration for his son.

"George, whereas I once thought it better for you to complete your medical training if you were able, I know you have to do what you think is right and it is an honourable decision. You will be able to pick up your studies when it's all over."

Rose too had heard the conversation; if she hadn't had Polly's children to negotiate down the stairs, she would have let her feelings explode. Instead, they froze inside her heart and remained there. George helped her bring the children down into the hall and looked to his father. He wanted answers; his boyhood friend was gone. His father had always been able to put things right, only this time, he knew he was powerless like everyone else. He had to retaliate; kill the Hun responsible; do something to give meaning to Francis' life. All those men dead from battle; all someone else's friend, not his. But now it *was* his friend that was dead; destroyed by more failed objectives. All he could do was embrace his sister and support her numb body while barely able to hide his own grief and anger.

"Try not to be angry, son," said Estelle, "it will not serve you. Revenge and retaliation won't bring him back. We need to stay strong and wait for a resolution to this slaughter, for it will come one day."

"I do hope so Estelle, I do hope so," said John.

"I have to do something," said George.

"Then help as many as you can to stay alive," said Estelle and squeezed her son's arm. She felt bewildered; what else could she say to him?.

Rose was kept busy enough with her school studies but put her mind to little else and took to moping about the house alone rather than being with her friends. By the Christmas holidays, nothing having changed, Estelle thought the best thing was to keep her occupied so she would spend less time thinking of Francis. She sent Rose off to Tiplin to help the nurses in their care of the wounded. As she always wanted to train as a nurse, this direct experience would make or break her. Estelle went with her initially and found some comfort there herself. If she could help the recovering men, someone might do the same for George, if ever he were injured.

Rose excelled in her duties; it had been completely the right decision. "Francis was their brother in arms and now I'm helping them too and it makes me feel connected," she explained to her Grandmother. Lady Peters was in awe at her stamina, wishing she could do more herself; it was frustrating for her that she could not. Most of her time was taken up with Austen, who was becoming very frail. He had developed a heart condition and since his last attack, he could not do much for himself. It was only a matter of time; he was aware of that, but he wanted to see the war out if he could. He wanted to see England come back to normal; all this change was too much for him to accept. One positive thing was that his home had been put to good use, he didn't mind that at all..."and it means I have the doctors and nurses at my disposal should I have the need. The Duchess's nurses nearly all have titles so they will know precisely how I need to be looked after."

"I'm sure they do Austen, but they are very busy looking after our guests; you mustn't distract them." He let her continue to think she was right, as she always supposed she was, and sent word via his valet that they must be provided with an adequate supply of wine. He liked to see that any guests in his house were properly looked after. He believed a little alcohol was always pleasing and would improve the monotony of the repetitive fare at the dinner table. The gatherings Tiplin held these days hardly put a mark on his vast cellars; their contents needed to be reduced and he would never be able to consume it all himself.

The war was grinding on, and after the release of a government propaganda film, most people at home were more committed to it than before. Everyone was trying to do his bit. Alongside obstetrics, John was working extra hours in general practice to support other doctors while they were away at the front. Jason had secured a very large contract with the British Army to make convalescent blues for all the wounded soldiers in recuperation and his factories were working day and night to keep up with demand. As well as the various fund raising activities for the war fund which kept her engaged, Vicky was also busy with the suffragists. She was involved in setting up an employment register so that the jobs of those who were serving could be filled.

Estelle stayed on the committee at the maternity hospital but it tested her patience; the health and well-being of the women giving birth seemed to take second place to its rules and regulations. She understood now how John had felt at The Royal and pestered him to take a more prominent stand in administration. He replied that he was too busy with his consultancy and teaching to deal with the day to day logistics of ward activities.

"But you used to get incensed about substandard care," she argued.

"But I don't think the care is substandard," he replied. "It's not to your liking, that's all. If the midwives choose to run their wards - very successfully I might add -in a regimental fashion, then who am I to change them? I know you disapprove of their insistence on feeding the babies by the clock, but surely that is to mould them as early as possible, so that bad habits are not allowed to be formed? I know that Sister Hewer is of the firm belief that regularity in feeding is one of the most important factors in successful baby-rearing, and that the long rest to the digestive organs, when there is no night feeding, is of great value. What do I know of these matters anyway? I'm an obstetrician not a paediatrician."

'And that discipline,' thought Estelle to herself 'is precisely what was fed to Polly and why little Freddy became half-starved. But who am I to have any say in the matter?' She felt frustrated but it was out of her hands, there was little she could do.

Chapter Nineteen

Charlie knocked on the library door and waited for John to call him in. It was easier for John to examine him here rather than at the clinic. His leg was healing well, but was noticeably shorter than his other and still weak. He required a stick to help with walking but refused to see it as a disability and expected, with his usual stoicism, to be back soon with the Pals. John however, changed all this during their consultation. "Put simply, you are not fit. You will slow your friends down and that will be no good to anyone. I can't even see you in a job away from the front, that shrapnel could cause trouble at any time and the medical staff are far too busy with the immediate concerns of battle trauma. I'm sorry old chap, but your war is over." John signed the papers and put his pen down. "There is something else we need to talk about. You understand I'm sure, that times are changing and unfortunately I have not the same need for a valet as I once perhaps did. The concern now is finding a suitable future occupation, so you are able to look after your wife and family. I have given this great consideration. I know you enjoy tinkering with automobiles. I believe the time has come for you to set up your own garage business and I know just the place."

Charlie remained with his head bowed until John mentioned automobiles. He didn't know whether he felt relief or revulsion at being pronounced unfit. Inside, he was ready to do his duty, but the thought of staying at home with his beloved family was intoxicatedly alluring, as was the thought of mending cars for a living. He continued to listen to what was being said, not in the least caring about losing his job as a valet; he knew the good doctor had little use for him these days, Estelle usually sorted his clothes and most of his other duties had been absorbed by employing local tradesmen when necessary. "Those disused tennis courts along the road attached to old Lenny Grey's place," John continued, "they are the ideal location and I know who owns the land so renting won't be a problem. There's some sort of building there already which will serve as your workplace. You may of course continue to live above the old coach house but I expect you will soon have enough to afford somewhere larger. Well," said John when he received no audible response from Charlie, "come on now Charles, what do you say?" Charlie had remained quiet while his animated mind busied itself. What would he say? Should he say he felt bad at having a gammy leg and could no longer serve his King, or be thankful to the Hun for giving him the gammy leg enabling his lifelong ambition. He knew the answer and would have jumped for joy if he could.

"What I say is, when do I start?"

"That's a jolly good chap. Shortly, shortly; I will sort out the renting issues and we'll take it from there. Excellent, excellent." John left Charlie in more of a state of shock than when he had gone into battle. His adrenalin had spurred him on that occasion, but now he felt as if a feather could knock him down. He tottered over to Polly and regaled her with his news. She would at last be married to a man who had a business, no less, which was surely better than a mere shopkeeper. She was going up in the world, and she also thought she may have some other news for Charlie. Better wait for another month before telling him, just to be sure.

The house was quiet these days. Rose was at Tiplin most of the time, John busy at his and everyone else's work. The household staff; well, it could hardly be classed as staff any more, Estelle decided. She liked it this way, the place to herself, no menu problems, laundry issues, cleaning duties. As soon as Polly had announced she was expecting another child again, Estelle forbid her to attempt any housework, declaring she had enough running her own household; with two young children, one still a baby and now another one on the way. Charles was working all hours in his new enterprise leaving little time to help.

She sat down to relax after doing some cleaning herself and was waiting for the kettle to boil. She looked around at her kitchen. 'Yes, it really was her own kitchen now that Mrs. Cook has finally admitted to herself that she can barely even make the walk there, let alone lift any heavy pans and cook,' she mused. She leant back in her chair and smiled contentedly. The walls, in desperate need of new paint, largely hidden by heavily-laden shelves of crockery pots and implements, were hers to do with as she liked. The kettle spluttered its lively contents onto the range and Estelle stirred herself to make a pot of tea. 'Maybe,' she thought, 'now the household is smaller; maybe it's time to do some renovations? A kitchen placed upstairs would be far more convenient than running up and down the cellar steps all day.' She drank her tea and wondered how she might broach the subject to John. She assumed he would drag his heels due to the upheaval.

"Well you had it in you to design a whole hospital, then surely a domestic kitchen would be a mere trifle." She hadn't thought he might respond like that! Thinking he would need a lot of persuasion she had begun the conversation explaining the strain on the knees from continually climbing the cellar steps. He interrupted her chatter as he turned away from her saying, "Whatever you think my dear," and fell immediately asleep. She hadn't expected that either! She spent yet another empty bedtime interlude thinking of how her kitchen would look. Of course it would replace the parlour; hardly used these days, but still a lovely room, and the obvious place. She lay on her back and stretched out contentedly, thinking about the built-in cupboards, soapstone counter top and a double wet sink which gently occluded John's persistent snores. She knew exactly how it would look; thoroughly modern and something built to last.

The next morning John awoke and was still in weary mood. He had not felt like this for years, not since before he met Estelle. He looked at her lying next to him sleeping. Her hair, still full of colour and curling over the pillow and across her face. He loved her as much now as he ever had. He wasn't getting any younger and, with so many of his colleagues serving at the front, his days were kept long, after which all he wanted to do was go to his bed and sleep. His inclinations toward Estelle had been lost somewhere along the way, and in order to keep her bright he had not thwarted her desire to move the kitchen upstairs. He would do anything to keep his wife happy; anything to arrest her need to run away from whatever it was she had been avoiding since he had known her. What Estelle concealed from him; for he was sure she had not suffered any lasting memory loss, was not for him to uncover. If she wanted to keep those years between her abduction and his finding her to herself, then so be it. He had realised this as soon as Rose was born. He had no desire to upset her and preferred to leave Estelle to resolve her inner conflicts alone and when she was ready. Over the years he had seen her struggle, especially since war had been upon them, but she had always managed to hoist herself up. He was encouraged that she had found a new occupation. Planning a new kitchen would help take her mind off the war and George.

With that thought he decided he might raise his spirits by taking a walk through the park. He set forth after breakfast and entered the park by the stone circle and headed for the small lake. Estelle had mentioned the other day she had counted nine little chicks that had been added to the duck population and he wanted to see for himself. Babies of any sort were special and they would be a pleasure to observe.

If they had been blessed with a house full of children like his sister; Estelle would have been fully occupied. His biggest fear now she was passing her child-bearing years, hysteria might creep in. He had seen plenty of that in his clinics; husbands not knowing what to do with their frustrated wives. Did they not know it was their responsibility to keep them satisfied and then this needless condition would not arise, or did one have to be medically trained? Maybe he had been lacking in that direction of late himself. He would have to take steps.

Regrettably, Estelle had never borne another child. Not that he ever imagined she would, as he had sustained such a bad attack of mumps after Eleanor passed away that it most certainly would have rendered him infertile. When Estelle was expecting Rose, he had hoped, that by some miracle he was potent; but she arrived early looking full term and he understood something. Rose had belonged to someone else. Following that, although he was an active man, he never produced any offspring. He had seen how Charles had taken Polly's first-born and saw only love in his eyes, the same as when he held Rose for the first time; not of his flesh, but no less his daughter. He reminded himself that Estelle had taken George into her heart from the beginning and that they did have two children between them.

He reached the lake and studied it intently. There was plenty of duck activity at the other side, some sort of altercation with a dog, but no little fledglings. John waited, still deep in thought. George, his only boy, was so big and burly now. How proud he was of him. They were fortunate in that they received letters from him often, their comforting but concise contents revealing he was normally a sufficient distance away from the battle fields to avoid the shell fire. His work was to receive the injured from the stretcher-bearers and either treat them so they were able to return to their unit or stabilise them prior to evacuation to a casualty clearing station. His cryptic text implied his work varied from the mundane to the manic and anything in between. John prayed quietly, hopeful that he would come through the war unscathed and be able to continue his medical studies when it was over. The war would at least provide a wealth of experience to the medical profession and a new breed of young doctors would emerge, with not a green one among them.

Thanks to Mr. Walkpast who dealt with the dog, the ducks quietened down and resumed their daily business. The lake deemed safe again, a lonely mallard materialized out of the reeds and eight regimented chicks appeared one by one in line astern formation behind her. The clouded water reflecting the grey day emphasised their bright yellow feathers as they swam inside their mother's wake, safe for now. So she's lost one, John thought. He watched nature's fluffy gifts for a few moments and in the stillness beyond the constraints of time, he found peace. Nodding a 'good morning' to Mr. Walkpast he sighed deeply and moved on with his day. Parenthood; it was a tough road, whatever the species.

Builders were engaged who worked quickly and efficiently fashioning a pantry. Although she tried hard Estelle had not persuaded John to purchase an electric refrigerator. She would have to settle for the cold slab. She dispensed instructions to the carpenters and the fitted cabinetry and built-in cupboards looked clean and bright after coats of white paint had been applied. "Very sanitary Missus," declared the head craftsman. "You can see the dirt now see. There's no way for them bacteria to hide."

"Quite so," Estelle replied. He had forgotten that the idea of painting had been hers and not his own. After they had finished she kept herself busy cleaning up and filling the cupboards with utensils.

"You have done marvels Estelle, marvels," said John. "Just the place to eat one's breakfast and keep warm next to the new range. It's so cold first thing in the morning in the dining room now there's no one to light the fire. This little eating booth is just the thing. However did you think of such a thing?"

"That's easy to explain. I've seen it done before."

"Where? Vicky and Jason haven't got one have they?"

"Oh you know, magazines and such, it's the latest thing."

Estelle was happy with her new kitchen. She spent hours there busying herself, cooking and baking at the reliable new range and chatting to Rose when she was home from school and not repairing off to Tiplin. She felt she could almost stay there forever; fall asleep like Sleeping Beauty and wake up in a hundred years, everything still the same.

"Hey, less of the beauty, she was young, not old like you," laughed Rose.

"Beauty is in the eye of the beholder I'll have you know," retorted her mother "and for all you know she was an old hag whom the prince thought to be gorgeous."

"I believe you, thousands wouldn't!"

Chapter Twenty

John was delighted his revived bedroom tactics were working. Estelle was so much happier these days and was always obliging. He thought he might write a paper on it, if only he had time. Still it wasn't her husband's actions that were pleasing Estelle particularly. Spring was almost upon them and even though the war showed no signs of any conclusion she felt positive that the end was coming. "It simply cannot go on for ever," she told Vicky who had called in to ask if she would mind the children for a few days while she accompanied Jason on a business trip to London. While there, she was hoping to attend a victory party at the Queen's Hall with the suffragists to celebrate the Representation of the People Act.

"I said you would get the vote eventually, didn't I? And if I was right with that then I will surely be right about the war ending."

"Don't forget that includes you too and every other woman over the age of thirty."

"That's only because the politicians think at our age we are most likely to be married with children and therefore less likely to belong to radical movements with radical ideas. They obviously haven't heard about you though."

"Very funny," retorted Vicky. You know I've been more involved with organising finance for women's hospitals than in any militancy, and anyway don't forget we're suffragists not suffragettes."

"Whatever."

Jason arrived with the children. They burst through the front door before Estelle had managed to open it fully and knocked her off balance. "Steady there," bellowed Jason after them, but they were already gone, racing up the stairs shouting for Rose to play. Only the young Elizabeth remained with her father, not quite two years old and clinging to him like a limpet. Estelle suggested they might go into the kitchen so Elizabeth could settle in. While the two adults spoke, the small child's inquisitive nature got the better of her and she soon uncurled herself off her father's lap and toddled over to a plate of enticing buns. A rare treat, but Elizabeth knew nothing of the austerity of war. First one and then another small chubby hand filled themselves up with little pink and white cakes, the right one trying, but failing to manage two at once. Butter-cream was licked out of each in turn. Estelle smiled; her ploy had worked; she had never known a youngster be able to resist. They both let Elizabeth indulge without restraint.

"She is such a pretty little thing, as are all of your offspring. You must be very proud of your lovely family Jason." But Estelle began to feel mischievous and before Jason could reply, she carried on. "You must be losing count now of how many you have, seven now isn't it! I don't suppose you would even notice another one."

"My God! Do you have news that I should know about?" He was shocked, but only for a moment; he knew Estelle too well. "No, that's not it, you're laughing too much."

"I'm watching your daughter, she is so adorable, look." Elizabeth was getting into difficulties, she couldn't manage to eat the remaining bits of bun without their paper encasements getting into her mouth. She was just getting to the point of giving up and starting again with knew buns when her father felt it was time to intervene. He performed the sticky task of pulling remnants of cake out of their cases and putting them on a plate with great dexterity. He then helped himself to a pink bun that took his fancy. "Ah! Now I know what you are thinking."

"And how could you possibly know that my dearest brother-in-law?"

Jason paced around the floor, cake clutched in hand. Twice he put it to his mouth, but that was as far as it ever got. "It's difficult for me, but I will say it anyway. I always feel compelled to tell you what is on my mind." His thoughts were elsewhere and not on consuming cake, tasty as it may be. Rose had made them and he was usually partial to Rose's baking. In the end he gave it to Elizabeth whose mouth, already crammed full with crumbs falling from her lips, was seeking to refill her empty hands. Estelle thought it better that Elizabeth be the recipient of the cake as she was a growing girl; Jason was becoming larger every time she saw him and it could not be good for his health. She had spoken about his increasing waistline to Vicky more than once but his doting wife seemed unconcerned, passing it off as a sign of a healthy constitution. Estelle thought she knew better and told Vicky he had been eating too many of those pork pies he was so partial to than was good for him.

Jason cleared his throat as if starting to make a speech. He paced some more before eventually beginning to talk. "Not that I mind, in fact I am eternally grateful but every time Vicky and I have a child I am reminded, with some dishonour, that it's because of your tactics."

"Tactics? I'm sure I have no possible notion of what you mean."

"Well if you choose to have forgotten about our little, how should I put it, tête a tête in the tea rooms all those years ago, when I was so disillusioned, let me assure you, dearest sister-in-law, I never have. I sometimes wonder how things would have been had you not brought me to my senses."

"Nonsense, I'm sure you would have sorted things out eventually."

"Eventually, maybe, but how long might that have been? Anyway, thanks to you, I was... well, lets just say I now have all these lovely children to show for it. Yes, I am very proud, thank-you."

Estelle wasn't sure how to respond. He must really think he had undergone some kind of cure. Well, when she thought about it, she supposed he had, but not the kind he thought. Then she saw Jason was near to tears; he was such a sensitive fellow underneath the confident, booming persona he normally portrayed. She loved him dearly; he would never know nor understand how important it was for her that he and Vicky should have had children, she was near to tears herself. She gave him a sisterly hug. "Dearest brother-in-law, please, no tears. Quick, go now while Elizabeth's eyes are fixed on the cakes." Successfully overlooked by his daughter whose finger was busy poking into the butter cream of the surviving buns, Jason slipped out.

Estelle took charge of the seven children for the two days Jason and Vicky were in London. She liked the company of her nephews and nieces; there was so much banter between them she could barely keep up. "It's 'cos you're old Auntie Estelle, it's not your fault."

Old? Yes she supposed she was, she hadn't thought about it much. The years were passing surprisingly fast, life continued unrelentingly, despite the fact they were grappling with such a great war.

"No, you have it all wrong, I'm not old, it's you who are too young. I bet you can hardly remember a time before the war, can you."

"I remember that picnic in the park and the band was playing," said Algie, "It was the best picnic ever."

"And I remember you giving me rides on your bicycle," added Stevie.

"Ha yes, I bet you're almost big enough to ride it yourself," said Estelle.

"I'm nearly up to Algie. Look." Stevie went back to back with his older brother.

"So you are, then you are certainly big enough."

"Yey, quick, happy dance everyone," said Stevie. John narrowly missed one of them knocking him over as he arrived home. The prancing ended abruptly as they switched to formality. "Hello Uncle John, we've been dancing."

"Is that what you call it?" Estelle tried to get him to join in. He gave a half-hearted attempt and then excused himself. He wanted to finish some work in the library before dinner. Oh heavens, dinner? She hadn't even started the children's tea. Obviously she was old if she couldn't even remember meal times!

"Oh my goodness, they've got him."

"Pardon?" said Estelle responding to John's exclamation. They were both sitting in the breakfast booth in the kitchen and John was buried in the newspaper. April twenty-first had heralded the first official day of spring, coincidentally the same day Baron Von Richthofen died.

"The Red Baron is no more. He was shot down over the Somme. A Canadian captain got him." He spoke as he read the printed information.

"There, what have I been saying, we are going to win and the war is going to end soon, especially now we've shot their best pilot."

"Not us, the Canadians."

"Well he's still dead."

John had read out many lurid headlines during the years of the war including the murders of the Russian Tsar and his wife, and then their children. "Terrible things happen sometimes, it's the way of things and someone has to pay the price, there's nothing you nor I can do, unfortunately." Estelle's answer surprised him, she was usually so sensitive to such matters.

"Who could do such a thing?" He was truly shocked and it wasn't just the death of the poor innocents. If the Bolsheviks were able to do that to those so great, then what else could they do? "Is it possible for that to happen to our King do you think?"

Murders weren't the only thing John was concerned about. Influenza had started innocently enough during Spring. They had news from George that he had a bout of 'flu which laid him low for three days before he had begun to feel better. "Nearly everyone has had it;" he wrote, "no appetite, sore throat and headaches."

"That sounds about right," said John as he read his letter. "Easy for him to diagnose though." By May however it was obvious that its effects were worsening. He had received a letter from a contemporary in Glasgow that caused him so much alarm he went straight to The Royal to organise an isolation ward. "Look at this," he yelled as he slapped the letter on the table in front of the professor who looked at it in distaste and declined to read its content. "If you cannot be bothered to read it then I will read it to you." John was always exasperated by hospital authorities and especially this one. He had had so much opposition in his youth. He started to read out loud, "When brought to the hospital, patients very rapidly develop the most vicious type of pneumonia that has ever been seen. It is only a matter of a few hours then until death comes and it is simply a struggle for air until they suffocate. It is horrible."

"Glasgow you say?" said the professor. "Then don't let us become too hasty, a few isolated cases I expect, no need to panic people, and if I remember my geography, I believe Glasgow is nowhere near here."

The professor was clearly unimpressed and John banged a clenched fist on the desk. "You are not listening. We need to prepare wards here for those who succumb to what sounds like a dreadful epidemic." But his words fell on deaf ears. The professor turned in his chair and feigned to read the correspondence on his desk; an act which made John only more furious. He tried again. "You would prefer I use the maternity hospital and put new born babies at risk?" He stormed out in rage, mumbling that nothing would ever change in that place.

"Can't they see that the virus has mutated and the soldiers are bringing it home with them?" he asked Estelle as she handed him some whisky. He spent the evening on the telephone to the maternity hospital trying to persuade the duty sister to clear a ward.

His fears were founded, the disease was spreading and had become rampant all over the country. He ordered everyone to stay inside or at least away from public places where they may be infected by someone. George had returned from the war but had gone straight to Glasgow to help treat the affected at the hospital and worked to breaking point. Estelle was desperate to welcome him home arguing he had already had the 'flu. "He is needed there more than to appease your emotions," answered John dispassionately. Surely she was not to be denied seeing her only son when she hadn't seen him in so long she argued.

"Don't be so melodramatic woman. The war is ending, he'll be home soon enough. Be thankful we still have him when he could so easily have been killed over there. If only I had been able to give you children, then you could have been occupied with them." He realised at once he had said too much. He had never told her he was infertile. He waited for what sort of effect it had made. It took a few moments for Estelle to realise what he had said, and then longer to understand its implication, and had already begun walking away. 'So he knew Rose was not his child.' She stopped mid motion and turned to look him face to face but said nothing. What could she say? She couldn't deny truth. "Yes." He said it gently. "I have always known. I cannot have children."

"But you have George."

"Yes, I have George. I should have told you Estelle and I am sorry for that but you wanted so much for Rose to have a father and I loved you so much, and still do." John came over to Estelle and took hold of her hands. I had mumps you see, after George, after Ellie, and well, that was that. Then you had Rose; we had Rose;" he corrected himself, "and we were a little family albeit somewhat unconventional. I didn't care though, you meant everything to me. I was still glad to have married you whatever the circumstances." Estelle pulled away and paced the floor rubbing her hands together. John's words had shocked her. She had lived with her lies all this time, and he knew!

"I deceived you, I'm so sorry." She started to cry as the reality hit and all her past emotions began engulfing her. She wanted to run and run as far away as she could from her shame. She started for the door.

"No Estelle, don't go outside, you must not go outside." But it was too late, she had gone.

John thought to leave her to let her recover herself but then thought better of it and set out to find her. He headed for the park hoping she was there; it was the place she went for comfort and at least it was an open space. He walked the entire perimeter and all the way through but found no sign of her and in the end gave up his search, hoping that by now she had returned home of her own accord.

She hadn't gone far, only reaching the standing stones before giving in. She sat on one and wept openly. Eventually she calmed down and looked about her. There was no-one there to see her, fortunately; people had acted on the advice to stay indoors. She imagined she must look very silly and then wondered why she had stopped by the stones; she usually skirted round them, but this time they had been so inviting, a place almost where, she thought, she might feel as if she were somewhere else, the circles her protection from the rest of the world, keeping it away. However, there she was, sitting on a cold stone on a cold Sunday morning the day before the Armistice was to be signed to officially end the war. It was what she had been waiting for, the end of all that futile killing, but instead she was filled with remorse and tears because of her deception. She felt so stupid, he had known all along. How could she live with herself now?

Estelle started to feel the cold, she had left without a coat and was now shivering, she thought it best to return and face the music. As she rounded the corner into her road she noticed Mr. Walkpast coming towards her from the other direction and as they passed each other he raised a hand towards his head to lift his hat. It never got past his face because he started to sneeze and kept it over his mouth. "Bless you," she said as she passed by.

"Thank-you," he said as he searched for his handkerchief. As soon as she got home she made for the range in the kitchen to put the kettle on for a cup of tea and to warm herself. She was cold through and through. John returned and they sat in silence holding hands. He wanted to tell her there was never anything to forgive and but for her he would never have had Rose as his daughter. She wanted to tell him what a good man he had been to her and how she had always felt safe and wanted.

She didn't feel inclined to make any lunch, she wasn't feeling her best; the cold of the morning had penetrated right into her and she thought she might go and lie down for a while. Rose prepared some toasted cheese sandwiches for herself and her father before he retired to the library to complete some paperwork.

Rose looked in on her mother later that afternoon. She didn't look well. Rose called her father, her urgent voice mustering him quickly. He saw the tell-tale mahogany coloured markings dotted across his wife's cheekbones and for the second time in his life was helpless in warding off the inevitable. He pulled his daughter back out of the room. "What's wrong with her?" Rose asked but didn't want to hear the answer, she already knew.

"You have to stay away from her now Rose, I'm sorry."

"Stay away? How can I stay away?" Rose clutched at her father. "Not Mum. Please not my Mum." He held her close but he could not stop her going to her mother. Estelle was still conscious; she had seen her daughter wriggle away from her husband and come towards her. She looked into her daughter's eyes and tried to motion her back but Rose would have none of it. Estelle looked at John; he would be broken, afterwards. She saw him tie something round Rose's face, a handkerchief, she thought. Yes, he had to protect her now from her own mother, it wasn't safe to be near.

"I will get water, her mouth will become dry."

"Yes Dad, I know that."

Estelle saw him leave the room and she turned to Rose. It was quite a struggle even to move her head; everything ached, she felt so ill. It was hard to get her breath and she had such a forceful cough it felt as though she was tearing her insides apart with the force of it. Blood foamed at her mouth and down her nose. Rose wiped it away.

"Rose," she gasped, "dearest Rose." Her eyes closed and Rose straightened the sheets as best she could to make her more comfortable. John returned with some water and a small sponge.

"I'll try and get hold of George," he said and left again, he could not bear to watch. Rose sat alone with her mother trying not to focus on her loud and laboured breaths so much. It wasn't easy. Perhaps she should open a window and let some fresh air in? Perhaps not; it would make it too cold. Perhaps she ought to light the fire and then open the window? She found more blankets but her mother was sweating; she folded them up and put them back. She wet her mother's lips as they looked a little dry and squeezed out some of the water into her mouth. She watched her mother's chest heave and struggle for air and wiped at the blood now oozing from her ears. Rose thought how blue her skin was becoming.

Estelle was weak but she managed to open her eyes and look at her daughter. "What day is today?" Her rasping throat forced the question out.

"The day before it all ends, it's the very last day," said Rose, trying to be cheerful. She was perturbed her mother had forgotten, but so pleased she had spoken. She saw her mother's lips quiver into a tiny smile.

"Remember me, on the last day." She said no more and Rose held her hand while her mother's gasping lungs suffocated.

"I have sent a telegram to George, it was hopeless trying to raise him on the telephone, no one could find him." Rose hadn't heard him come in; she was still holding her mother's flaccid hand feeling its warmth leaving for ever. John walked over to the window, he didn't want to look at his wife and face reality. Polly was outside; she saw Doctor John close the curtains and ran straight upstairs and into the room. She was too overwrought to knock; closed curtains meant only one thing; death. And it was Madam's room. No not Madam, it can't be her.

John was still at the window with fists white, and clutching the back of a chair. Rose was sitting by the bed crying silently. Madam was half sitting up in bed. She ran to her; Madam was dead. She looked at the doctor who was staring at the wall blankly. She looked at Rose and moved to embrace her; the poor girl, another tragedy for her. And for him, another wife as well.

"Doctor," said Polly. "Doctor John, I think we must come out now." She tried to lead him from the room.

"I can't. Not again. It can't have happened again."

"You go on down and call for Charlie, Rose and I will see to her."

John and George dug her grave; they were lucky to have a family plot in the cemetery. So many had died from the vicious viral attack. The morgues were stacking bodies in the corridors and mass graves were being dug to free the town of rotting corpses. Charlie built her a coffin; there was not a carpenter to be found without work. It was better that way; they felt they were doing all they could for her. Lord and Lady Peters wanted her in their plot at Tiplin but John overruled them and put her next to Ellie.

Armistice day had brought further tragedies. For the last few months everyone had been warned to stay inside and away from public places, and the strategy had been working. The dance halls and theatre doors were kept closed and the streets sprayed with chemicals to keep the disease at bay. But the celebrations for the end of the war only served to fuel another wave of infection. The people gathered together in their hordes and the virus swept through them. Thank goodness thought John, that none of their household had the inclination to celebrate. He realised then that if Estelle had not succumbed they would all now most likely be dead.

The family laid low and in mourning and followed the government's guidelines to combat the 'flu until the spring when it looked liked it was clearing. John was a broken man and incapable of dealing with the household responsibilities. Rose found she was stepping into her mother's shoes more and more. "What will you do?" she asked her brother.

"Return to my studies in Edinburgh and then work alongside Dad I expect. I can't see much else I want to do."

"But surely you want to break out, get married, have your own house and family?"

"No chance! Marriage is not for me; not when I've seen Dad suffer with Mum. And my other mother, he's had to go through it twice; there's no way I want to do that."

"Do you remember your first mother?"

"No. She died giving birth to me. That's another reason I don't want to marry. Anyhow, you are going to look after me and Dad, I know you aren't ever getting married, not after Francis."

"No, I don't suppose I will ever marry, but I do want to nurse."

"And you will make an excellent nurse Rose. I will get Sister Hewer to have a word with you." Rose flung her arms around her father. He had entered the kitchen at just the right time to hear her. "Your mother would have been so very proud of the both of you." He broke into uncontrollable tears, the first of many he would shed.

"No Dad, she will be proud of me, when I am one."

"A good nurse should possess a strong love for children simply because they are children, and should prefer being a nurse to anything else. A person who has this characteristic is rarely lacking in the second all-essential quality; that of patience." Sister Hewer had looked Rose up and down as if she were a specimen for examination. Nevertheless she accepted Rose into the next training school.

"Patience," thought Rose, "I'll need plenty of that. I have a long way ahead." She spent a little time before she started her training at Tiplin. Her Grandfather was failing and she wanted to help. After he died and the family had gathered for the funeral, she looked at her aunts, Lily and Violet and saw her mother in them, but then thought of something she had never considered. They were both called after names of flowers, as was she and she thought to ask her grandmother if her mother had ever been named before being stolen away. Later, when she thought the house should have a name, she got Charles to build a wooden gate at the side of the house at the entrance to the back garden. She painted its new name at the top of it. It was next to where the jasmine grew up the side wall.

PART TWO

Chapter Twenty-One

1970

Glenda had left her job as a teacher of English and drama some weeks previously, throwing herself into her new role of 'heavily pregnant lady.' However the role had proved lately to be rather too demanding and she was fed up with it. She had no care for the bright spring sunshine that normally provoked her usual sprightly step. Her hair, usually in a neat French pleat, hung loose; she hadn't even bothered to put on her make-up. Normally she wouldn't be seen dead without it; thick foundation, heavy lines of black eye liner and mascara to frame her almond eyes, pillar-box red lipstick to emphasise her full mouth; she liked to be the centre of attention. Today, feeling dreary and dejected, she began to waddle away from the antenatal clinic and into the park, each faltering step slower and heavier than the last. Her dark frame of mind spread around her like a cloak, clinging to her, clouding her judgement; she felt alone in the blackness as her head pounded in time with her feet. Her tired and weary legs took her underneath the canopy of cigar-like buds in the avenue of copper beeches that lined the main walkway of the park. She felt the need to sit down.

Glenda had always looked forward to her antenatal clinic appointments; each visit bringing the birth a step closer, a marker of the time left to go. The doctor and midwife who often took the clinic together had always given her the reassurance she needed with their professional expertise and encouraging smiles. They took it in turns to examine her growing bump with expert hands and, as if in friendly competition with each other, discuss which way round the baby was, how much it was going to weigh and where the head had got to. They listened intently to confirm the presence of a strong heart beat and bantered about whether it sounded like a boy's or a girl's and Glenda would leave feeling happy and hopeful. Today had been different. Glenda was in distress. Her middle had been expanding so much lately that to do anything at all was such an effort, even getting dressed. The simple task of putting on her clothes had fast become a major tactical operation. Reaching her feet was proving very difficult; bending down to put on shoes and socks and still having room to breathe was impossible. She needed to lie down and rest afterwards because of all the effort involved. The issue of the shoes had been the last straw for Glenda and she had arrived at the clinic desperately hoping they would send her to the hospital to set things off.

"Blood pressure needs watching but otherwise everything is as it should be; we'll check it next time," the doctor had said as he helped her struggle up from the examination bed.

"See you next week," was the midwife's parting cry. 'Another week of this?' she panted to herself as she plodded her way home through the park and the blackness turned to red. She was feeling hot because of the weather and hot because she was pregnant and hot because she was cross with the world in general, oblivious that her pregnancy hormones were the cause of her emotions running wild. The chaotic sea of her subconscious had stirred, brewing and bubbling irrational thoughts that strained for position before bursting through into her brain. 'Why does no one understand?' she seethed inwardly, 'My baby needs to be born now! No one realises! Nobody cares!' She stood still and stamped her foot in rage. She stayed in the same position for several moments doing nothing but staring into space and then sighed deeply. 'It's just not to be then, there's no reason for them to induce me on medical grounds. No saving angel to shout, "bring forth the child!" no all-seeing wise woman to say the baby must be born today. There's nobody to help me at all.'

Glenda was exhausted. She had nearly reached her home, it was just across the road from where she was, but she could not walk another step. She eased herself down on an available park bench to wallow in self-pity. It was quite comfortable as park seats go and her tired swollen legs were feeling easier by resting. Slowly as she took in the ambience of the day, she began to stop feeling so sorry for herself and her heavy mood melted in the warm sun. May blossom was everywhere, carpeting the neatly-kept grass in great swathes of pink all the way down to the lake where she counted seven tiny ducklings, their mother quacking protectively at onlookers to keep their distance. Glenda sighed again, rubbed her stomach and waited for a kick whilst watching the day go by.

She had a good view of the standing stones from where she was sitting, a slightly different one from what she was used to; one of the outermost stones being only a few yards from her front door. From where she was sitting she observed a little plaque with the written words 'ancient monument please respect this site' that had been set into the grass near to her feet. She watched as two small boys clambered over the larger ones and jumped over the smaller ones. A cigarette was shared between two older youths who sat in the inner ring, using one for a backrest. Glenda smiled to herself as she considered what one had to do in order to show a few old stones respect. Her mood brightening with the pleasantness of the sunny day, emotions stilled, Glenda's thoughts began to turn to food. Heaving herself up, she set off to go home. However, as her attention was still with the stone circle, Glenda did not notice the elegant Victorian-style lamppost projecting proudly upwards nearby, and the direction in which she took made her abrupt introduction to it inevitable. Her tummy being so large, protruding forward before the rest of her got a direct hit, absorbing the full force of the collision. Glenda gasped in surprise and shock, her hands automatically reaching forward, one clutching at the post for support, the other over the point of impact, her baby. She stood still, panting and worrying about the baby, hoping it was all right. Minutes passed, she held her breath while rubbing her tummy, waiting hopefully. Finally she felt a reassuring thud from inside. Standing gingerly upright, cursing herself for not looking where she was going, she set off for home. She would normally have passed through the stone circle and stepped over the small wall that separated her flat from the edge of the park, but she did not want to lose her balance while going over the wall and instead, passed through the east gate and lumbered across the road.

Glenda, along with her husband Tony lived in a small flat on the ground floor of what was once part of a much larger house. It was situated on a curve of the road, the park wrapping it on two sides as if it were its grounds. The front door of their flat was in fact a side door of the big house, but they did not use it much, preferring to walk round to their small garden at the back and enter through the kitchen door. Bruce, her dog was barking loudly as she went in showing his pleasure at seeing his mistress by standing on his hind legs and pushing his paws at her in welcome. "Hey careful, I've just had a knock there and it's still sore, I don't want another one you great daft dog." She pushed him down and patted him affectionately and let him out into the back garden where he bounded about, pleased to be let loose. Lately his morning walks had been cut short, just enough to attend to his business then back home. It was all Glenda could manage. He would have to wait for his master for a longer one in the evening. She watched Bruce romping about after the stick she threw for him and worried whether he might be jealous of the baby. Glenda resolved to do miles of dog-walking to make up for things after the birth. She turned back inside and to the front door to check for post, sighing as she went. There were a couple of letters that had fallen onto the mat. It was too much trouble to bend and pick them up and shuffled them with her foot but then gave up on them; she couldn't be bothered with correspondence. Back in the kitchen, Glenda switched on the radio and started making something to eat. She didn't feel up to cooking anything and placed a slice of beef left from the Sunday roast on the top of some bread, eased herself down at the kitchen table and started to eat. She only nibbled at it though, her normal appetite seemed to have inexplicably disappeared, and when she thought about it, she even felt a little nauseous. Her back was aching and after sitting uncomfortably for a while and failing to finish the sandwich, she heaved herself up, turned the radio off, gave the remains of her lunch to Bruce, and went upstairs to lie down almost slipping on the letters lying at the foot of the stairs. Her stomach felt so heavy. Glenda drifted off to sleep but awoke sometime later in such horrendous discomfort that it took her breath away. Lying still, she hoped it might pass. However, it only got worse, boring into her relentlessly, her tummy felt as hard as a rock.

It came in waves, one wave on top of the next, no respite, no rest, always there, always pain, excruciating, all consuming. Clutching at herself, doubled up, she tried to get out of bed in an attempt to go downstairs and get to the telephone to ring the midwife for advice for this was not the way labour had been described to her. She had been to all the classes; she knew the onset should be gradual. This was not like that; this did not feel right at all. Glenda could barely move as she tried to get out of bed and had such an intense feeling of pressure. She needed to get to the toilet. It was as she pulled off the bed clothes and saw all the blood she knew she needed help.

When trying to piece it all together later, Glenda realised at some point she had managed to dial for an ambulance but had no clear recollection of any of it. She had a brief memory of clinging onto the stairs, her whole body bearing down as if she had a severe attack of constipation and diarrhoea at the same time, the dog barking continually, a baby crying as if it were far away, but that was all. She had drifted in and out of consciousness for much of it, but her memory of events was clearer when the afterbirth had come away; she felt it plopping out onto the floorboards.

Her awareness coming back, she began looking around and found herself halfway along the hallway clutching the telephone receiver, with a trail of blood in front and behind, telling the story of what had happened. Glenda was sweating, and her pulse was racing but the pain had gone and she knew it was over. She was aware of baby noises coming from the bottom of the stairs and looked over in that direction. She could see a towel moving as if something was inside. Tentatively reaching over, her eyes filled with joy as they saw tiny arms and legs kicking the towel undone. With renewed strength, she managed to pick up the baby girl and began to study her, counting her fingers and toes, stroking her tiny body. Her umbilical cord was cut and tied. Glenda wondered why she could not remember doing that and looked back at the afterbirth. She could see the umbilical cord coming out of it and stretching round the back of the stairs and out of sight. Glenda followed its length, managing to crawl around the corner, but the tragic scene laid out in front of her imprinted itself like a photograph in her mind which she could never completely cover up, remaining there forever. Her heart broke into tiny pieces.

There, in a pool of green slime, another baby lay, a boy. He had no towel to keep him warm; no kicks coming from his arms or legs, no cries to be heard. Glenda regarded his quiet, lifeless little body; nothing but complete stillness. She tried to take everything in, the shock and realisation almost tangible. She grappled for any sense of reason. There was nothing. Managing to keep some presence of mind, slowly and carefully she picked him up. His limbs limp and hanging, his mouth open, his desolate mother cradled him to her bosom and rocked him gently. She reached for a towel from the pile of laundry sitting on the hall table that had been abandoned earlier in the day, and wiped away some blood that had started to spill from his mouth. She reached for some twine and scissors from her mending basket, she tied and cut his cord, trying to care for him as best she could. She did not know how long she had been there before help arrived, one baby pink and warm and suckling greedily, another blue, cold and still. However long it had been, those moments when she had held him, those very precious moments, united for the first and the last time, were brief.

The kitchen door opened and Bruce bounded out followed by two ambulance men. "He's dead," she sobbed as soon as the first ambulance man was through the doorway. He cautiously came toward her, absorbing the scene in front of him. The other kept Bruce at bay.

"Let me take him," he said softly "It's the other one that needs you now." Glenda reluctantly gave up the boy, sobbing quietly. It was the last time she saw him.

After the ambulance men had checked her over they covered her with a blanket to keep her warm and considering her stable enough to travel, they stretchered her into the ambulance. "Bag the placenta up and bring it along," one said to the other.

"Oh my God!" said the other.

"What?"

"The bloody dog's eating it."

"Well just get what you can of it and let's go, see if a neighbour will look after the dog."

While they were retrieving what they could of the afterbirth to the disappointment of the ever-hungry dog, an inquisitive crowd had gathered in the street. Glenda was in her own surreal world of shattered mosaic pieces not quite fitting together and oblivious of prying intrusion. She clinched her baby close, perhaps a little too tightly and shook uncontrollably, she was totally lost.

There was movement in front of her and she followed it abstractedly. She noticed how the gnarled veins resembled the branches of a tree and how impressively they twisted their way over a prominent tent pole like framework. How beautiful the texture of the transparent skin, speckled with colours of reds, browns, purples and stretching across majestically from one tendon to the next, like an exotic tent. An elderly lady, her withered eyes loving and kind was beside her and, touched her cheek with her hand. Glenda was brought back into the present and looked up feebly. The lady took off a cloak she had been wearing. "Here," she began tenderly, "let me put this round you, it will keep you warm."

"Thank you," replied Glenda faintly and allowed the woman to fuss over her, having no will to do anything else. Satisfied Glenda was tucked up sufficiently, the woman then looked at the newborn she was clasping closely.

"Your baby is beautiful," she whispered as she kissed her own fingers and touched the sleeping infant's cheek with them lovingly. "Have you a name for her?"

"No, not yet."

"My Grandmother wanted my mother to be called Jasmine, but it wasn't to be."

"What a pretty name," replied Glenda. It made the old lady smile.

"Yes, isn't it. I never had children of my own, you are very blessed. Take good care of her, none of this was her fault." A tear trickled from the old lady's eye.

Glenda, already fractured and now bemused by what she had just heard, wondered if the old woman was some sort of mystic. What did she mean that it wasn't her fault and how did she know she was a girl? There was no time to find out as the old woman retreated into the crowd and the ambulance doors closed. Maybe the ambulance men had said something, but she never found out.

The police and coroner's involvement that followed had only added to her torturous experience, leaving a guilty sense that she had done something wrong. Her grief was ongoing, consuming every waking moment although she tried her best not to let it show. Tony, her husband, tried to support her but ultimately she felt isolated and alone. He had shifted through his own grieving experience quickly, and did not understand how or why she could not move on. Glenda struggled by, handling her baby daughter as little as possible in the fear that she might do her harm.

Two years later, she gave birth to another baby girl. It happened in hospital this time and among caring professionals. Everything was straightforward from a medical point of view and even Glenda felt it gave her some form of closure; she could cuddle this baby without any fear and the two little girls grew up well enough even though they always knew there was a missing brother. Glenda's former theatrical personality returned and Tony was not sure whether to sigh with relief or not.

Chapter Twenty-Two

...Twenty-five years later.

It was early evening in another part of town. Steve arrived back home after honeymooning with Jasmine, his bride. The heat of the day had lessened but the sun, still with generously textured warmth, had moved around enabling shafts of gold to shoot through the windows, arousing the sleepy rooms of the north-facing flat. The rays, like accusatory fingers, highlighted not objects but spaces, capturing within them a myriad of tiny specks swirling lazily along on their perpetual journey to nowhere. Around and about and back again, the tiny particles' continual inconsequential wanderings were the only movements within the silent room. "Welcome home wife," Steve said with a glint in his eye as he opened the door of the flat. The particles of dust changed direction agitatedly, as if startled by the sudden intrusion. Scooping her up in one swift movement he carried Jasmine over the threshold. She played along and feigned a swoon. However, by the time they arrived in the bedroom the weight of her was making him strain a bit. Not that Jasmine was large in any way; on the contrary; but the effort of carrying a body around corners and through narrow spaces and then up the stairs onto the mezzanine, his original designs were becoming less and less appealing.

Steve had seized the opportunity to prove how romantic he could be but was now slightly regretting his impulsiveness. He ended up almost dropping Jasmine onto the bed and collapsed next to her sighing loudly. Jasmine, realising his valour was fading, started to giggle in between placing gentle kisses over his face in attempt to make him feel better. Looking into her eyes, he began to ponder what it was about her. How beautiful she was, to him, how his chest swelled every time he saw her. How he loved just being around her, holding her, loving her. How different life would be without her, if he had never known her. Her eyes were bright with mirth, he couldn't resist. Taking hold of both of her hands in his he slowly pulled her towards him, not taking his eyes off her, not even for a second. Jasmine wasn't giggling anymore, in fact she was barely breathing, anticipating what was to come. Looking at each other and still holding hands, they kissed.

How full they were of excitement and hope; their flood of feeling complete in that moment of their unity and how glorious they felt life might be, as afterwards they lazed luxuriously in the glow of the sunbeams, the two of them together, forever. The dust settled back to its former leisurely drift, a moment of time absorbed into all other moments of time; of little consequence to its meanderings.

Steve and Jasmine had known each other from when they were very small, experiencing the same things, playing and learning, side by side, and a strong bond had formed between them. He had always loved her, right from the start. The first time he saw her was when they were both about six years old at a birthday celebration. How pretty she had looked in her pink party dress with trailing ribbons in her unruly yellow hair, a perfect vision. His little heart had faltered and before he knew what he was doing, as though a force was propelling him forwards he had given her a hug and placed a kiss on her cheek.

"I'm going to marry you!" he had exclaimed but then flushed with embarrassment as he realised what he had done and backed away. From her bemused perspective a strange boy had jumped on her out of nowhere and almost knocked her over. She had tried to straighten her dress, sort out her uncontrollable hair then sniffed, stuck her nose in the air, and walked away, hands on hips. However, her eyes were on him for the rest of the gathering, part of her wanting it to happen all over again and her already strongly-defined chin jutted out determinedly. Afterwards, when she discovered they were near neighbours, Jasmine seized every opportunity to be with Steve in case he might want to kiss her again. Their initial embarrassment was soon forgotten as they became friends but she never did get another kiss, that is, not for a very long time.

As the awkwardness of puberty beckoned, its differing perception brought a new timidity to their relationship. They both chose to keep their feelings to themselves. While he enjoyed improving his expertise in football and sparring with his mates; she was content to watch, giggling with her girlfriends, embraced in sisterhood. They kept a close distance, alert to where the other one was, always wishing, never daring. There was unfinished business between them.

Meanwhile Steve's family was on the move. He knew he had to say something about it to Jasmine but he did not want to believe it was really happening. It had been the top topic of conversation at his home for the last few months but he did not know what he thought about it and had hoped the whole thing might just go away. It was not until almost the last minute before he managed to say something.

"I'm leaving to live in the States next week," he coughed out one day when they were on their way to school. He turned into a side street and lit a Silk Cut, his eyes firmly fixed on the ground as he took a furtive drag.

"When did you ever smoke?" Jasmine quizzed, attempting to shut out what she had just heard, the weight of it landing like lead on her chest. It was hard for her to remain composed; dizziness and nausea swept over her as she reeled from the life-changing information he had imparted. "Put it out, it's making me feel sick."

"Sorry," he said, not knowing if he was apologising for the cigarette or for going to America. Steve pulled on the cigarette, threw it on the floor and stamped it out.

"Now you're littering the place!" she shouted aggressively, not knowing how to handle the situation.

"Sorry," he said again and picked up the squashed tab and put it back in the pack.

"Yuk!" she exclaimed. "That's disgusting." Steve was feeling exasperated. Whatever he did was wrong.

"Well what am I supposed to do?" he said, unaware he was addressing both topics at once. They continued on their way to school without talking. Steve was thoughtful; he loved Jasmine as though she were a part of him, but he just could not tell her; he was still young, too shy, the time was not right. He knew that in going to America he was able to avoid the matter. For the first time he realised he was actually looking forward to going. He suddenly found his voice.

"Yeah, my Dad's landed this great job in a university there. He'll be on secondment for a couple of years on some scientific research about black holes or worm holes or something. It's all a bit weird and sci-fi but Dad's really into all that and he's really excited about it. He's tried to explain it all to me but he gets into complicated maths stuff and I can't follow it.

Anyway, I'm all sorted out with college there and there's massive sports facilities and other stuff, so er, you needn't worry about me." He flashed a glance at Jasmine but her face was fixed firmly on the ground. All the words she wanted to say to him were left unsaid and the rest of the journey was silent. They reached school. "See you later then," said Steve, relieved he had managed to tell her and now able to disappear into his lessons.

"Bye then." She watched him go, waving feebly, wondering if it was all real. Two years was a long, long time and it felt like a whole lifetime for Jasmine. After a few moments, eyes wet, she turned round and ran. Running was good; her breathlessness gave her the distraction she needed as she headed for her class. And the running never stopped after he had departed. When Jasmine ran it helped to numb her pain. He had gone on his big adventure far away and left her as though one half of her was missing. She was barely able to make sense of life. There was no spark, no glow; a void, emptiness. When not out running, in her misery, Jasmine took to spending many hours gazing out of her bedroom window. She could see most of his house from there. For anyone else, the view was the same as it always had been, the weeping willow in the corner, the white colour of the rendered walls, the long roof incorporating the garage. Not for Jasmine. For her the outlook was now completely different. There it stood; his house, bleak, lonely and most of all, empty. No Steve in the garden playing football, no Steve sitting at his desk under his bedroom window, no Steve waiting at the gate to set off for school together, no sign of life anywhere; nothing. Whenever Jasmine went past it, she slowed down and took as long as she possibly could. She caressed the gateposts and dragged her hand along the fence, she would breathe in the scents of the house, the garden, the flowers, hoping any essence of him that may still linger might be pulled inside her. For Jasmine, life had almost stood still for two long years. Everyone else seemed to carry on as normal but she felt stuck as if in some sort of time warp; stuck in an invisible force-field that would not let her out to enjoy life. Nonetheless, her self- imposed protective bubble was about to burst.

It had started out like any other day, Jasmine was finishing her usual five mile run and customary slowing down as she reached Steve's. Today, however she noticed his house was somehow different. Jasmine, already alert with the adrenalin boost she got from running, studied intently, hands on hips sucking in air, trying to see why. The answer soon came. It was life. There was something moving inside and she suddenly saw what she had been waiting for, the reason she had spent all those long hours, days, weeks, months, years in that same position. Her heart began to beat even more furiously. There he was! Steve stood waving feverishly at her and she waved back almost swooning with happiness.

Steve had been thinking of the 'Jasmine reunion' the moment he re-entered the country. The girl he had left behind. The girl he had wanted so much but had not dared do anything about. Jasmine, the girl he had run away from but had never completely left his thoughts. Unsure of her present feelings and apprehensive of any confrontation, his nerves were jangling more incessantly the nearer he got to home, part of him hoping she might have moved away. Once back, Steve relaxed a little, breathing in the familiar atmospheres of the rooms, one by one. He came to his bedroom door, opening it eagerly, but was not ready for what faced him. He saw the juvenile posters on the Blu-tac marked walls, his childhood books pushed onto the floor usurped by football memorabilia, his out-dated music collection on old cassette tapes. He had effortlessly stepped through time; back to the days of his boyhood. He stood and looked. It was just as he remembered and it was good to be back but yet it was as if he were a stranger in his own space. He wound up his old alarm clock that lay precariously on the edge of the bedside table and watched the minutes tick by, feeling almost trapped by the time capsule his room had become. In his two years away he had slowed down for barely a second, there had been so much to explore, so many exciting things to experience, so much knowledge of life to learn; he had grown up leaving his younger self as a formative but non-returnable memory.

Steve opened the drawer of his bedside table and pulled out some photographs that he had left there. An old faded image of Steve's great-grandfather fell to the floor. He picked it up and looked at the face staring back at him. He must have been fairly young when it had been taken; late teens possibly. What fascinated Steve about the picture (and why he asked his mother if he may have it, the other, in case she might throw it out like she did everything else) was that he could have been looking at a photo of himself; the family resemblance was uncanny. From being a small boy this one image had given Steve a sense of the continuity of life; like a great wheel turning slowly and constantly, linking everything and everyone together. It made him feel how important his great-grandfather Jason and other ancestors were to him. He appreciated his very existence was because of them. He didn't want to follow the same path as his favourite ancestor though; apparently his nickname had been Humpty Dumpty because he was so paunchy. He put the picture down hastily in a move to separate himself from any fat genes he might have inherited, and looked at the others photos.

There were plenty pertaining to football that his father had taken during matches. He could remember that pass, and his Dad had taken the shot perfectly. He remembered Jasmine had been watching that particular match and had candidly looked for her reaction when he scored that goal just before the final whistle. He found one of his old dog Bess. Before she became arthritic he and Jasmine had walked her everywhere. Jasmine, he had a photo of her somewhere. She had given it to him as she thought he might like the setting as the Wembley football stadium could be seen in the background, just! Jasmine! She was back in his thoughts again. On reflection, he had come home and there was nothing to prevent him from picking up his old life and just enhance it with all that he had embraced over there. He found the photo in the wallet he had forgotten to take abroad with him. Jasmine; he had to see her again, scene or no scene. He had to meet her. He moved to his window and looked out and saw her in the road. She hadn't changed a bit and she was stunning. He gasped loudly. An old familiar feeling lurched inside him and he knew he had to do something about it this time.

They easily caught the attention of each other and he sprang downstairs, leaping over the bannister in his haste, but when he was out in the street, he walked towards her as nonchalantly as he was able. Jasmine waited, still in the middle of the road, her t-shirt wet with sweat across her heaving chest. Steve grew closer and closer and they both bathed in the face of the other; his, chiselled and sharp with the fairest of skins that as yet had barely been introduced to a razor and eyes, gentle, and the bluest of blues; hers, large featured, with full and ruddy lips pulled into a wide smile, hazel eyes dancing animatedly, her pale skin glowing red. For a moment, for each of them, the whole world stood before them. Steve was the first to break their silent communication. "Hi there." It wasn't what he really wanted to say and he knew what he craved but his nerve was beginning to falter. His own chest rose and fell as she watched him catch his breath, still panting for hers, and the muscles on his torso filled out his shirt more impressively than she had remembered. He was so near to her she smelt the scent of his body and it was intoxicating.

"You've grown." She wanted to say and do so much more. A car's horn beeped. The moment had passed and they moved off the road to safety.

"Let's go and have a drink somewhere this evening?" Steve quizzed.

"I suppose we could," Jasmine replied, disappointment sweeping over her. She would have to do more waiting, but she was used to that.

"Right then, see you later." Steve dared not look to her eyes again and went back indoors to remonstrate with himself in private. His old feelings from before their enforced separation were not only reawakened but were multiplied a thousand-fold. He wanted their relationship to move forward. He had to find the courage from somewhere, he had to be brave; he did not want to lose her, their bond was too precious a thing. He looked through his window over at her house and saw Jasmine come out still in her running gear. His eyebrows flickered slightly as his resolve came...

"Why did you never write?" Jasmine chastised. They were sitting in the local pub where they could be by themselves and had settled down with a couple of drinks.

"When did you start running? I thought about it but never actually got around to it, writing, not running," he replied after tasting the beer, using the time taken to swallow as an excuse not to reply straight away giving him a moment to formulate his answer. 'Just being in his thoughts was good enough wasn't it? She wants letters as well?'

"I would always write to you if we were ever separated," Jasmine replied, "and I've been running for the last two years."

"Well why didn't you then?" He did not feel he should take the whole blame and felt justified in giving some of it to her.

"How was I to know where you disappeared to? You never left any address." she retorted.

"Hmm! I suppose you wouldn't have known. I apologise. My penance will be to buy the next round." He did not want to argue with her, his mind was thinking of something different entirely and it was difficult to remain calm. This time he did not want to keep his feelings to himself. He needed to know if she felt the same. "So, have you missed me then?" he said, leaning over towards her, his new confidence coming with help from the beer. Jasmine decided to take a sip of her drink for exactly the same reason as Steve had done a few minutes earlier.

"Of course I've missed you; there was no-one to do my maths homework."

"Hmm!" he repeated. He wasn't really listening, he was too busy watching her, looking at her; the way she moved, the way her long curly hair bobbed about her face, just as it had the day he had first seen her. He took hold of her glass and placed it on the table. He put his finger under her chin and lifted up her face. He moved closer and put his lips onto hers, softly. It was their first proper kiss. She had waited such a long time. "I'm going to marry you," he said as they pulled apart.

"You said that once before, a long time ago," said Jasmine, his fervent kiss leaving a fire burning fiercely inside her.

"I haven't forgotten, I am merely reminding you of my intent." He could hardly wait, but this was not the right place.

"Oh," was all she could muster. She wanted to marry him too but she knew they were too young to be contemplating something like that. She took another gulp of Pinot Noir in an attempt to quell the heat that was bubbling inside her. No, it wasn't marriage she was thinking about, particularly. They did not talk anymore, each other's presence was enough. Before their drinks were finished, they both rose as one and went in search of seclusion in the nearby wood. The noisy, smoky pub was in complete contrast to the temptations among the trees. Their lungs breathed in the sweet air, their ears soaked up the sounds, all the while their intentions unfaltering as each heart throbbed for the other. In complete silence they ventured down a moistened path that took them deeper and deeper into the wood; they trusted each other to know which way and how far to go. When they came across a small clearing that lead down to a brook they paused. This seemed like the right place. Steve took hold of Jasmine's hand and led her to the water's edge and she leant against the trunk of a great tree and it gave her the support she required. The canopy of branches and dappled sky above covered them, the dewy meadow grass grew soft and thick below. The temperature in the air was palpable to them both and the sap continued to rise in the heat. It was there they felt they had discovered paradise.

They spent the summer barely apart. Their friends nicknamed them 'the love hearts', it was as if there were tiny little heart shapes passing from one to the other, pink and fluffy. "It's so pathetic," laughed their friends, trying to conceal their envy. Lucy, Jasmine's younger sister, and completely unlike her in both looks and personality, painfully threatened to tell their mother all she knew unless Jasmine let her permanently borrow her hi-fi. "Whatever," Jasmine had replied, she didn't really care. "Keep it if you like, I'm going soon." She was soon moving to another town to start training as a nurse and would be able to do as she liked. Her father, usually oblivious to such matters, had also noticed Jasmine was not as moody as usual.

"Excited for your course coming up, is it?" he asked her one day, his tired eyes peeping over his perched reading glasses as he raised his balding head above the Evening Gazette.

"Yes I am, very much," Jasmine replied.

"You know we used to live there, and not far from the hospital where you are going to train, don't you?" said her father.

"Yes Dad!" she said sighing with exasperation, she had heard the story repeatedly. "And yes we used to live opposite the park and no I don't remember."

"I was just saying, in case you didn't know." He turned over to another page subconsciously attempting to stifle the words that were filling his throat. They were left unsaid but a series of small coughs ensued.

"I tell you what, I will go past the house and see if I can remember anything." Jasmine added, wondering if she had inadvertently upset her father. There was a long pause before he said anymore.

"There was a sadness to that house; first there was what happened to us, but then there was some tale of a child having been kidnapped years ago. No, it didn't hold happy memories; it's why we moved in the end."

"I know Dad. I'm sorry." Jasmine felt awkward, she never knew what she was supposed to say when her parents hinted about the baby they lost.

"Don't be sorry dear, it was never your fault. Anyway, it was all a long time ago now." He folded up his paper and moved away, in attempt to busy himself with other matters. As her twin brother had been stillborn there had always been a huge shadow hanging over them and it was times such as these that Jasmine would feel as if she may have been somehow to blame. She sometimes wondered if her mother felt that too, she knew that Lucy had a much closer relationship with their mother than she ever had. Lucy's birth though, had been straight-forward, unlike her own arrival. She had never known for sure but perhaps all this had influenced her decision to move away. She was harbouring a feeling that she did not belong with them, that she had to get away, to find herself. Steve would be leaving anyway, and so she had little reason to stay.

This was all so far away now. Jasmine had attained her ambition and was now not only a nurse, but had also undergone training to become a midwife. Steve had chosen a university in the same town and they had stuck together and Steve had found a job teaching in a local secondary school. It had seemed inevitable that the next step was for them to get married and now they had just returned from honeymooning overseas.

The sunbeams disappeared, the dust invisible once more and as the air cooled, thoughts of food came into their heads. Steve pulled on his jeans and went out to get some fish and chips while Jasmine got out the plates and cutlery. She found a lonely can of beer at the back of the fridge which they shared and settled cheerfully into married life.

Chapter Twenty-Three

Jasmine's morning began as usual with pressing communications from her bladder overriding any excuse for languishing in bed. Still half asleep she grabbed at some clothing and stumbled into the kitchen, pulling a t-shirt over her head just as the postman was passing the window. The letterbox squeaked and the morning's post landed heavily on the floor of the communal hallway as she waited, well hidden (as only her top half was clothed), till the postman went away. Startled out of her sleepy state and keen to see if any property details had been delivered, she peered round the door of her flat. A pile of envelopes lay provocatively at the front door and she ventured out towards them with excited anticipation for potential details of their own future home. It had been a couple of years since their wedding day and they had been saving hard, hating the fact that they were throwing money away each month paying for rented accommodation. They loved their flat but it never felt as if it was really theirs.

Half way along the hall, almost at the bottom of the stairs, Jasmine stopped, rooted to the spot. A sharp rush of air, chilled by its haste, entered her open mouth as she froze. She had heard a noise from the landing and now stood as if in the middle of a game of musical statues, desperately wanting the music to start so she could move away. She had forgotten that one of the upstairs flats had been re-let. They had been empty for some time and they were used to having the place to themselves.

Skipping innocently down the stairs, the new neighbour's eyes popped out for the briefest of moments; he could not help but enjoy the view. "Good morning," he said by way of a greeting. "Lovely t-shirt," he added as he took everything in, directing a wide smile towards her. Too far away for a hasty retreat inside her door Jasmine, becoming animated again and trying desperately to act as if everything was normal, dived quickly to the front door and hastily grabbed as much of the post as she could and held it in front of her, forcing a grin on her face that looked more like a grimace, and saying nothing. "Oh, by the way, I'm Trevor," he added, extending his hand towards her whilst thoroughly enjoying the experience.

"Er, Jasmine," came the reply as she looked down and wondered how she could manage to spare a hand.

Trying desperately not to laugh, Trevor withdrew his hand and continued, "Don't worry, no need to open the door for me, I'll get it. You seem a little preoccupied with the post. Is there any for me?"

"Er, I don't know. Er I was just er, I'll look through it in a minute," was all Jasmine could manage. Not wanting to reveal any more of herself to Trevor, she made her way backwards down the hall with a magazine and a large brown envelope covering her modesty. Her face reddening by the second, she really wished she had the ability to vanish.

"'Bye then, I'll see you later, nice meeting you." he said as he opened the front door to leave. "The pleasure was all mine!" he added, the smile still on his face.

"Oh God!" was all Jasmine could say as she got back to safety. "Oh my God!"

Later, fully dressed this time, she peeped out of her door and made sure no-one was about before quickly dashing over to the rest of the post, sorting out what was hers and dashing back, apprehensive of bumping into Trevor again. It did indeed contain what she was hoping for. There were several details from various estate agents of properties for sale. Steve and Jasmine had spent several weeks tramping around potential dwellings, viewing big, small, expensive, new, old and utter wrecks but nothing they had seen so far had felt right. After this morning's episode, Jasmine was more than ever ready to move, and she was hopeful that this latest batch of details would bring something interesting. She spent the rest of the morning studying all the information, the time passing so quickly that she ran the risk of being late for work. Grabbing an apple from the fruit bowl, she picked up her ironed uniform and stuffed it into her bag and fought with her hair to get it to stay tied up on the top of her head before making for the door. She left the new consignment of house particulars on the kitchen table with a comment of 'looks hopeful' on one of them for Steve to see when he got home.

Once at work, all thoughts of moving house were erased as she immersed herself in her job. The old maternity hospital had recently closed and its services moved to a newly-built wing at the main hospital. Jasmine had not taken to the move; from the beginning of her training to be a midwife, she had felt at home at the old place; much more so than the imposing Royal. There, amidst the smaller wards and their sun terraces and the private labour rooms there had been a more gentle atmosphere. Every nook and cranny oozed history and had seeped into her, moulding who she had become. In comparison, the new maternity wing at the main hospital had no soul; characterless and impersonal was how the staff described it when they had first moved in. Not a patch on the friendly and nurturing age-old Reid Street, but all part of improving services and modernisation and the babies would keep on coming regardless.

"Just push a bit if you can!" Jasmine encouraged gently.

"I am pushing!" the woman shouted back full of exasperation.

"Yes you are doing very well, just a little bit more."

"I can't do it!"

"Yes you can, just a bit more," replied Jasmine with more support.

"No I can't!"

"That's it, you're doing it. Now breathe, just breathe, you don't need to push anymore."

A blood curdling scream escaped from the non soundproofed room and reached the pricking ears of other midwives. They waited and listened because they understood. Nine months of hopeful anticipation and now the resulting agonizing and noisy climax pre-empted another sound, so joyous in resonance that it demanded notice. "It's nearly here. One more tiny push. Here it comes!" Jasmine began drying the baby with a towel, welcoming it into the world. "Hello baby!"

"It's a boy!" said the woman's partner, his eyes wet with tears of wonder as the baby accepted life and began to take up its cry. Those other midwives who had been listening now smiled, and got on with their business. Jasmine also smiled, remembering why she loved her job, what it was all about; that moment of birth, when life begins. Another soul is entering into the world; a vibrant being is adding its own unique sound and a new note is playing alongside the rest of the universe, joining in with the great cacophony of all that exists. Jasmine knew how privileged she was to be there, to be able to witness the miracle of birth time and again; nothing ever bettered it.

"Would you like to cut the cord?" Jasmine asked the woman's partner, coming back down to earth and thinking of more practical matters.

"Of course he does," insisted the woman, speaking on his behalf. Jasmine put the cord scissors into his reluctant hands and motioned how to cut it.

"You've done it, well done," Jasmine said happily. A few minutes later, placenta delivered and checked, baby weighed, maternal observations dealt with and the proud new mum made comfortable with baby suckling contentedly, Jasmine began to clear up. She collected a cup of coffee and sat down to the mammoth task of documenting the whole episode on various pieces of legally necessary paper, booklets, charts, and swearing at the computer as it refused to speak to the printer.

"Can you come and check some antibiotics with me please?" asked Kelly, the midwifery sister on duty. Jasmine followed her to the treatment room, knowing it would be at least ten minutes before she could return to her work.

"Funny how penicillin is just a load of mould," Jasmine mused.

"It's like so many of the medications we use," replied Kelly as she drew up water to dilute the drug. "Take ergometrine for instance. We use it to contract the uterus but did you know that it too is a fungus?" Kelly was always a mine of information. "It grows on rye. In the middle ages people were poisoned by eating infected rye bread. Their limbs would drop off through gangrene or they would have convulsions."

"No wonder we're wary of giving it to those with high blood pressure."

"Exactly!" Kelly replied. "They are already in danger of having fits; we don't want to make matters worse. Talking of high blood pressure, did you know what magnesium sulphate is, the drug we use to ward off an eclamptic fit?"

"No idea."

"Epsom Salts!"

"Never!"

"As I tell you no lies," replied Kelly. She finished preparing the antibiotic and as they went to administer it to the patient, Kelly asked gleefully "By the way, did you know LSD is a derivative of ergot of rye?"

"No way!" Jasmine enthralled.

Penicillin given and signed for, Jasmine returned to the computer and took a slurp of lukewarm coffee but it was soon abandoned and left to grow cold on the work station, forsaken for more pressing matters. "Crash section!" someone shouted. Jasmine's adrenaline began to pump around her body as she pulled on theatre blues and arrived in the operating theatre just as a woman with fear written all over her face was heaved onto the operating table.

"Its okay, you'll be asleep in no time," said the anaesthetist by way of reassurance. The woman was becalmed by gas and the operation commenced. Five minutes later the baby complained bitterly of being thrust into the world so suddenly while his mother remained in enforced oblivion. Following a tacit sigh of relief from all present, the frantic pace of the proceedings and everyone's heart beats slowed down, the operation continuing in more relaxed fashion. Later, Jasmine was back battling with the computer, bashing its keys in the hope it could be beaten into submission and understand how to communicate with the printer. She decided the alleged computer meltdown in the year two thousand would be a Godsend if it happened. 'No more wrestling with stupid data processors!' What a thought. Jasmine had barely finished her paperwork when the emergency buzzer sounded. Heart racing and adrenalin pumping again, she and every other available member of staff rushed to answer it.

The sudden assembly of bodies in the delivery room was alarming for the poor woman on the delivery bed. "What's wrong, what's happening to my baby?" she screamed, full of fear and dread.

"Your baby's shoulders just need a bit of help to come. Listen for what we tell you to do."

After agonising moments, and with all hands on coordinated deck, the baby's shoulders were freed.

"She isn't crying. Why isn't she crying?" said the woman, and then held her breath for the most part of the next torturous moments. After the deft implementation of a towel, an oxygen mask and a cold stethoscope the baby gave a reluctant cry, tired out by its challenging arrival. Panic over, Jasmine went back to woman number one, leaving a much relieved but traumatised new mummy in the capable hands of other staff.

The labour ward doors were flung open and two ambulance men burst through with a woman on their trolley puffing for all she was worth on the gas they were giving her.

"Are you pushing?" Jasmine asked. She began to work quickly and ushered the party into an empty room.

"It's coming, I can feel it!" cried the woman in between her contractions. The baby's head was visible just as the ambulance men moved her onto the delivery bed, relieved that they had arrived in time. "Don't push, just breathe, breathe, breathe, that's it, well done!" Jasmine was back to the script. "Watch, your baby is coming. Did you know what you were going to have?" Kelly came in armed with needle and syringe as Jasmine brought a baby girl up to land on the woman's abdomen.

"Not another girl! That's four of them now," the woman sighed. The baby cried. "That's a lot of weddings to organise," she said, smiling now she had heard the baby cry and gathering her up into her arms.

"Oh well, at least there won't be any men's shirts to iron!" quipped Kelly while winking at Jasmine as she injected the woman with a synthesised version of ergot of rye to aid the contraction of her uterus.

Another hour later and Jasmine's shift was over. She trudged home wearily and fell into a chair. "Busy day dear?" asked Steve bounding into the room to welcome her back.

"Oh, you know, the usual stuff," she shrugged.

"Never mind, you've got two days off now. Here, let me pour you a glass of wine and we can talk about tomorrow." Jasmine accepted the wine and spent the next few minutes listening to Steve chatting about his day. She was just wondering if she should mention her unfortunate meeting with their new upstairs neighbour when he piped up. "Oh I nearly forgot to say, I met the new bloke from upstairs earlier."

"Oh yes?" replied Jasmine tentatively.

"He was just unlocking the front door as I came home. He seems very nice." He took a sip of wine and then added, "Trevor said he already met you this morning."

"Yes, I bumped into him in the hall." She began to giggle nervously.

"What's funny?"

"I suppose I'll have to tell you," she said.

"Tell me what?"

"I went into the hall to get the post with only my red top on and nothing else and he was there. I didn't know where to turn. Stop laughing, it wasn't funny."

"Well you were laughing about it a second ago."

"That was nervous laughter." She started hitting him as he became helpless with mirth.

"No wonder he said what he said," he managed to splutter. "It did seem odd at the time, ha ha!"

"Tell me what he said." She was still hitting him playfully.

"He said, now how did he put it? Oh yes, he said it was a joy to meet you and he thought you showed great poise with the morning's unwieldy post."

"Oh God!" said Jasmine as she covered her mouth with both hands and slunk low into the chair." I'm just going to have to avoid him from now on."

"Don't worry about it. He just got an eyeful and enjoyed the experience. He won't hold it against you!" he added playfully.

"Shut up!" Jasmine retorted and hit him with a cushion.

"Anyway, you have a lovely bum, especially from behind."

"He didn't see me from the back, well I hope he didn't anyway."

"Don't get me wrong Jas, I'm not entirely comfortable with it but there's no beating about the bush so to speak, it's happened and it can't be changed."

"Just be quiet, no more, please!" Jasmine beseeched. They settled down with the wine and the subject changed, Jasmine was wound up enough with the present one. "What did you think of those house details I left out? I barely had time to look this morning but it looked okay."

"I thought it was very interesting," Steve said, taking Jasmine's glass out of her hand. "But *you* are far more interesting at the moment. I think I'd like an eyeful of your behind right now, especially that bit, right there," he said as he pinched the left cheek.

"You leave my bum alone, you know I'm self-conscious about it, especially because of, well, you know. He probably saw everything for all I know."

Over breakfast the next morning they read the details over and over. On paper it appeared to be just what they had been searching for. They rang the estate agent, hoping for a viewing that day. "Fantastic. We'll be there in an hour." Steve put down the phone and related the conversation he had just had with the estate agent to Jasmine. The house apparently was empty and they would be able to pick up the keys from the agent and go to look at it by themselves. Jasmine decided to ring her parents and tell them of their plans.

"Hi Mum," Jasmine greeted over the phone as Glenda picked up.

"Oh hello how are you? I was meaning to ring you. Lucy is coming to stay for a few days shortly and I am sure you two would like to get together. I wondered if you wanted to come to lunch one day." Jasmine already knew about the proposed visit, she had heard it all from Lucy already. They had already arranged to meet up. Now she was going to have to be diplomatic.

"How long will Lucy be up? Maybe she will have time to stay with me as well."

"Oh I don't think so dear, she only has a few days, and you know how busy she is. How marvellous she is to have got that design contract. She is such a clever girl. You do know about the design contact don't you? I'm sure I must have told you."

"Yes Mum you have told me, this must be the third time now," replied Jasmine. She could easily have been envious of the praise, but was proud of her sister as well and over the years had become immune to her mother's constant preoccupation with her younger daughter.

"Yes I thought I must have. She will be meeting all those wonderful people, how exciting! I don't know how she manages it all I really don't. It's going to look so theatrical, I cannot wait to see it when it's all finished."

"I'm sure you'll get an invite," Jasmine replied. "Anyway, the reason why I am ringing is to say we have been thinking of buying something rather than renting and we're going to look at a house this morning that sounds promising."

"Oh so you're not moving back here then?"

"No of course not, we're both very settled with jobs here and anyway, we like the town."

"Yes I'm sure you do but you could easily move back here, Steve could easily find a job in a local school and you will surely be starting a family soon won't you and so you won't need to work anymore. Lucy of course has to live in London because of her type of work otherwise I'm sure she would live here if she could."

"Mum, it's not that simple to change jobs and anyway, why would Steve want to, he loves his job and has no intention of leaving."

"But don't you want a baby?"

"What's that got to do with anything? Look Mum, I just rang to say what we were planning. Anyway, I need to go now; I will speak to you later about coming for a meal." She put the 'phone down with exasperation. Speaking to her mother was never straight-forward. She needed to go for a run to calm down.

"Forget about it Jas, you know what she's like. Come on, there's something about this one, this time." Steve tried hard to make her shrug off her mother's protestations for once but she still wanted a run. They compromised, she would go later and they set off to pick up the keys to the property feeling as if they were starting on some sort of great adventure.

Chapter Twenty-Four

The house was set in a peaceful road fairly close to the park and coincidentally the same area that Jasmine had been born. Steve and Jasmine had always liked the locality. They had discovered it shortly after they arrived in the town several years earlier after Jasmine had wanted to see where she had lived when very small. She had no recollection of the house but vaguely remembered the standing stones in the park. She must have played on them or been able to see them from the house, she did not know; but there was definitely something familiar about them. A glimmer of a memory had surfaced of an old woman always sitting on a seat near the stones. Then another picture came into her mind. It was the woman's wrinkly face talking, smiling, eyes wet. She was saying something about a flower. Or was she calling her name, Jasmine? No, not Jasmine, she was mouthing an 'oh' sound. What was it? What a funny thing to remember after all these years. She made a mental note to ask her mother.

The estate agent's details stated that the house required some refurbishment. "Only some?" remarked Steve. He was looking up at the windows with their flaky paint and rotting frames, and the guttering at one end which was coming away. "Damp issues," he said as he pointed up towards it. Up for a challenge, neither had been daunted. They both had a feeling. "Something about this one, don't you think?" Steve said. 'So, well, lovable,' he thought. It was the way it looked, the windows either side of the door, the door in the middle. Silly really, all houses had doors and windows, but this house had *those* windows and *that* door, and then they saw the gate. Well, that did it. It was meant wasn't it? There, on the battered and somewhat rotten wooden gate that led down the side of the house to the back garden were two words in faded paint, 'Jasmine House'. "This is my house!" Jasmine had exclaimed after she read the words. "Wow, that's unbelievable! Oh Steve, we just have to have this house."

"Lovely house isn't it?" They both turned in surprise towards the unexpected voice. "Been empty for a while now, I've been watching its old glory fade; it's a shame. Needs someone to love it."

"We've come to look at it as we are wanting to buy something in this area and yes, it is lovely," Steve replied. "Are you a local, do you know this house?" he added, hoping for some information about it.

"I don't know it as such but I've been around a long time, seen the comings and goings so to speak."

Jasmine could not contain her exuberance, even with strangers, and gesticulated to the gate. "That's my name on the gate, 'Jasmine', it must be a sign for us to buy it!"

The passer-by looked directly at her looking a little baffled by her outburst but then seemed to come to recognise what she meant. "Of course, yes, I didn't realize at first." He looked back at Steve and made a small bow. "I wish you every happiness."

"Thank-you," they both said in unison. Steve decided not to quiz him for information, he didn't want to confuse him further and they watched him doff his hat and walk on his way.

"What a quaint old man," Steve said as he turned the key and tentatively opened the front door. They stepped over the mound of junk mail that lay unclaimed on the mat and into another world. Steve and Jasmine had been informed by the agent that its previous occupant, an old lady, had lived there for a long time and had not done much with it. Consequently the place was in a sort of time warp, looking as if nothing had been touched for years and the air inside was stale, the house having been shut up for some time. It was as if they were visiting a museum with room settings entitled 'how we used to live'. They went from room to room without saying a word, enthralled at what they saw. "Incredible!" said Steve at last. "There's stuff from every period of time, Georgian, Victorian, Art Deco; oh wow, look at this juke box! What on earth would that be doing here?"

"It's just amazing," agreed Jasmine, in awe. They both knew they had to live in this house, but then they had known that even before they had set foot in it. Somehow, it felt full of love; they could feel it seeping out everywhere, waiting for an embrace. They were smitten. "Why has no one bought it?"

"Because all they see is a load of work and a pile of old junk, they haven't seen the potential," Steve answered as he motioned Jasmine into the back garden. The garden turned out to be a veritable jungle and impossible to go into.

"I can see why it's called Jasmine House, there's jasmine all up the side. It's so lovely," she said as they stood. They also noticed a climbing rose full of hips. Jasmine looked very thoughtful. "Rose! She was saying rose!" she blurted out triumphantly.

"What on earth are you on about?"

"Oh nothing. I just remembered something from when I was little. I remember an old lady sitting on a bench in the park saying something about a rose, that's all."

"Okay, how much shall we offer?" He took it as read that Jasmine was in agreement.

"Well no one else seems to want it; we might get it for a good price," said Jasmine. They chatted about what sort of offer they would make on their way back with the keys but then decided to stay calm and not make one immediately. They deposited the keys with the receptionist without comment about the house but spent the weekend thinking of nothing else. It was another week before they made their offer.

Three months later the stale air from inside greeted them, hopefully for the last time. It was theirs! Finally, it was really theirs! Their offer had been accepted and after a whirlwind of solicitors, mortgage application, paperwork and worry they felt exhilarated. Steve grasped hold of Jasmine's hands and pulled her inside and danced her round and round, laughing. "What on earth are you doing?" she gasped.

"Dancing the happy dance of course."

"The what?"

"The happy dance. My family has always danced it when they are feeling really happy, it's sort of traditional. The story goes my Great-grandfather Jason danced it when his first baby was born."

"So now I understand why you did that funny jig every time you scored a goal in football games at school," she puffed.

"Well I wasn't going to start dancing it with my team mates, was I? They might have got the wrong idea and anyway, it's sort of private, just for family."

They danced around for several minutes, Jasmine learning the steps. When Steve finally let Jasmine go she ran into the nearest room and wrestled with the window trying to get it open. The dance had made her breathless and she wanted to let in some fresh air. "Here, let me do that," said Steve. "Could do with a new sash," he deduced when it finally moved. They went around trying all the windows and managed most of them when a bit of brute force was applied. The rest would have to wait. Back in the kitchen they turned on the water and made themselves a cup of coffee with supplies they had brought, trying to postpone decisions on the enormous task ahead of them. It was in a dilapidated state and money, time, effort then more money was needed to bring the house up to date. Despite that, they had followed their hearts and bought it. Rewiring, plumbing and new timbers were the primary requirements, but they wanted to get a feel for the house before they started ripping it apart. Their parents were worried it was a money pit; their friends decided they were just plain crazy.

"There are some wow-factor, brilliant, state-of-the art new-builds in the area and you went and bought this?" they had exclaimed. So there they were, young, in love, and from their friends' view point, blissfully bonkers. At least the roof was sound. Someone must have persuaded the old lady who had previously lived there to do something about it.

Chapter Twenty-Five

"I've had enough of this, do you fancy an ice-cream in the park?" Steve asked throwing his wall paper scraper down. They had been pulling off wallpaper for most of the day, stopping only for a sandwich and coffee at lunch time. Progress had been painfully slow as the paper, of which there were several layers, was coming off only bits at a time and the task which had begun with enthusiasm was now arduously boring. They were in one of the bedrooms at the back of the house, the one that looked as though it had been used as the nursery. They had both decided to make this their bedroom as it belonged to a suite of rooms.

"Look, that can be the en-suite, and that can be made into an enormous walk-in wardrobe." Jasmine had enthused when they were planning the upstairs. "It has such a lovely view of the garden."

"You mean it *will* have when the jungle out there has been tamed," added Steve.

"Come on Jasmine, hurry up let's go to the park." He got up and ran on ahead knowing he was faster. He turned around and watched her as she ran breathlessly towards him, laughing.

"Stop leaving me behind all the time," she cried as she caught up.

"But I love it when you chase me!" he joked and caught her in his arms pulling her into some nearby bushes and started to kiss her. They were both relieved to be in the fresh air and away from wallpaper stripping. She responded to the kiss by closing her eyes and wrapping her arms around his neck enjoying the moment but as his hands pressed harder, pulling her to him, she broke away.

"Not here!" she protested. Steve responded by taking hold of her hand and pushing further into the rhododendron bushes.

"There's no one about," he said. "Anyway, there's no time like the present." Later, when they had finished wriggling through the undergrowth of the thicket, they came onto the wide-stretching path and walked hand in hand towards the ice-cream van that beckoned with its familiar melody. They looked at the pictures of the ice lollies. The choices made them laugh. Steve fancied a 'screw ball' but Jasmine was torn between a 'big juicy' or a 'dipstick'. She eventually chose neither and went for a plain cone with a

190

cherry syrup topping. Feeling sufficiently cooled by their excursion to the park, they carried on stripping the wall paper, still giggling at the choice of ice-creams.

The house buzzed with activity from electricians, plumbers and carpenters. It was as if it were embracing the intrusion; the old musty atmosphere gradually disappeared as it shook awake after its long slumber, welcoming life back into its body. It had readily thrown up some of its secrets. The cellar, which had housed the original kitchen complete with range, was like an Aladdin's cave. There were old copper pots, Victorian kitchen utensils, a beautiful set of old crockery, and a large dinner service hidden behind a cob-web enriched rickety door which looked as though it had been shut up for the best part of a century. The plumber had unearthed a fancy teaspoon which had turned out to be solid silver with the name 'George' inscribed. A beautiful dress that Steve thought must be at least a century old had been found under floorboards in a bedroom wrapped up in very old brown paper along with some enamelled and silver hair brushes. Jasmine loved the dress and its inset handmade lace-work. "I would love to be able to make lace; it's such a lovely thing to do. I just cannot imagine why someone would want to hide something so beautiful under the floorboards."

"That's obvious! They put it there just so that we could find it of course!"

"Ha ha, very funny," retorted Jasmine.

Little by little, room by room, the house took shape. They quickly decided that the kitchen was fine as it was. The cupboards were built-in and looked as if they were from the Edwardian or Arts and Crafts period and far too good to destroy. A new coat of paint and they looked as good as new. Once they had a working bathroom, they gave notice on their flat and moved in, Jasmine giving a brief but relieved goodbye to Trevor. She had found it difficult to look him in the eye properly since their first meeting. Steve had not given the matter another thought and he and Trevor had found a mutual interest at the local pub, and took time to help each other prop up the bar there. According to them it was of great importance they should test out the different beers, carefully considering their selections, checking they were always up to scratch, remembering the subtle differences of taste, holding every glass with appropriate reverence, picking over the good and not so good points of each and only wending their befuddled way home when satisfied they had successfully completed their mission. Steve had decided that it was still going to be his local. After all, he did not want the standard of beer to drop in his absence.

Furnishing the rooms was never a problem; there had been a wealth of stuff to choose from, dusty and forgotten. It was evident that the old woman who had lived there had closed off many of the rooms, using them for storage. There was evidence of a family having lived there at one time as there was children's paraphernalia dotted around; an old high chair, bits of furniture for 'small people' and a magnificent vintage coach-built pram "From the Edwardian period," Steve described. One of the downstairs rooms was very impressive with mahogany-clad walls and shelving to two sides A few old books lay in thick dust ranging from old very heavy medical publications to modern paperbacks. Jasmine and Steve had often considered getting in touch with the old woman to ask about the history of the house; they wanted to keep its chronicle alive, it seemed important.

Meanwhile, they did not want, or need to keep all of the house contents, there was far too much, they preferred to be more minimalistic and there were years of clutter. It was yet another daunting task but Steve felt he was capable especially as he rather enjoyed learning about antiques and their history. It had both upset him and annoyed him as a child that his parents had rid themselves of all their old and 'hand me down' furniture in favour of the more modern stuff. The kitchen table that he had known all his life, with its familiar dents resulting from childhood tantrums and other traumas, had disappeared one day and in its place, as he got home from school, was his dad sitting cross-legged on the floor poring over meaningless line diagram instructions, bits of wood scattered around him, an Allan key in his mouth and his mum counting screws trying to make the amount she was counting the same as the amount required in the instructions. The resulting new table wobbled and was never big enough for their needs. "But it's Scandinavian, it's modern!" therefore it suited his parents who were ever in search of anything innovative, especially since returning from America. The very comfortable and, what Steve believed to be a technological masterpiece of engineering design, swivel and tilt chair that he loved to curl up in and read a book? "Gone to the tip," his mother had snapped as if relieved by its departure. In the space of a year nearly every item of furniture had been replaced, which he could only think was some sort of madness or frenzy his parents had been overcome with. He had heard the term mid-life crisis and perhaps that was it. It was a phase that 'grown-ups' had to go through, like he had to go through phases, or so his parents told him. "It's just a phase," his mother explained when his back and face were covered in spots.

Some of the new stuff however, Steve thought was flash; the new coffee table for instance; completely sculpted out of glass! Well it was fine as long as it remained visible; it developed the illusion, in some lights, of having disappeared completely. Cries of pain, curses and bruising of the shins were reminders that it was there and completely solid. Steve had developed the habit of searching antique and junk shops in the hope of finding his beloved furniture and out of that sparked his interest.

Steve liked antiques but it didn't mean he was stuck in the past. He was very interested in new technology and had been one of the first to own a home computer, soon discovering the new auction site *ebay* on the internet when it emerged in 1995. Steve had been amazed at what people were buying, making him hang on to some of the stuff that he would have previously thrown away regarding it as rubbish. Any sale, no matter how small, would be profit and help pay for all the work on the house. When he was tired of decorating, he would be found sorting the unwanted items, dragging them around to get a decent photograph, and listing them on the *ebay* site. He could not believe the interest in old chipped tea cups. He was unaware people still drank from them. 'Aren't they the *mugs?*' he chuckled to himself, admiring his own wit.

Chapter Twenty-Six

Time marched on methodically and the couple slowly made headway in the house renovations. Jasmine spent months during her spare time stripping marble fire surrounds of their layers of paint despairing of her dirty nails as she blackened the hearths.

"Beautiful!" said Steve.

"What me or the fireplace?" Jasmine retorted. "It's the floors to sand next and then we can start painting."

"We? I thought you were the painter. I choose the colours, it's a very important job, and if I get it wrong you will have to paint it all over again!"

"Very funny I don't think. Go and cook me dinner or I'll go on strike and you will have to live in a building site." Believing Steve was jesting Jasmine continued happily until he called that the meal was ready. "Mmm, smells delicious won't be a moment, just need to scrub all this black off." By the time she had come downstairs again, there was a visitor lounging languidly at the kitchen table that was housed in its own little nook.

"Hello there, just passing."

"Hello Trevor, how are you?" Jasmine asked politely. Trevor was the last person she wanted to see.

"Absolutely fine, thanks for asking. However, can't stay." He got up abruptly. "I'll call you when I know."

"Okay then, cheers Trev. I'll see you out," answered Steve as he followed Trevor to the door. "I think Trev's got himself a girlfriend," he winked knowingly when he returned.

"Really? What makes you think that? "

"Oh he's been a bit evasive recently and now he's just cancelled our night out this Friday."

"How do you deduce from that that he has a girlfriend?

"What bloke would cancel a night out with his mates for anything else?"

"Well it's a big jump from a pint of beer to that sort of conclusion."

"Certainly is but I'm sure of it, it's the way he was acting."

"Well thank goodness for that, I shall be pleased if it's true." Jasmine was relieved, she always felt Trevor fancied *her*. Another girl would give him something to think about. After eating they lit a fire in the gleaming fireplace and studied colour-scheme brochures. "Do you think we could make a start in the library room next; it's one of my favourite rooms with its wood panelling, so cosy," Jasmine mused. "In fact I think it should become a formal dining room, considering we got rid of most of the books and have no use for a library."

"Can't we just stop for a bit and do something else?" asked Steve hopefully. "We do nothing but decorate."

"I don't think it needs much work, just a lick of paint to give a limed effect and lots of wax polish and, oh yes, a nice rug."

"Whatever." Steve was weary of endless decorating but knew when he was beaten and looked forward to bed time where he held out some hope of getting his own way.

A few nights later Jasmine was on her way home mulling over the events of that evening while waiting at some red traffic lights. She had been picking up paint and wax polish and the said items had triggered her memory. However, the completely satisfying recollections were quickly replaced by an intriguing scenario in the Italian restaurant over to her left. Her eyes had been drawn by the collection of little coloured lights clustering underneath the low hung roof line and her mind had followed them abstractedly. She thought how pretty they looked as they cascaded down the apricot rendered wall between the arching windows. The restaurant looked full as she peered through the not yet shuttered glass and then just as she felt the need to take a sharp intake of breath, the lights changed abnormally promptly and Jasmine reluctantly moved on to continue her journey home.

"Guess who I saw at D'Agostino's this evening!" Jasmine said with relish.

"Go on then," replied Steve as Jasmine seemed to be waiting for his response.

"Trevor, with a girl!"

"Told you! It's the only reason he would cancel our Friday night out. At long last he's pulled! Well done Trev! Ha-ha, he'll be in for some ribbing."

"I wonder what she's like."

"Time will tell," replied Steve as he moved the paint pots off the kitchen table where Jasmine had deposited them and took them into the library where he presumed Jasmine would want them so she could make an early start in the morning. "Do you fancy going out to eat tonight? Er, I appear to be free!"

"Not D'Agastino's."

"No, I was thinking more on the lines of a curry. Fancy the Mumtaz?"

"Yes, that would be great, I'll get my coat, we can walk through the park. It's not a bad evening, not too cold.

On the way home they took the long way round past their old flat and were just in time to see two silhouettes at the front door before it closed. "Look, its Trevor again. He's taken her home!"

"The dirty bastard!"

"Steve!"

"Sorry! Boy is he going to get some stick when I see him."

It was several weeks before Steve had a call from Trevor. "Been busy?" asked Steve.

"You know how it is, something came up." Trevor answered casually. Steve tried not to laugh.

"I'm sure it must have."

"Yeah! Nothing much one can do about it. Just got to get on and do the business."

"Absolutely. Successfully I hope?"

"Er, yes I think so. Fancy a pint?"

"Absolutely."

"Do you know much about black holes?" asked Trevor as he swilled the last of his beer around in his glass creating a whirlpool effect.

"Fancy another?" said Steve as he gestured to the barmaid to be served and deliberated the question. He believed Trevor was attempting to change the conversation in such a direction that it would make it impossible to steer back onto relationship matters. He had got nowhere when probing for information about girlfriend activities and soon gave up trying. Trevor was clearly not ready to divulge anything.

"Not really," Steve answered. He took a sip of the pint of Landlord that had just appeared in front of him and then continued, "but I know a man who does. My father was into all that. We spent some time in California when I was in my teens where there was some research going on into black holes. Dad went to help with the maths. He's had a lifetime's interest in Einstein's theories on relativity and when the opportunity came up to study further, he couldn't resist."

"What has Einstein's theory of relativity got to do with black holes?"

"Lots apparently but I'm not sure I can explain. Dad was forever trying to make me understand but, not being a mathematician or scientist, I found it difficult to follow."

"You've got my interest, try." Trevor rearranged himself on the bar stool ready to be educated.

"Are you sitting comfortably? Because it's a long story."

"Then begin!" Trevor quipped.

"Once upon a time then, back in the 1960s, there was this mathematician who was able to describe a black hole by mathematics and, that if the said black hole were to rotate, a Polo mint type of formation would occur and it would become possible to jump through the hole in the middle and arrive in a different place. Are you following?"

"I think so, go on."

"Anyway, no one took him seriously until real black holes were discovered in the Milky Way and other places. That was where my Dad came in. He was part of a team that followed Einstein's general relativity equations about space-time singularities and set out to prove that such a thing was impossible."

"Space-time whats?" Trevor spluttered as he drained his glass.

"Yeah, I know! Polo mints basically. Or that's how I saw them. Have another beer and it might seem clearer." Steve got the next round. The conversation continued after they judged the beer to still be on form.

"Well that's a shame; it was sounding as though H. G. Wells' time machine could actually work, providing it resembled a mint."

"Just wait, the story isn't complete. Apparently they had no choice but to conclude that if one was able to manipulate a black hole, there was nothing in the equations to stop you time travelling."

"So what are we waiting for?" asked Trevor as he almost slid off the stool. "Let's buy a packet of Polos and go for it."

"Ah well. There's a catch."

"I might have known. There's always a catch. Don't tell me; the world's stock of Polos is all used up?"

"No, it's obvious really. Put simply, we haven't got the technology to time travel. Fancy a peanut?"

"Well what a surprise," concluded Trevor. "Never mind jumping through black holes, we haven't even got a handle on how to fly the buggers. No holes in peanuts. Yeah, I think I'll be safe enough with a peanut."

"Thank goodness for that," said Steve as he lay down to sleep that night.

"What?" Jasmine asked, curling up next to him.

"Trevor's back to normal."

"Oh right." Jasmine remained nonplussed. "Goodnight! It's late and the clocks are moving forward tonight."

"So they are. We'll be time travelling without any black holes in sight."

"What on earth are you talking about?"

"Nothing, nothing at all. Goodnight."

Chapter Twenty-Seven

Several months later...

The noise of the ride-on mower caused Steve to look up. The fresh-cut grass had been wafting its perfume into the classroom through the open window. He could sense it in the air; the atmosphere was almost fully charged as the summer sunshine beckoned. Term was nearly over, the pressure of work winding down. He had set his afternoon class their final piece of group work and they were keen to get it finished, knowing it was to be their last. He had been walking between the various groups, offering help and advice where needed. Steve loved to teach, he had discovered he wanted to make a career of it when he had helped a neighbour's son with some homework whilst at university. For him the greater challenge had been getting through the dreaded curriculum, rather than keeping the kids under control but now, with a few years of experience behind him, he found he was even improving with that. His main subject was history and he had the ability of bringing it to life by his enthusiasm and his love for it.

The droning mower was somewhat distracting as it made its continual presence felt. Steve started closing the window in an effort to kill the noise. As he did so, he paused as his eyes were drawn to two figures leaving the sports hall. He recognised the larger figure; Adrian McDermott, the headmaster, and he was very much aware that the other was most definitely all female. He finished closing the window and was moving away when he stopped in his tracks. There was something about the woman's physique, and the way she walked. He recognised that body; he recognised that walk, it was unmistakable. It took a few seconds for his memory to compute. He hardly dared turn round. An old flame of desire spluttered and sparked into life. Torrid scenes from years ago burned in his head. He could not help but take another look. He gasped inwardly and swallowed hard 'Suzie? Oh my god it can't be Suzie, here? Now?' The two figures disappeared from view but he had seen enough. It was definitely her.

The rest of the period progressed in spite of the lack of input from Steve, and the sound of the school bell brought the relief he was waiting for. Class dismissed, he sat down at his desk, his hands clasped at his forehead, his eyes closed. Minutes ticked by, he did not move. Memories were welling up fast, free from their long-enforced suppression and Steve allowed himself to bathe in them luxuriantly. He had all but forgotten about Suzie, but she had dominated his time in the States. He met her on campus, bumping into her by chance while searching for the library. Suzie, captivated by this interesting but altogether rather naive English boy with his 'cute' accent, lost no time in introducing him to America in her own inimitable style. He could only bask in awe at her apparent knowledge and maturity. She was living away from home in rented accommodation, and was a year ahead of him in age, which was of enormous benefit to Steve, enabling him to romp his way through his education, relishing every moment. Preferring to 'seize the day' he managed to quash any guilty thoughts of Jasmine. After all, she was the girl he had left behind, the girl, he believed, would always wait for him, so he reasoned with himself. Whatever happened in America was irrelevant to his relationship with Jasmine. However, from the moment he had arrived back in England, Jasmine was the girl he wanted. All trysts with Suzie had been conveniently kept well hidden; secrets sweet in their savouring, stories never told, tales perhaps left unfinished.

Steve opened his eyes and remembered where he was. The groundsman was evidently still busy on the playing fields cutting the grass, the voices of children to be heard both indoors and outdoors. It was lunchtime. Steve put his thoughts away and made his way, first to the staff room and then to the dining hall. Unusually his appetite had disappeared and so he headed to the vending machine for a cup of black coffee and a bar of chocolate.

"Oh Steve, there you are, I have someone here I need to introduce to you." Adrian McDermott's voice made Steve freeze on the spot. Either time had stood still or he was standing at the edge of a great chasm not knowing how to cross; he did not know which as he steadied himself, realising precisely who he was about to be introduced to. He watched his hand moving as if in slow motion as it carefully put down the full and hot cup of coffee that had already slopped as he had brought it out of the machine. He braced himself and turned around, his mouth full of dairy milk, ready to face his past. "This is Penny Smith; she will be joining us next term in the science department."

"I am so very pleased to meet you," replied Steve with all the excitement of a screeching chimpanzee and with the widest of chocolate grins. He took hold of her hand in both of his and the suspended moment of time jolted forward causing his animated reaction to look like he was going to kiss her as it leapt across the void.

"Well, what a greeting," she replied nervously, ducking away from the over enthusiastic welcome. He did not care. He really was delighted to meet her. Her posture, her chemistry and body language, it was exactly the same and he could not believe how relieved he was. It wasn't her! It wasn't her! He wanted to jump in the air and shout aloud. It wasn't her!

"Are you feeling all right Steve?" asked Adrian McDermott showing mild concern over Steve's slightly bizarre behaviour.

"Yes, sorry," began Steve, "I thought you were someone else, but you weren't, and I was relieved that you were you and not someone else, as I had first thought." Steve was starting to feel ridiculous.

"Ah yes, I see, I think." replied Adrian McDermott unable to hide his worried expression. "Well, come Miss Smith, we should be getting along, lots to see yet." Steve watched a puzzled-looking Miss Penny Smith throw a backward glance as Adrian McDermott swiftly bundled her away.

"Well that went well," Steve muttered to himself as he picked up his coffee squeezing the cup enough for more to slosh out. "Ouch, bastard!" he exclaimed as the hot liquid ran over his fingers. Roll on the summer holidays, he thought as he saw a couple of pupils sniggering at him. He sat down at an unoccupied table, sipped the coffee and finished the bar of chocolate, happy in the knowledge that he had escaped the dreaded dilemma of working with someone he might still desire, while married to the love of his life.

"What's all this?" Jasmine asked as Steve arrived home with an enormous bunch of flowers and a bottle of wine.

"Just presents for my gorgeous wife."

"How lovely, thank you very much, they're beautiful." Jasmine busied herself with arranging the flowers in a vase while Steve sat regarding her.

"Jas?"

"Yes."

"You must never stop looking, you know, er, don't ever let yourself 'go' like some other women do."

"I beg your pardon? What on earth are you talking about?" Jasmine had affront written all over her face "Do you think I'm getting fat?"

"No, not at all. No I just don't want you to, that's all."

"What's brought this on? You've never said anything before."

"I was just thinking how lovely you look and that I love you." Steve was feeling rather awkward, wishing he had not opened his mouth.

"Well I would hope that you should still love me whether I were thin, fat, tall, short, or anything for that matter. I should still love you whatever you look like because it's the bit inside that counts, isn't it? Maybe it doesn't with you; maybe it's all superficial with you." Jasmine was upset. Despite the early hour she opened the bottle of wine and poured a glass, but paused before taking any. "What were the flowers really for? Hello Jasmine, these flowers are to soften the blow, but I think you are turning into an old hag? Is that what they were for?" She felt like pouring the wine all over him.

"Can't I buy presents for you then?" Steve blustered, retaliating from the outburst from Jasmine. Without saying a word, Jasmine disappeared upstairs, clattering down after a few minutes in running gear.

"I'm going for a run in case anyone might like to know," she stated as she left noisily. Steve reflected in the quiet she left behind. He hated any upset and did not understand quite what he had done wrong although he felt that guilt must surely be dripping from him. He thought women were supposed to like flowers as gifts, maybe chocolates would have been the better choice, but under the circumstances, perhaps not. He was at a loss. He opened his computer to see how his items on ebay were doing. Before the hour had turned he heard Jasmine return. He hoped her mood had mellowed as he met her in the kitchen.

"I'm sorry, Jas, I was thinking aloud, I should not have said what I did," he began apologetically as he handed her some water and tried to put his arms round her, but she was having none of it.

"No don't. I'm all sweaty." She wriggled away.

"So you are, but I like you just the way you are and I don't want anything to change." He kissed her neck and Jasmine pondered, sometimes men could say the worst things. Her run had produced plenty of endorphins and she was feeling less maligned.

"Well don't think that this beer gut can develop anymore." She tapped his tummy lightly.

"This is a beer gut? You think I've got a beer gut?"

"I'm going for a shower." She left Steve sucking in his tummy and checking out his abs.

"Of course we could both grow fat together chewing the cud in our lovely garden," she mused later as they sat outdoors together in the evening sunshine. The air was rich with the scent of the climbing rose and they both felt content, inwardly warm with the wine they were drinking.

"No, just you, when you have our baby."

Jasmine gulped, Pinot Noir spluttering out of her mouth.

"Did you just say the 'B' word?" She had never dared broach the subject of pregnancy. She had thought the 'blood and gut' tales that she brought home from time to time had surely put him off.

"Yes, I think I did," Steve had even surprised himself.

"Wow!" was all Jasmine could say and as they watched the sunset together in contented silence, the softest of evening breezes caused a blanket of fragrant petals to flutter around them.

Chapter Twenty-Eight

The summer break was quickly over and Steve was back at school with pupils new and old, using every ounce of his mental energy to navigate them through the curriculum; essay structure, exams, time management and maybe even teach them in the process. That was in the classroom. The staffroom held different challenges. It was the fault of the new science teacher that the unwritten code of behaviour among red-blooded males was lost as they all scrapped for attention. Providing more than just sultry looks, she managed to engage them all with affable conversation and dippy personality, probably brought on, they wondered, by long hours spent in chemistry laboratories creating bubbling potions over the hot blue flames of a Bunsen burner. Steve, although not uninterested, preferred to keep his distance, reminding himself that firstly, he was a married man and secondly, he was still embarrassed from their first meeting and thirdly it was fun to watch the idiotic spectacle of grown men vying to be her errand boy. By sheer coincidence one day, he bumped into her in the park. He had gone out for some fresh air as he felt nauseous after spending his entire Saturday morning with wax polish putting finishing touches to the renewed library, now the formal dining room.

Pleased to be out to capture the remains of the beautiful but dying summer, he sat on the bench near the standing stones, watching the fallen leaves blowing around and when coming to rest, form shapely golden mantles around each of the monoliths. He saw her walking slowly and carefully in and out and around each stone holding a metal rod in each hand. Steve watched her absent-mindedly noticing how lovely she looked, a strand of her wavy hair over her face getting in the way of her eye; he wanted to touch it, he wanted to hold it back for her. He suddenly became aware of his thoughts and felt ashamed that he could be thinking like this. He loved Jasmine and always had; they were a team going through life together. Then he realised. Penny reminded him of Suzie who reminded him of Jasmine because he could see Jasmine's mannerisms in the both of them. He was merely projecting the bits he loved about Jasmine onto them, not desiring them for themselves. He breathed a sigh of relief; he could converse with his colleague without feeling that basic instincts were giving him an ulterior motive. "I thought you were a proper chemist. What sort of alchemy is this?" he called out to her with a laugh when she had noticed him.

"It's an interest of mine, something for the weekend if you like, and I like to take conventional science a step further."

"It's a bit of a weird step," replied Steve deciding she was most definitely dippy. Penny sensed he was ridiculing what she was doing and felt affronted.

"From my point of view what I am doing is perfectly natural. I am more than merely a secondary school science teacher who, incidentally, does not want to bury her own misgivings of accepted truths like most who simply accept them because they find them so difficult to understand. Where is the scientific spirit when one is so totally uncritical?" Steve agreed with her. There had been occasions when he had questioned whether there had been manipulation of some historical facts to propagate the misinterpretation of information. However, he was a victim himself when it came to dowsing; propaganda about the art had certainly left him sceptical. Before he could reply Penny was off again. "For those not involved in teaching, this may well be of little consequence but for those who are, it is irresponsible to look the other way and almost criminal to teach nonsense rather than discover and put right any misunderstanding on their own part." Steve was, as usual, when confronted with persuasive persons, lost for words. This beautiful spirited woman would knock his hormone-rich male colleagues for six. They really did not know what they were dallying with. The reply came after several minutes of sheepish deliberation.

"I did not mean to upset you; I did not know dowsing had such a close link with science that's all. I have evidently got a lot to learn." Penny sat down beside him as a friendly gesture, she did not bear grudges for long.

"Would you like to try?" she asked handing over her two inoffensive rods and before he knew it, she was teaching him the ancient art of dowsing.

"As far as I'm aware, stone circles were constructed over the earth's ley lines."

"What on earth are earth's ley lines?" asked Steve, watching the same strand of hair fall across her exquisite face every time she moved her head and again reminding him of Jasmine in its unruly quality, but not in texture. Jasmine would tong her hair into poker-straight submission; she had hated her curls.

"You have heard of acupuncture?"

"Of course," replied Steve wondering what the relevance was.

"What about meridians?"

"In association with geography, yes," he said tentatively. He was already lost.

"Basically meridians are energy channels which run along our bodies, each one associated with an organ and it is along these that acupuncture points are located."

"Right," replied Steve attempting to understand.

"Sorry, I was trying to relate it to something I thought you understood. Its okay, I'll start from a different point." Penny could see he was baffled. "Simply speaking, leys are part of an energy grid system covering the earth with a logical geometric structure. It's like a deep current of power that runs through the earth as if the earth were a living thing, like the meridians of our bodies. Along these lines are power spots where there is a vortex of energy that can increase the power of chi through the land. All will be clearer as I carry on, bear with me." She could see his eyes glazing over again.

"I do hope so."

"You must have heard of *chi* as in *Tai Chi*?" Steve nodded that he had. She carried on.

"The Australian aborigines call them song lines, sung by the chorus of nature, a story of the land. Leys become stronger by building on the song's memory and with the cohesion of both natural and human action, the messages of occurrences are told. By these actions more notes are attracted and the chi constantly changes, free flowing here, collecting and getting stuck there.

"Notes?"

"Yes notes!"

"You're losing me again."

"The notes are the throb of the cities, the screech of war as it sears and scars, the deep rumbling of the hills, the high notes coming from things like church spires and sky scrapers. They weave the song from deep in the ground right up to the ionosphere where the songs are reflected around the world like waves."

"I think I understand. You mean the way radio signals are transmitted."

"Exactly, you've got it."

"And you're picking them up with those."

"Look! So are you! Can you see the rods moving towards each other?"

206

"How is that happening?"

"You are picking up a change in the energetic field, it's very strong here." Steve played around with the rods for a while in amongst the stones but then got tired of it and sat down.

"Well it's a good party trick but how is it helpful?"

"From a technical point of view it is a relatively unknown science that needs further exploration and testing and there are many sceptics. However, perhaps we understand the energy more than we imagine. For instance, why were the standing stones erected here? Was it because the energy was strong here?"

"Maybe it's the stones themselves that are creating the power," Steve answered and made Penny laugh.

"Now you are talking as though you understand the energy."

"Actually, I was half joking," he replied.

"Only half? Let me try to explain the other half. Why did you come to the park and sit on the bench?"

"Oh I love the park, it helps me to de-stress and I come away feeling refreshed."

"Full of energy?"

"Yes."

"Now go back and listen to what you have just said. You come to the park to let go of stress and fill yourself with energy."

"Yes !"

"So where do you get this energy from?" Steve began laughing; he could see now and answered in his monosyllabic way.

"The park!"

"Exactly!" continued Penny. "The park, just like the standing stones, has been constructed on a ley line. Like the aborigines say, the song of the earth has attracted both to be constructed right here, which in turn, attracts us. People gravitate to the chi energy as if it were a power source. That's why churches were built on ley lines."

"Incredible!"

There happens to be a ley line in Trafalgar square actually, take some rods and dowse for it next time you go.

"Not likely." Steve could not imagine for one minute dowsing in the middle of Trafalgar Square.

"Hello?" Jasmine said questioningly. They had both been so engrossed in conversation they had not noticed her arriving. "I came to see where you had got to, are you feeling better?"

"Much better thanks. Oh, this is Penny, the new science teacher I was telling you about."

"Good God!" Jasmine exclaimed when she looked at Penny properly. "I mean pleased to meet you." They shook hands but Penny noticed Jasmine seemed a little edgy, so made her excuses.

"I have been keeping your husband too long, I didn't realise how the time has passed. Nice to meet you but I must get back, see you later."

"What was that outburst all about? You were very curt with her," said Steve.

"Please don't be annoyed with me, I didn't mean to be, I just wondered what had kept you. Oh my God Steve, I know who she is."

"Yes so do I, it's Penny, she teaches chemistry."

"She may well teach chemistry, but she's also Trevor's girlfriend!"

"Really? No way! He's a sly one! That explains why he has been trying to gain so much scientific knowledge. All is now clear! Well well well! Good one Trev!" Steve said approvingly.

'Lucky sod,' he said under his breath and gave a long sigh as he followed Jasmine back indoors and picked up his paint brush. He tried to think of a jibe about dowsing rods that he could use during Friday night drinks in the pub.

Chapter Twenty-Nine

Apart from the attic, there was one room in the house that they had never really touched since moving in. The furniture had been moved to one side of the room to take the floorboards up to plumb in a radiator and thread in new electric wiring, but that was all. Today was the day, however, that Jasmine had earmarked for its history to reveal itself. Every room in the house had seen a treasure trove of delights uncovered and she trusted that this one be no exception. The old four-poster bed wobbled on its wooden legs as they sat down to make a list of the contents in Steve's pocket note book. They had realised by now that cataloguing was the best way to organise what was to stay, what was to sell and what was to be thrown away.

The bedroom stood at the front of the house and although not the largest of spaces, looked as though it had been of some importance as there was an inter-connecting door to the principal bedroom. The faded blue patterned wall paper was practically stripping itself from the walls; the damp had been particularly bad in there. It didn't look as though it had been in use for a long time. A mahogany wardrobe stood empty apart from a lovely silk dressing gown hanging on the back of its door. It looked very old, but with a careful wash, Jasmine fancied wearing it; just the exact colour that she liked. The bow-fronted mirrored dressing table in the window had hairpins, broken beads, an assortment of hairbrushes and combs on its top. Steve had started pulling the drawers of the dressing table out to look at its condition more closely. One of the drawers did not close properly and after satisfying himself that the drawer was sound, Steve stretched his arm into the chest, felt around and pulled out a bundle of old papers tied up with a bit of ribbon, and a photograph of a young soldier. He hurled the papers towards the bed, glanced briefly at the photo as he aimed it in the same direction and replaced the drawer. "That's better," he said satisfied with his work. "Cleaned up and lined with fresh paper, it will look the business. Can you help me move it out to the landing? We'll clean it there and then it can go straight into our room."

That was easier said than done. A pile of thick hard-backed books were in the way which needed to be moved first, but the books proved far more interesting to Jasmine than furniture manoeuvring. "These books are on obstetrics from years ago." She sat on the bed and began browsing through them. "How fascinating," she deduced.

"They look in better condition than those we found in the library."

"Oh yes, I'd forgotten about them, they were falling apart with damp weren't they. Did you get much for them?" asked Jasmine.

"I took them to that bookshop in town but the bloke there thought they were too far gone to be of any interest," replied Steve as he resorted to dragging the chest of drawers across the room by himself.

"Take the drawers out first, you might find it easier."

"It would be easier if you helped as planned, or has your enthusiasm for decorating again waned?"

"Not at all, I'm coming." She helped push the chest but she was thinking about the books. "These books are too old to have been the old lady's."

"Maybe she just collected them like the rest of the stuff that was in the house when we bought it. We really must get to see her."

"What a good idea. Those books must have belonged to someone interested in medicine, a doctor most probably. Mind the door." Steve pushed the door out of the way and the chest of drawers was placed on the landing ready to clean. The rest of the furniture was catalogued into Steve's note book. They had not wanted to keep any of it but it might be of use to someone. Jasmine wanted to hold onto the books, at least for a while as she was interested to learn how obstetric practices had changed. The grainy monochrome photographs within the heavy volumes had sparked an interest in her of how things used to be. Steve shut his notebook and looked across at Jasmine who lay on her stomach across the bed engrossed in one of the books, and then around the room. The scroll of papers he had salvaged from the old chest and tossed carelessly away caught his eye. The ribbon binding had loosened by his careless act unfurling its long-kept secrets. He picked up a couple of the leaves of aged paper, sat on the bed next to Jasmine and started deciphering the rivers of words scrawled upon them; no mean feat as lakes of ink had made sterling attempts at obliterating them.

April 1900

My love,

Much has happened since my last brief note but here I am, ensconced in this house! Who would have thought it! I will try to fill you in. They found me collapsed in the street by the park near to the stone circle and carried me home! Doctor John Brown, who lives here, believes that I was knocked over by a passing horse and cart. My memory of the events is foggy. I can remember walking along beside the park and then nothing more than having a tremendous pain inside my head.

The house looks magnificent, so grand, and with servants! Words cannot explain what it feels like to be living here. At first I slept in the blue room. I suppose it is called the blue room, on account of the décor being predominantly blue. The wallpaper is a William Morris trellis design, in blue; the bed is dark wood with hangings that are guess what, blue and very floral. Even the chamber pot is decorated in blue! The fire was always lit making it cosy and I felt cocooned while there, safely away from the reality of my situation. However, life has to move on and I had to work out what to do next. There was no question in my mind that I would stay, where could I go? How could I come back to you and then I was so afraid that you loved her! I saw you before I left, kissing. Luckily John, who is a widower, has a young son who needs looking after and I have become his nanny. The nursery is now my personal domain and I managed to look ahead for the first time since I arrived here.

I am still amazed at the improbability of the circumstances I am in and I am finding it hard to get to grips with it. It has been so difficult to keep quiet about where I came from but even harder to blend in with the current situation. I feel like a total outsider and blunder about making one bad gaffe after another. I think John believes it is a result of some concussion I might have.

There are several other people who live here. The first person I saw as I woke up that first morning was Polly who is a maid in the house. She is only about twenty, but thinks she knows it all. I can tell she does not like me very much; she thinks I am some sort of imposter. She knows nothing! Then there is Charles, the 'man servant' or valet or whatever he is supposed to be who is slightly older. He fancies Polly but she keeps him at arm's length. Mrs. Cook, Cookie as she is known, is the cook, obviously. She bellows and bawls all day long, giving her orders to everyone, including John. Apparently she has known him since he was young and still treats him as though he were still a boy. Poor Fay gets the brunt of most of it though. She is just sixteen and in between scrubbing and washing, helps prepare the food. I feel sorry for her; she has left her family to live and work here and has no life outside of that kitchen and always looks so drawn and pale.

I try to avoid them if I can now; they make me feel unwanted in their presence. Popping into the kitchen for a snack is 'improper' as Mrs. Cook puts it. Apparently I have to ring the bell and wait for Polly to come but Polly just sticks her nose in the air and sniffs when I ask her for anything as if I am the scum of the earth.

Thank God for John's sister. She came and helped her brother as soon as she heard of his 'latest acquisition' by sorting out clothes and domestic arrangements. I think at first she viewed me as an activity, giving her something to occupy her days but, we actually get on really well. When we first went shopping for some of my own clothes in Rushworths it was such an experience. I felt like a V.I.P. Assistants were running around fetching armfuls of underwear; camisoles, chemises, drawers, petticoats and nightgowns, all edged with lace and broderie anglaise. I am now the proud owner of two corsets you will be pleased to know and I even have a boudoir cap. I will describe one of my new outfits for you. The shop assistant assured me the dress had come straight from a collection in Paris. It is pale green and has such a sweeping skirt because of the godet at the back and so long that I will have to lift it up when I walk to keep it clean.

I have the tiniest fitted jacket in cream to go over the top and the smallest of hats trimmed with flowers and a veil with an umbrella to match.

I have other things to tell you, but I cannot bring myself to say anything yet. I will write again soon and tell you more.

All my love, always yours, missing you x.

"My God, I really have to go and see the old woman, this is amazing."

"What was that?" asked Jasmine, deep in one hundred year old obstetric practices.

"Nothing, just some old writings the same as what you are looking at." Steve stopped reading and let his consciousness drift and a sensation of timelessness was over him. It was similar, he remembered, to when he had returned from America and went into his bedroom. Then, he had felt his room was a storage place for past events but now he felt he was stretching through time; no beginning and no end, a circle round and round. Maybe it was the correspondence he had just read, bringing life to a long dead past, maybe it was the vintage sense of the room itself, the same William Morris wallpaper, the old chipped and peeling paint, each layer revealing another untold chapter of history. Maybe it was the books that Jasmine had found, their musty aroma spilling out from the opened leaves and speaking of their age, or maybe it was Jasmine herself who had always been there, with him, for him. However he had got the feeling, it made him speak his mind. He was not ready for any more changes to the house and gathering up the rest of the yellowed blotchy papers and putting them carefully into one of the drawers of the old chest, he returned into the room. "Jas, do you think we could wait till after Christmas before we do any more with this room? I am going to have lots on at school, I would rather just chill if I have any spare time left if that's all right with you." Jasmine turned over onto her back surprised by Steve's change of plans.

"Oh, really?" she retorted. Secretly she was relieved as she had not met the thought of stripping yet more wallpaper with much relish. Perhaps it was a good idea to wait until the New Year and put away the unsightly row of dirty paint brushes soaking in spirit-filled jam jars. They had blotted the kitchen window sill for months and clearing them suddenly seemed the right thing to do. She imagined the ledge adorned with some of their pretty pottery." Yes, of course, if that's what you would rather. Let's close the door to this room for now and do it next year, perhaps in the spring. Actually, do you think it would make a nice child's room? Maybe we should wait until I'm pregnant."

"Fat chance of that!" Steve laughed, "we're always decorating."

"Well not anymore!" giggled Jasmine as she edged closer to him on the rickety four-poster, and put her arms around his neck.

Chapter Thirty

The cold-snapped November air heralded the wintry season and Jasmine and Steve, wrapped up with scarves and each other, took a walk in the park enjoying their time-out from decorating. Their thickly-socked and booted feet, kicked through the frosty and crisp autumn leaves as they went. Above them, the last straggling foliage clung on bleakly in the mighty branches of the now copper-less beech trees that lined the main walkway.

Their memory as fragile as the flowers themselves, the flamboyant annuals had been plucked ruthlessly from the summer beds, their places usurped by hopeful wallflowers. Lawnmowers, their cold motors silenced, were garaged in workshops ready for their yearly overhaul; the park was taking on its winter mantle. The sensational firework display had delivered all of its usual vibrancy and the safety barriers were now dismantled and stored; the preparation for the Christmas season had begun. Jasmine and Steve watched as workers who were puzzling over a knot of fairy lights dropped them hastily to rescue ladders that were leant against the tree trunks in the way of a large road sweeper. "That looks as if it doesn't take any prisoners!" remarked Steve. "Come on, I'm freezing, let's go to the café and grab a cappuccino."

"You would think they might want to buy some more contemporary lights. Those look as though they have been churned out year after year," said Jasmine after they had settled in a window seat at the café where they were able to carry on watching. "Perhaps something on the lines of Blackpool illuminations would pep things up a bit."

"When did you last go to Blackpool? I can only remember a tediously boring and very garish display when I last went. Anyway I quite like the look of our park lit by these tiny lights."

"Tiny," replied Jasmine, "being the operative word. They throw no light out whatsoever."

Their coffees arrived and they both took a spoonful of chocolate sprinkled froth into their mouths before taking a sip. "I don't think they are supposed to, they are just there to look pretty, like stars from a distant galaxy." Steve explained then added grinning mischievously, "just like your eyes." Jasmine chose to ignore the flattery.

"Well it still won't tempt me in on a dark night; I find it too foreboding on my own and so for me I see no point in putting them up." She took another sip and watched as they succeeded in untangling the lights. "Hurrah! They managed," she said a little patronisingly.

"Well they could look quite charming when I take you for a romantic walk underneath them." Steve had largely ignored Jasmines feisty ways, putting it down to their failed attempts for a baby. He hated upheaval and each month her despairing moans had been met with his steadfast support. His aspirations were simple; to keep Jasmine happy to guarantee that life ran smoothly. It was why he had been so long suffering about her obsession of 'doing up' the house. In the beginning he had been just as excited but it had taken over most of their lives lately and they had done little else. Steve could barely get through the front door after a full working day without some sort of decorating tool being thrust in his hands. He needed a rest and the old woman's bedroom had been the last straw. Thank goodness she had agreed.

"I can't wait," she replied indifferently. They sat in silence and were warmed by the dark and delicious nectar and watched the progress outside the window. Jasmine was thinking about the lights. "Don't you think our house would look nice with fairy lights around the outside?"

"No," was Steve's concise response. He could not think of anything worse than adding to the tasteless assortment of flashing monstrosities that adorned other houses.

"Yes I suppose you are right. Do you remember when Trevor insisted on putting those plastic snowmen on our wall?"

"Don't remind me, they were hideous, like Blackpool illuminations."

"You have a thing about Blackpool illuminations, that's the second time you've decried them."

"Not really, it's just that they are so brash; I prefer subtlety." He finished his coffee and watched Jasmine's eyes as they appeared to pop out, just as they always did when she was scheming. He could read her well. "Perhaps that's why I like you so much."

"What do you mean?"

"Well," he continued slowly, "you are very good at getting what you want by working in subtle ways." He tried to tread carefully as he did not want to upset her, he was not sure which way this could go.

"Oh you mean I am delicate and restrained. That's nice, thank you." Steve breathed a sigh of relief. She had misunderstood his slight criticism of her. "Anyway," she went on, "I was thinking about the jukebox. Isn't that bold and brash?" Steve hooted with laughter. She had just proved herself Machiavellian.

"That happens to be the iconic 1015 Bubbler. Don't you just love its brightly coloured arching shape?"

"Yes, like an illumination from Blackpool!" Steve could never win, but usually managed things to his advantage.

"Come on, let's go home and put it on, we haven't played it in ages."

The hour had not yet come for the park lamps to be lit but the autumn dusk rapidly approached as they stepped back outside and faced its bitter embrace. The gnarled branches of the trees fully dressed now with strings of unlit fairy lights reached up to clutch at the near-full moon. They hurried along quickly past the paddling pool, its freezing surface projecting icy reflections of lunar light and on up to the mound of the standing stones where they paused for a moment to stare at them. "They look like gravestones in this light." commented Jasmine. "You can just expect Dracula to come leaping out from behind them." Shuddering, she linked her arm under Steve's and dragged him onwards and out of the park and into the road where a few of the street lights had come on. "That feels better," she said as they were a few yards further away.

"I still cannot imagine why the old woman would have a juke box." They were back at home where Steve had opened a bottle of beer and was listening to the music the juke box was churning out. "Jas, I've been thinking, I would like to pay her a visit." Jasmine took the beer out of his grasp and took a gulp. "Hey, what are you doing?" He tried to grab it back but she skipped out of his reach.

"You are always saying you are going. Perhaps one day you will." She gave the bottle back. "You never know, she might have all sorts to say to you."

"I will go one day." The phone rang. Steve picked up, listened and held it out for Jasmine. "It's your mother." Jasmine took the phone and walked out of the room to leave Steve and the music but gesticulating to him to open a bottle of wine for her. She knew she would need something afterwards; her mother always seemed to rile her. However, she was back in the room sooner than expected.

"Mum wants to visit next month," she said as she took the glass of wine that Steve was holding out for her.

"Oh God!" said Steve as he grabbed it back and took a large gulp. "For Christmas?"

"No, before. We're going to theirs for Christmas, and yours on Boxing Day. Remember?"

"How did I manage to forget Christmas with the in-laws?" Steve asked Trevor in the pub the next day. Trevor did his best to console his friend by saying he would have New Year to look forward to; Trevor was thinking about having a party at his flat. Not having in-laws himself, he didn't fully grasp how Steve was feeling. The customary festive excitement was of far greater intensity than usual because the twentieth century was nearing its close. Everyone was in a state of heightened expectancy of what was to come, not least the hyped-up media for inducing fears that the 'millennium bug' could disrupt every aspect of life. Companies were preparing for the computer meltdown that many experts had been predicting over the last few years. Steve was trying to explain it all to Trevor; how computer systems could be vulnerable when they ticked over from the shortened year number of '99' to '00' making some of them interpret the year as 1900.

Trevor didn't think it would be much of a concern; not that he bothered much with computers. There was one where he worked, he thought, to do the payroll. "As long as my money gets paid into my bank account at the end of the month, that's all I care about... and they can always go back to the way they used to do it, so what's the problem?"

"That's all very well for you; but what about going shopping, for instance. The tills might not work properly. They might forget how to add up; we would have to go back to mental arithmetic. How many gum-chewing shop girls will manage that? And what about the government computers, the big red button might be pressed because of a faulty programme. I think," deduced Steve over his pint, "that we need to be a tiny bit worried."

"I've worked on the tills in a supermarket in my time and I can add up. I don't chew gum either."

"Nor are you a girl." Steve thought his deduction skills to be in good order, especially after deducing that they would have to have another pint of the guest beer to further deduce whether it was worth going back to the usual Landlord.

"You're just being sexist," deduced Trevor. He took another sip of beer. "Talking of sex, I've met a girl."

"Oh really!" Steve tried to be surprised but couldn't bear the deception and started to giggle.

"Is that so funny? Did you think it an impossibility?"

Steve steadied himself by immersing his face in his pint of beer before answering. "No, its not that at all." He decided to come clean. "Actually Trevor, I believe I already knew."

"No, that's impossible; there is no way on earth you could possibly know. Okay then, how did you know?"

"I know you have brains Trevor, on account of your being able to distinguish the different tastes of beer, and of course the fact that you are a dentist, but sometimes I wonder. Have you ever asked your girlfriend what she does for a living? It doesn't matter, I will tell you anyway. In fact I will tell you all sorts of things about her. First, she is a science teacher. Second, she has a rather strange hobby of dowsing ."

"So you were the bloke in the park! She said she met one of her work colleagues; oh, you are one of her work colleagues."

"And third, you like to take her to D'Agostino's."

"She told you that?"

"No, you were seen there by Jas. Sorry Trev, but you have had no secrets from me, I didn't want to say anything as I thought you would tell me in your own good time, as you have. Anyway, I shall look forward to being formally introduced to Penny as your girlfriend."

"It's Penny who wants to have the party. She's er, moving in, so to speak."

"And so another one bites the dust. Never mind Trev, there's always beer."

"What do you mean by that?"

"My dear Trevor, she hasn't even moved in yet and already she's arranging your life for you, with a party. You'll learn!"

Jasmine's mother came to stay. Steve found lots of work he had to do at the school keeping him away till late into the evenings. "It's unfortunate," he said, "but can't be helped."

Jasmine had taken some annual leave days so she could spend time with her Mum. Glenda appeared to enjoy just going around the local area reminding herself of it, and Jasmine was happy to accompany her. She was ready for a change from work and visiting the shops as a leisure activity rather than dashing there and back was novel. Jasmine did not normally have the time to peruse all the clothes shops at length, but Glenda was determined to find 'the perfect dress' to wear on Christmas day. Jasmine found one she might like for herself. It was a very plain shift with three-quarter length sleeves and came in either electric-blue or rose-red. She felt very comfortable in it but could not decide which colour she preferred. "The red is more festive," insisted Glenda. She chose the red one; it pleased her mother.

On one of their excursions they ended up at the old maternity hospital where Jasmine had done her midwifery training and where Glenda had spent time after her confinements. Seeing the aged place was upsetting for both of them, but for different reasons. For Glenda, hoping to lay some ghosts to rest, it had reminded her of the tragedy of the loss of her baby. She also thought of those few days in that hospital with Jasmine as a newborn, beautiful and content, where she felt cared for by the midwives and doctors, but felt too scared to go home and accept what had happened and too afraid to love Jasmine in case she too was taken. With these thoughts and feelings from long ago stirred up inside her, she had inadvertently pulled Jasmine toward her in a hug and started to weep.

Jasmine too was crying, but for completely different reasons. This beautiful, but run-down building in front of which they were standing, had gently nurtured her as she had learnt her craft. From testing urine for its specific gravity to delivering her first baby as a qualified midwife; from cleaning bedpans in the sluice-master, to bathing babies; this fine structure had absorbed it all and stood its ground. Its old solid walls of blackened sandstone, its grand entrance hall with gated lift to the first floor and the Nightingale wards each with its own character and name, spoke out to her of their history. Linen League, March Ward, Hudson, Barran and Bartram; each had its own benefactor and every bed a plaque of dedication above, she felt part of that very fabric, for she had been part of that history, part of its contribution. But for what? The cries from the labour ward had long been silenced and the babies hushed. The building was considered too old for modern times and had been overthrown by a more contemporary usurper. And now with windows smashed and collapsing roof, she did not have long. The main entrance was boarded-up and a 'keep out' sign was fixed over the gates. The grand old lady had seen her day. It was too much for Jasmine and she was glad to feel her mother's arms around her as she sobbed for former days.

"Said goodbye to your Mother yet?" Steve asked as he tentatively put his head round the kitchen door after coming home from work.

"She went this morning," Jasmine replied. Steve gestured as if his favourite team had just scored and then went towards Jasmine to give her a hug. "Don't get too excited, she wants to come back in the New Year."

"Please tell me you are joking."

"Actually I'm not. I think she has really enjoyed her little stay and thought Dad might like to come and revisit old haunts. I think she's changed a little and I know Dad loves to come. Anyway, enough of them, tell me about your day."

Thankfully for Steve, Christmas came and went swiftly and he and Jasmine got on to thinking of Trevor's Millennium party. Trevor had announced that Penny wanted everyone to wear something from centuries gone by. Steve couldn't think of anything worse.

"What's wrong with a pair of jeans?" he asked.

"That's the trouble with everyone these days, nobody bothers to dress up for anything; that's probably why Penny has decided on a theme party."

"I think we should call it Penny's party; it has a nice ring to it don't you think?"

"It doesn't matter what you call it, I can't go to it; or rather I shall have to leave as soon as midnight has struck." Unfortunately Jasmine was on the early shift on the morning of the new millennium. She had tried for weeks to get it swapped, but nobody would oblige. "Who wants to be at work when a century is turning," she had complained relentlessly to Steve. Not even relinquishing her day off on the twenty fifth in its place had any takers. Numerous members of night staff had said yes to her plea; but their shift was worse than hers so no good at all. At least she wouldn't be at work when the actual hour struck, which was some consolation.

They decided to begin at the pub, have a few rounds and then go on to Trevor's flat for food and see in the new century at midnight. Jasmine's shift started at half-past seven in the morning so she wouldn't be able to have much to drink and would have to leave the party early, leaving everyone else enjoying themselves.

"Seeing in the new year is the main thing that everyone is bothered about; after that it will be all down-hill as everyone will be drunk. At least you won't be waking up with a hangover Jas, think of that."

"Some consolation."

Jasmine however liked the idea of a themed party and was looking forward to wearing the dress she had found under the floorboards; it was clearly old. She had shown the dress to her sister when she saw her at Christmas, who had thought it definitely Edwardian. Jasmine had always longed for the right occasion to wear it and the party would be just such a time. She had persuaded Steve to dress up, he was now going as Marley's ghost, which didn't really require anything special, just a hole in an old bed sheet for his head to peep through, and his jeans underneath.

Chapter Thirty-One

Steve rang the doorbell and stood back and waited. "Can I help?"

"I have an appointment to see Miss Brown," Steve spoke back to the box where the disembodied voice had come from. The large front door opened of its own accord and Steve walked in through the vestibule into a large but empty hallway. He looked round to see where he should go. To his left, an impressive staircase led up to a galleried landing above him, to the right, he could see two doors, both closed, and a corridor. Large double doors faced him and another smaller door was to the left, just before the stairs. All firmly closed. A nurse appeared from nowhere. Steve jumped.

"Mr. Bartram?" She looked him up and down with considerable curiosity. No-one ever came to visit Rose. "It doesn't shut itself," she hissed disapprovingly while going back to shut the door. "She's in here, follow me." Steve was led through the double doors and into a sizeable room with windows covering most of one wall. They looked out onto what might have once been a beautiful garden. The light from the glass was refreshing; it needed to be when he took in the room's contents. He followed the condescending nurse past a clutch of matching pallid-green chairs all occupied by shrunken, grey, sleeping beings. The overly-loud television they were clustered around was seemingly wasted on them. An arm reached out attempting to grab at him as he went by; he dodged it, unsure of the etiquette in such circumstances. He was led over to an alcove at the far end of the room. Another wizened creature was slumped into a different style of chair. It had a flowery print fabric covering, not plastic like the others. He recognised it, there had been a matching one at home which he had taken to the tip; it had been in better condition than the one in front of him now. "Rose, there's a young gentleman to see you." The nurse stalked off and left Steve wondering what to do.

"Miss Brown?" His communication got no response. He pulled up the wooden chair nearby. "Miss Brown?" he enquired again. She moved slightly. He placed his hand on her arm, remembering what the nurse had called her. "Rose?" Her face moved to his direction and her eyes opened. They took some time to focus and grow bright.

"What day is today?"

"The last day in December, New Year's Eve."

"Is it you, have you come?" The words formed and then churned in her chest. Steve watched as they came up and congregated at her throat; her neck arching so that her head could throw them out of her mouth. It was an extraordinary feat; as though they caused great effort to conjure forward.

"Yes, it's me. Did they tell you I was coming?" Steve was a little surprised she seemed so pleased to see him. He had explained a little of who he was and why he wanted to come when he had made the appointment but wasn't sure how much the old woman had been told. He expected that she probably did not have many visitors so any caller would be a diversion.

"I knew you would come, I've been waiting for you." Her body made the same manoeuvre as before to release the words.

"Ah, right." The words uttered by this strange wrinkly being had confused Steve and he was already feeling rather uncomfortable. He wasn't sure, but he thought perhaps she might be a little dotty. He wasn't used to really old people, his grandparents on his father's side had died when he was very young and he had never had much contact with his mother's parents. They had both died when they were in America and his mother had seemed to find it an inconvenience to return to England not once but twice to attend their funerals. And yet, there was something about this aged lady, he wasn't sure, something around her eyes. He got on with the reason for being there. "My name is Steve Bartram, I er, am living in your house. I wondered if you were able to tell me something about its history.

Bartram did he say? Of course, he was living in her house, right in the midst of the memories its old walls held. So many questions to be answered, he would have so much to ask, so much he would need to know. "She didn't say your name was Bartram, how lovely."

"Right," said Steve wondering why his name pleased her. He did not know how to respond, so instead he carefully pulled out the photograph of the soldier he had found in the old chest of drawers, from his jacket pocket. "I wonder if you know who this might be."

She peered at the photo. "I need my glasses." Her neck pulled out like a giraffe's. "Maria," she said as if calling for someone but the strength wasn't there to give any volume.

"Which one is Maria?" Rose smiled.

"She's my nurse. She brought you to me." Steve looked around for the nurse who had shown him in. He saw her by the door stooping over an old person gripping a zimmer frame. He went over and tentatively asked if Rose could have her glasses. Maria regarded him with more suspicion.

"She doesn't use her glasses, hasn't had any call for them."

"Well she needs them now," Steve said almost curtly. "I have something to show her." Maria sniffed at him and said she'd look for them when she had time. Steve thanked her and went back to Rose who looked as though she had fallen asleep, the photograph still held in her shaking hands.

There had been so much he had wanted, intended to ask her about the history of the house but now, none of that seemed to matter. It was all here in front of him in this little old lady. She had lived it all; had breathed it in and now at the end of her life, she was letting it go. Steve sat silently, an overwhelming feeling of respect for such an exploit had left him mute.

"I found her glasses, whether they'll be any good or not I don't know, her eyes have been bad a while now. I've given them a clean, we'll try them. Rose, let me help you with your glasses. How are they?"

"Wait a minute, don't rush me. Now then, what did you say?"

"Your glasses Rose, how are they, can you see better now?" Rose looked over at Steve and scrutinised him through the lenses. "Ah yes, of course you are, I can see the likeness."

'Of course I am what?' thought a bemused Steve while Rose regarded the picture in her hands. Her face changed into one of surprise.

"I didn't know you were to bring me this. Wherever did you get it?"

"I found it with some letters tucked behind a drawer in your house."

"Ah, the letters, it was very upsetting to read those, I wasn't who I thought I was. They changed me." Steve saw a faraway look on her face and he had to wait some time before she had any energy to speak some more. She was engrossed in the photograph. Finally she said something. "I didn't know she put this with them." She looked up. "Of course, she knew you would bring it with you." Steve decided she was definitely dotty but carried on with another question.

"When was the photograph taken?"

"He came home on leave and had it done. I never saw him again." Steve was confused now; the picture was of a boy, not someone old enough to be her father.

"Who is the picture of?" he asked. Rose held the photograph to her chest and sighed. Her eyes moistened. Steve had not wanted to upset her but curiosity was getting the better of him.

"It's my Francis. It's the first time I have ever seen this picture of him, thank you for bringing it."

"Francis?" Steve quizzed. He could see the look of love on her face now and deduced who Francis must have been but her expression changed again. She looked dejected, broken. After a pause her head lifted and arched forward preparing to deliver another communication.

"Francis took my heart with him to France. It was 1915 when he landed at Boulogne and he kept it with him till the Somme, almost seventeen months later. He never came home. I was sixteen, he was older at nineteen." The poignant reply had not been unexpected but still hit Steve straight in his stomach. Old at nineteen? He supposed when he was nineteen he had thought he knew it all but now, looking back, could there be any comparison? He thought not, Francis would have leapt straight from childhood into horror.

By the time Steve had left that afternoon; time was against him and he needed to hurry; he had learned all about the last moments of her beloved, but not much else. Felled by a grenade skirmish on the very night they had won the battle of Thiepval Ridge. How sharp her memory was when speaking of her sweetheart. They had been so young, just starting out, but war had shattered all their hopes and dreams. She had carried his memory in her heart all her life and had lived alone, never marrying, a testament to their love. She had kept his letters with all her family photographs safe in the attic for years but then a chimney had caused a fire there and all her mementos were destroyed. Steve would need to return and learn more.

"Couldn't be bothered to stay for a cup of tea then," deduced Maria as she helped Rose to drink. "Who was he anyway?"

Rose smiled smugly. "My mother knew I would know him, and I did!"

"Yeah right," said Maria realising Rose was as batty as ever. "Well whoever he was he certainly got your attention. I've never seen you take so much interest in anything for ages."

"It's today, and he came. It's the very last day today you know."

"That's what I was trying to tell you this morning Rose. Now get this tea down you before it gets cold.

Chapter Thirty-Two

Jasmine was trying on the dress she had found under the bedroom floorboards when Steve got back from the retirement home.

"I don't think they wore bras in those days, I wanted to see what it's like without one and decide if I can go without. You're just in time to do me up. How did you get on anyway, did you meet her?"

"You look tasty in that," said Steve eyeing her from head to toe, "it suits you."

"Thank you, always nice to get a compliment." Jasmine twirled about in front of the mirror. Steve watched.

"Didn't learn much about the house; lots about her boyfriend in the war."

"Which war?"

"First one. It was the only thing she remembered clearly. I don't think her mind was quite all there, she seemed to recognised me as if I were someone she knew. We were right about the new roof, turns out the chimney caught fire and devastated the attic. Her family photos had been stored up there as well and were all destroyed."

"That's a shame." Jasmine wasn't really listening as she was more interested in how she should wear her hair. "I don't think an Edwardian girl would have had her hair down do you? They would have done something like this." She twisted her curls into a French pleat and searched for something to secure it. "Yes, that will do, something easy."

"I hope you're going to be easy," Steve mumbled under his breath.

"What's that?"

"Nothing dearest."

"Help me to undo it then, it's too early to wear it yet and I need to clean the kitchen. I can't bear to think of leaving it in such a messy state when the century is about to change."

"Anything to oblige." An able assistant to help undress he might be, but cleaning kitchens...? He made his excuses and went to see what information he could find on battles of the Somme from the internet, he thought it better to get the information now while he could, before it crashed at midnight.

It took Jasmine so long to clean the kitchen that in the end they decided to miss the pub out and joined the party back at Trevor's flat. Trevor still lived at the same place above the one they used to rent and it was always an odd feeling to return there. They went through the main door into the communal corridor and up the stairs to the first floor. His flat, one of two upstairs, was quite small and all available space was taken by alcohol imbibed bodies. Jasmine soon lost sight of Steve while she got pinned by someone in a superman costume trying to pick her brains about the benefits of home births as opposed to hospital births. The last thing she wanted was to talk shop, it took her some time to find an excuse to get away. His wife must have been pregnant all of two days; it would be a long pregnancy; she reminded herself to steer clear in future. Eventually she really did need to excuse herself and made her way towards the bathroom. When she came out, she saw Steve chatting avidly to someone dressed as Lady Penelope but couldn't quite recognise who it was until she walked over. It was Penny. She wasn't entirely sure why a few jealous pangs ran through her; she was only his work colleague after all and anyway she was Trevor's girlfriend. Nevertheless she thought it best to go and break up their little tête-a-tête.

"Hello there," she said, interrupting their conversation.

"Ah Jas, where have you been? Couldn't find you anywhere. Penny is having to keep me entertained. What are you drinking? I need to refill my glass."

Interruption manoeuvre successful, they moved towards the drinks table. Steve asked if he had told her how lovely she was looking tonight and how long it was before midnight struck. Jasmine picked up his left arm and looked at his wrist watch.

"Twenty minutes to go." Steve changed his mind about another drink, his wife was looking divinely gorgeous tonight.

"We haven't got long then, come with me." He led her by the hand across the room, out of the flat and onto the landing towards the store cupboard. He looked round, put his index finger to his lips, opened the door and they went into the pitch-black, closing the door behind them. Keen to be inside, Steve thrust Jasmine firmly against the wall using all of his body and pressed up against her. In the course of the next quarter of an hour Jasmine hardly touched the ground. She was braced up off the floor as her legs were stretched across, and half way up the opposite wall. She pushed against it with her feet, and clung on to Steve for balance. Unable to see anything, they could go only by feeling the effects from each other and the sounds they made. And while in the darkness, a piece of equipment was disturbed and they rocked rhythmically in time to its rattles as they got louder and more frenzied, quicker and quicker, the intensity rising and then, just as suddenly, the frequency lessened, almost stopping before the climactic consequence of it all occurred. What turned out to be a ladder had clattered over the top of them, hitting Jasmine hard on her head and causing her to lose her balance. She ended up on the floor pulling Steve with her. While they disentangled from the ladder and each other, Steve had an irrational thought. "Oh, by the way, I didn't say earlier, but the old lady's name is Rose. You don't think she's the same lady that you met in the park when you were little do you?"

"Why on earth are you thinking, at this moment, of her?"

"No idea, she just popped into my head, that's all."

"Well she can jolly well pop right out!"

Minutes later Jasmine was back in the bathroom leaning over the basin trying to recover. Apart from the ladder, she was wondering what had hit her. The passion had been so intense, she had been so, well, abandoned! She decided it must have been the sudden and unexpected surprise of it that had made it so intoxicating. She decided that although it was hurting, the bang to her head wasn't serious and she could hear people counting down "nine, eight, seven..." She didn't want to miss it and rejoined the party to see in the new century. She had no toast and quickly poured herself a drink of something as Big Ben tolled from the television. She realised she had poured whisky and put the glass down, not daring to have any, and joined in the celebrations. 'Just for a while,' she thought.

They heard fireworks crackling and exploding; the whole party regrouped outside to watch. A night to remember; the world joined as one in exuberant celebration as the wheels of time had spun to a new mark; the next millennium. It was a spellbinding moment; they watched the heavens light up, and everyone felt on tonight of all nights, they could reach for the stars. Someone's phone rang; it was someone calling from America to wish them well. Jasmine felt her body warm from the inside out even though she stood barefoot, her arms entwined with Steve while watching the display. Slowly the fireworks diminished and they trooped back inside. Steve excused himself as he went to the bathroom and reluctantly, Jasmine thought about leaving.

"Happy Nnnew Year," someone said by her side. Jasmine turned round to see Dracula, or rather Trevor and managed to avoid his glass when he let its contents slosh out as he lurched nearer for a kiss. She proffered her cheek but he managed to get her full on the lips. She supposed she would let it go seeing as it was New Year and he was already very drunk. "Have yyou sseen Pennyyy? I need to inntroducce you."

"It's okay Trevor, Penny and I have met." She made her excuses, it was time to go; she needed a decent amount of sleep if she was to get up refreshed in the morning. She looked for Steve and saw him by the door. He saw her at the same time and waved and started to come towards her but hadn't got far when Penny was in front of him blocking his way. Jasmine saw him shrug his shoulders as if apologising for being stuck. She sighed; she couldn't be bothered to 'rescue' him again and instead went to find the cloak she had been wearing. It was in the bedroom. Trevor tried to follow her but she manually pointed him in the direction of where she had just seen Penny and went to get her shoes she had kicked off in the broom cupboard.

Back inside the flat there were sounds of claps and cheers and a circle had formed around a couple. Above them someone was holding a bunch of mistletoe. Someone saw Jasmine and pulled her through and into the ring and held another bunch of mistletoe above both their heads inviting her for a kiss but Steve had seen her holding her cloak and pulled her away. "Are you going already?" asked Steve.

"Yes it's already getting late and I still have to get home."

"I'll come with you." Someone was pulling at Steve's arm back into the ring.

"It's okay," shouted Jasmine, "Stay here, it looks as though you are enjoying yourself too much to leave." Steve did another shrug by way of apology before being led away. The last image she had of him was under the mistletoe obliging Penny with his kiss.

Jasmine gasped, she was bewildered and taken aback, she had the beginnings of a headache. How *could* he? There was nothing she could do about it and she had to leave; now. But Jasmine in her panic had misinterpreted the scene she had just witnessed. She was not to know that Penny had grabbed hold of Steve just to get back at Trevor. Penny had seen him kissing Jasmine and it had made her angry.

Jasmine heaved at the front door and it closed with its familiar clunk. It made her departure seem all the more poignant in its finality. She paused, one hand still touching the door as if trying to grasp at the distant murmurings from within. The street lighting was poor as usual and the darkness only helped in reflecting her mood. She sighed and looked upwards. The stars glinted in the vast space above her, the occasional firework peppered the skies, stragglers now from the recent midnight sound and light show. Resignedly, and alone in the quietness of the night, she set forth lost deep in her thoughts, only the occasional distant thunderous sound breaking the silence. She felt tired and vulnerable, her head smarted and it was late. She felt she ought to move more quickly, she only had a few hours before... well, she didn't want to think of that yet. Despite this her mind kept turning over the recent events and relentlessly came back to them. She had known for a while it would come to this and there was nothing she could change, but that hadn't stopped her finding it difficult to come to terms with the situation. 'Why did it have to be like this?' she moaned inwardly. But life's foibles can be so undeserved sometimes.

Then their parting; so unexpectedly quick in the end. She had wanted to say how much she loved him, but how could she under the circumstances? Seeing him with her had destroyed that. She hadn't even said goodbye; it had been too much to bear when finally she had walked away. Her footsteps slowed again at the thought. She was possessed with the thought of Steve back there enjoying himself while here she stood in the cold of the night all alone; the episode in the broom cupboard paled into insignificance, apart from the annoying ache from her head. She rubbed at a bump on her head where the step ladder had fallen on top of her only half an hour before, she was sure it was growing bigger. How mortifying, how ridiculous; a step ladder of all things. But she hadn't seen it and now she was bearing the consequences. Miserable and alone, she wished she had been able to talk with someone. She felt the need of company and fumbled in her bag for her mobile and dialled. Frustratingly it went straight to voice-mail and she was forced to leave a message. "Hello, it's just Jasmine wishing you a Happy New Year," she managed to say before her voice croaked, only adding to her dejection. The conditions had made any communication impossible, the network was jammed. She hoped it wasn't the millennium bug causing havoc already. She resolved to lighten her mood, put her mobile away and looked up and into the park, but it seemed deep and unfathomable in the shadows. Darkness and memories of love-making amongst the rhododendrons were her only reflections. She raised a smile, but it was to be short lived.

She did not have far to go, only round to the other end of the park, up the hill and she would be nearly home. Not far at all, but in her frame of mind of self pity, it seemed much longer. She walked along the road that edged around the park. She had first thought to walk through it, but after peering into its deep shadows she had changed her mind. It was not the place to be alone at night, the lights were always turned off at midnight as a deterrent, even the Christmas ones. The quietness was bearing down on her now, she tried to listen for something; was there a rustling? She was not sure. She looked about; most people had returned back behind their doors and apart from the intermittent lights from above, everywhere was dark and deserted. It once again reflected her mood and facing forward, she clumped one heavy foot in front of the other.

With the poor visibility Jasmine was finding it difficult to decipher much at all and at the same time the blackness of the park loomed like a monster waiting to pounce. A growing wave of nausea caused her to lurch about and a rushing sound was in her ears. A haze appeared in front of her eyes, swirling. Everything seemed distorted, she couldn't understand what was happening and she was feeling very giddy. It was only a silly bump to the head, nothing at all. She was making little progress. Trying to get a grip on herself she carried on as best she could, placing her feet apprehensively, fumbling her way forward. Nothing seemed clear now, her hearing was affected, even her footsteps were muffled, and so remote she had to persuade herself they were really hers. An occasional explosion, far off in the distance now, was her only reassurance that she was still in the land of the living. Her hands continued to feel about for any obstacles in her way as she inched along. The isolating murk was thickening, its only clarity being that she had no idea in which direction she was heading. She wished he had come with her; she wanted him now; needed him; she loved him so much, but he had deserted her, preferring to stay there, enjoying himself. How could he?

Her anger returned and distorted her reflections; she hated him for doing this to her. He had fallen under the spell of that predatory woman, couldn't he have shown a little self restraint? Jasmine recalled the day she had seen them together in the middle of the standing stones. She had seen

Steve under Penny's spell; he had been seduced by her with those ridiculous dowsing rods. Men were so easy to manipulate; why can't they see it? She had been so jealous; she hadn't understood why at the time but now she knew. Steve could be so weak willed sometimes. She pulled off her wedding ring and stuffed it into her handbag defiantly.

Jasmine began hating herself for feeling like this; her body shivered as it tried to rid itself of resentment. This present predicament had nothing to do with him. Surely she must be very near to the standing stones by now and maybe that was why these odious recollections were being triggered. That meant she was nearly home! She would ring him when she got there (just reassure herself he hadn't eloped) Jasmine peered for the ancient relics but couldn't see them; she couldn't see anything. They would be there though, standing and still, all the while soaking up the resonance of time. But something was definitely wrong and she was scared.

She stood in the silence rubbing at the bump on her head and trying to fathom what was happening, and began to hear a noise. The frightened woman listened; it became louder and louder; strangely different from the previous rumbles. It was coming towards her and it was growing to such a strength, her whole body began to sway to it, and her head hurt so much. It was in that one moment when the mist turned into a fog so dense and dark that everything changed. Maybe had she continued walking, had she thought to rummage for the torch she always carried in her bag but always forgot about, had Steve walked her home, maybe the outcome would have been different. Those maybes however were not to be and the consequence of that night affected all who loved her, forever.

Her breath came shallow and fast, her heart thumped as if making a break for freedom out of her chest but the thunderous sounds still clamoured in her head. She clasped her hands to her ears as they resonated violently, trying to shut them out. The whole street appeared to be shaking; everything seemed so jumbled up. She tried desperately to distinguish something, anything familiar. There was nothing. The deafening noise, the pall, the blackness of the fog and her vibrating head made her distraction complete. She was completely lost and hopelessly defenceless against the unseen menace...

It happened rapidly. The pounding noise in her head rose into a stunning crescendo, hitting her with an almighty force just as she took a step to steady herself. The unfortunate woman lost all consciousness and fell backwards...

Printed in Great Britain
by Amazon